HEATHER ANNIS

RINGERS

Cover photo: © Dan Dry/Power Creative

This is a work of fiction. Except for the three real racehorse trainers, and two photographers mentioned, all other characters, names, and incidents, are figments of the author's imagination. Except for those characters inspired by friends who gave their permission, any resemblance to actual persons, living or dead, is purely coincidental. Regarding the locations; almost all exist in some shape or form except for the dairy co-op, the strip club, and the cave on the river. Even the specific cabin in the woods of Vermont is real.

ACKNOWLEDGEMENTS

First and foremost, I have to thank all the assholes and dickheads who have made my life so challenging, without the trouble and strife you caused, this book would never have been written. So go suck eggs, you know who you are. If this book is successful and sells well, perhaps in the next one I can afford to thank you by name.

I would like to sincerely thank Dan Dry for the awesome cover photo; Stephanie Puckett, one of my physical therapists at Naval Hospital Pensacola for getting me over a serious hump when I got writers block after writing my self into a corner; John Sicca of Brook Ledge Horse Transportation, for the travel schedule; Trainers Todd Pletcher, Bill Mott, and Michael Maker, Thoroughbred trainers whom I admire and respect, and who trusted me on million dollar horses like Left Bank and Speightstown, for allowing me to use their names in this story; Tibor Szlavik because he actually goes out of his way to be a good friend; Val Annis, for editing most of my essays in college, and editing this book; my awesome son Oliver, for making life worth living, keeping it interesting, and giving me so many reasons to be proud of the man he has become; and my Navy buddy Jason Valadao, his terrific wife Danika, and their girls Elle and Siena for being supportive throughout and for inspiring the military past of the main character and his friends. Last, but not least, thanks to Orthopedic Surgeon, Dr. Stan Ragon for the bloody marvelous reconstruction he did on my knee.

DEDICATION

This book is dedicated to all the men, women, and children who have lost their lives in Iraq, Afghanistan, and now Syria, since 9/11 and to all the grieving loved one's of the servicemen and women who gave their lives in the name of freedom.

NOBODY ACTUALLY WINS IN WAR
Everyone is somebody's child.

MITCH AND ISABEL

CHAPTER ONE

Somewhere in Vermont – The Friday after Labor Day

The well-hidden man sniffed the air. The scent of the expensive perfume hung like a curtain in the crisp morning air. He had been following the four women for three days and had their routine down pat. Tonight he would put his plan into action.

The women were all between thirty-one and thirty-nine. One was a plump, short, bottle-blond, wife of Isabel's brother Justin. She didn't seem to fit well with the group and was often just a bitch.

The second was extremely skinny with shoulder length mousy brown hair, and the bandiest legs he had ever seen. She was a very good friend from Isabel's college days.

The third, also on the short side, with dark hair, and a wild laugh, was a more recent friend from the Connecticut riding circles. She and Isabel had bonded over a mutual love of horses and mutual problematic husbands.

However, it was the fourth woman, Isabel Lebedev, who was the focus of the hidden man's interest. She was about 5'7, 120 lbs, with long dark red hair that hung in large, soft waves framing her face and cascading down behind to the small of her back. He knew the women well from the profiles he had been given to study and had been watching them closely.

He had first seen the women as they bathed naked in the dark swimming hole at the bottom of the small cliff that jutted out below the trees. Isabel had been standing naked with her back to him. He had admired the taught muscles of her toned back and her small round buttocks that gleamed like white marble. Slowly she had sunk into the water and swum towards her friends.

Mitch had sat and listened to their laughter as it tinkled in the air. The women had drifted back to shore and he had held his breath when Isabel rose out of the cold water, her nipples seeming to point right at him, erect in the centers of the most beautiful perky breasts he had ever seen. His eyes had taken in her long slender neck and then dropped to admire the tiny waist and smooth flat stomach. He had swallowed hard as he stared at the neatly trimmed triangle of pubic hair. He knew he was going to love this target and had mentally stroked her lean muscled thighs while he chastised himself for his unprofessional thoughts.

The camouflaged man, hidden in the trees watching the women, was Mitchell Hammer a thirty-seven year old ex-Navy SEAL. This brown haired, blue eyed, all American college wrestler had spent thirteen years in the US Navy, before joining the FBI. For the last two years he had been assigned to the Department of Justice Special Task Force for Organized Crime. He was not a particularly large man at 5'10" and 175 lbs; and had frequently been underestimated by the enemy in hand to hand combat. He had tried marriage in his early twenties, like so other young military personnel are prone to do, but it had ended in divorce without children and the quiet, dedicated, agent was comfortable being single in light of his often dangerous assignments.

Mitch had deliberately watched the women for three days before he set the plan in motion, he needed no surprises and was a trained judge of human behavior. He heard the noisy talking involved with readying camp for making dinner upon their return. Soon they would be off for their routine evening swim.

As they left the camp, Mitch reached into his pocket and removed the vial of chloral hydrate. "Time for a Micky girls." he thought as he tipped it into the quietly simmering pot of coffee staying warm near the fire. He went into Isabel's tent and opened her back pack. The soft, dark green, silk G-string beckoned him but instead, he caressed his face with her night shirt as he breathed deeply, smelling her scent.

Mitch replaced the nightie and left the camp, glancing around for any telltale signs of his presence. He slipped back into the obscurity of the woods and watched as the woman returned, framed by a pink and purple sunset. The women hung their towels over branches to dry and settled around the fire to drink the coffee.

Once they actually started drinking the coffee,

Mitch crept closer just in case one of them tipped forward toward the fire; he wanted to be close enough to save her from harm. Within fifteen minutes Isabel, Janine, Sarah, and Fran were sprawled around the fire breathing deeply and slowly.

Mitch quickly collected Isabel's belongings, placed a note through the handle of the empty, rinsed coffee pot which read, "J ,S, & F, please forgive me but I awoke this morning with diarrhea and a severe migraine and decided to pack up and go home, will catch a ride. You guys were sleeping like logs and looked so peaceful, that I didn't have the heart to wake you. See you soon, Issy."   Then he lay the other three women in their cots, and slung Isabel over one shoulder, and her backpack over the other, before melting into the trees.

Mitch carried her down to the river and made his way down the shallows toward deeper water where he had hidden the inflatable Selvylor kayak. He dropped the bag and lowered Isabel's limp form into the inflatable. He tossed the bag in and jumped aboard pushing away from the shore. The boat drifted slowly downstream and once it was well out of earshot, he started paddling and followed the river along the tree line and into a small gorge. He sat listening to the sounds in the woods around them. Coyotes yapped, owls hooted, and often he heard the scurrying of a small animal or deer spooked along the stream bank. So far so good he thought.

Mitch floated them downstream for a about an hour before Isabel started to stir, and he glanced down at her, the buttons on her shirt had popped off and her lacy red bra firmly confined her breasts. Mitch reached into the toolbox and removed three cable ties. He placed one around each of her wrists and connected them with the third. He tied her wrists in front of her so that he could tow her if they capsized. He longed to touch her but he wanted her to be awake, wide, wide awake when he touched her, and to do so before hand would be unrelated to his work and thus unacceptable behavior.

Just then her eyes opened wide and Isabel stared at him in fear.

"Don't scream," he said, "Nobody will hear you this far down the gorge and you will only tire yourself out. Behave yourself and I won't hurt you." Guessing her fears he continued, "Oh yes, we are going to do that and when I am done with you, you will be begging for more." Isabel began to squirm and whimper trying to get her wrists out of the ties. They dug into her skin and tears welled in her eyes. "Stop struggling and don't cry, you can't get away and your only chance is to do as I say and keep me happy."

"Why are you doing this?" she asked swallowing hard to prevent herself from crying.

"Because you want me to." Mitch replied. "I heard you girls chatting at the fire, this isn't just what I want, it's what you want too."

"We were just kidding around." Isabel sobbed "and why me, why not one of the others?

"Well," said Mitch, licking his lips "I just had to have your hard, lean, muscled body, bucking against mine. I want to feel your strength as you fight me, and I want to hear your groans of pleasure when you beg for more. Anyway, you are a rose among those thorns. You have some might homely friends"

"Bastard! Bastard! How can you say that? You are going to rot in prison when they catch you."

"My name is Mitch, not bastard. Nobody is catching anybody except for me catching you sweetheart; so shut up and stop whining before I give you something to whine about!"

They traveled in silence until Mitch suddenly swung the boat toward a large overhanging rock. To Isabel's horror, the boat slipped under the rock and she had to duck sharply as darkness engulfed her. As her eyes became accustomed to the dark, she could see the dim outline of a small cave with only the moonlight coming in through the narrow slit they had used as an entrance. Mitch maneuvered the inflatable up against a ledge and threw Isabel's backpack out of the boat. He climbed out and tied up to a ring embedded in the rock. He put out a hand and when Isabel didn't take it he bent down and roughly dragged her out onto the ledge.

"Listen little one, you had better be a little more pleasant or neither of us will have much fun!" he said in mock anger as he shoved her ahead of him toward the end of the ledge.

After securing his own backpack, he switched on a flashlight and Isabel saw a dark shadow ahead. Mitch threw her backpack at her, and she gave him a pathetic look. Realizing she couldn't put it on herself, he cut the ties, helped her into the backpack and replaced a cable tie, securing her hands once again. He then shoved Isabel in the direction of the shadow. As they approached, the shadow became an opening in the rock revealed by the glow of the flashlight. As she ducked into the passage, Mitch grabbed one round butt cheek from behind. She lunged forward jerking up and hitting her head on the rock with a sickening crunch. Isabel fell on one knee holding her head as she battled to fight the waves of blinding pain and nausea.

"Don't pull away from me you little bitch, you're mine now! He swore at her, mentally kicking himself for his stupidity. He gently kicked her tight round butt, "Get a move on, we don't have all day. Isabel rose slowly and placing her hands on the walls as she gingerly moved along the passage.

She noticed a dim light ahead getting brighter and brighter and soon found herself on a small ledge behind a waterfall. The full moon shone through the water making it look like molten silver as it cascaded by.

"You better be careful here or you will fall." Mitch warned. He tied the two of them together at the waist with a short length of rope, mainly to discourage her from pushing him off the narrow ledge. "Follow me and keep a tight hold of my belt." Isabel grabbed his belt and allowed herself to be dragged precariously up the steep path to the top of the cliff. She looked around. All she could see were trees and more trees. It was very dark and scary in the woods and she wasn't at all sure that there weren't bears around. She contemplated running; but quite frankly didn't think she would be any better off if she did because she couldn't ditch the heavy backpack. Mitch walked off up a narrow path through the woods and Isabel followed, angry that she didn't really have much choice.

CHAPTER TWO

The cabin in the woods

Two hours later, after climbing steeply along the rocky trail, crossing a road, and a lot more trail, Isabel saw a clearing ahead, lit by the bright moonlight. There was a fairly large expanse of grass and at the near end, hidden partially by the trees, was a decrepit looking log cabin. The cabin, she saw as they neared, had two floors and a deck overlooking the small grassy valley that stretched up the hill on the other side. Mitch walked up the steps and opened the door.

"Welcome to my humble abode." he said as he went inside where he grabbed a lantern and fired it up.

Isabel stood at the door and looked inside. There were cupboards around the sides and a range in what appeared to be the kitchen area. The rest of the cabin consisted of a few horribly old, dirty, threadbare, brown, armchairs and an ancient kitchen table surrounded by some even older wooden stools, one with a leg held on by duct tape. The whole place smelt a little funny, damp and moldy. "Come on in and close the door." said Mitch, "I want to show you the rest of the castle." Isabel sullenly did as commanded and quietly followed him as he carried the lantern upstairs. Again, the walls were lined with waist high cupboards but this time the room was filled with mattresses; disgusting, dirty, smelly, stained mattresses that desperately needed burning. Mitch hurled her bag into a cupboard.

"You won't be needing that for a while. Now let's get back down and get some coffee brewing for later."

Isabel turned to go down the steep wooden stairs, tripped, and had to throw herself back against Mitch to prevent herself from falling head first down the stairs. He curled one strong muscular arm around her and buried his face in her hair, breathing deeply as he steered her down the steps. Isabel stood rigid with fear as he moved his hands to cup her breasts. She was so confused. She knew she should make a show of fighting him off; but she also knew that she stood less than a snowball's hope in hell of succeeding and might get herself killed in the process.

Mitch took out a knife and cut the connecting cable tie, leaving the ones around each wrist. He walked over to a chair and plopped himself down.

"Come a little closer." he said reaching around the back of the chair and retrieving a long thin riding crop. Isabel stepped forward. "Now take off your clothes and I want you to start with your shirt." Tears welled in her eyes. She felt the sharp burning across her leg as Mitch struck her lightly with the crop, and she screamed in fright more than pain. "I said get them off, what's wrong with you? Listen when I talk." Isabel still couldn't get herself to comply and again felt the crop across her legs. Slowly she peeled off her shirt. "Now the bra." Mitch commanded with a smile.

Isabel hesitated only long enough to feel the crop rake across her legs again and, now crying openly, she undid her lacy red bra and unleashed her perky little breasts from their prison. "Now the jeans, and get a move on." Isabel undid the button, pulled the zipper down slowly and wriggled her hips free of the jeans. She dropped them to the floor and after removing her sandals, stepped out of the jeans noting how dirty her toes were. Isabel stood naked except for a red silk G-string.

"I want you to turn around and show me your little round butt, and then I want you to bend over and slide your panties to the floor." Isabel stood as still as a rock, mortified, and cried out as the riding crop flicked across her thighs. Tears were dripping as she turned away and started to comply. "Wait!" he commanded. I am too tired right now. Maybe we keep the best for a little later."

She stood really still, waiting for his next command. She tried not to move as she felt the cold metal tip of the crop's handle stroking across her buttocks. "Now turn around" Isabel turned and stared at Mitch. In silence they studied each other. She couldn't help noticing his beautiful blue eyes surrounded by the most innocent looking, cute, almost fatherly looking face. How could a man so sweet, and innocent looking, be the brute he so obviously was. Had she met him under normal circumstances, she would have been mesmerized by those eyes and seriously attracted to his toned, muscular build. His brusque "Go make the coffee so it is ready for the morning. It's almost four am and I want to get a couple of hour's sleep." pulled Isabel back to reality and she turned toward the range. "Don't get any ideas about throwing hot coffee at me," he warned her.

While she was preparing the coffee, Mitch walked up behind her and started massaging her shoulders. She instantly became tense and went rigid with fear. As the fingers deftly kneaded her tired muscles and the aroma of the fresh brewed coffee filled her nostrils, she slowly began to relax. Mitch's hands moved down her back and Isabel put her hands on the counter to balance herself.

When his hands reached the small of her back, she was horrified when his touch sent a tug through her groin. Isabel was mortified, Oh God! How can that happen? she thought. The feeling intensified as he dug his thumbs into her butt muscles. Isabel was terrified. What if he thinks I want this raced through her head. She tried to fight the feeling but she felt weak at the knees it felt so good. She felt him stroke her thighs. She wanted to cry out for him to stop, but the words just wouldn't come. Mitch placed his foot between hers and moved her feet apart

"Please don't!" Isabel pleaded.

"Don't start whining now or you will just make me angry. I don't want to hear another peep out of you!" he answered gruffly. Mitch spun her around. He stood before her and looked into her eyes. "I know you want me, it's just a matter of time before you admit it," he whispered. Isabel closed eyes not wanting to acknowledge his existence. He bent and kissed her neck.

His lips moved down and he took a little red nipple into his mouth. He sucked gently felt it stiffen against his fluttering tongue. He took it between his teeth and bit down until he heard her groan. While his lips kissed their way across the hard flat stomach, his fingers caressed her thighs and buttocks. Each time his hands slipped down around the soft butt cheeks, he felt Isabel fiercely grip them together. Isabel started to reach behind herself to try and grab the coffee pot but his strong hands grabbed her arms pinning them to her sides.

He stared straight into her eyes and shocked her with a warm kiss to her lips. He took her arm and led her up the stairs. At the top of the stairs, Mitch steered Isabel in the direction of the cleanest mattress against the far wall. She wondered if she was going to die anyway, whether or not she complied with his wishes. She tried to weigh the odds, knowing that she would be scorned for her compliance by all who had never been in this situation.

Isabel decided that she would only try and escape when her odds of succeeding were heavily stacked in her favor. Until then she might be signing her death warrant. If it began to appear that she was going to die anyway, then she would attempt an escape despite a possible negative outcome.

"Sit down!" Mitch commanded. Isabel sat on the mattress and Mitch sat down opposite her. "I want you to listen and I want you to listen well." he said.

"I am going to lie down and relax and you are going to follow my every order. If you try and get clever in an attempt to escape or injure me in anyway, you had better make sure I'm dead or your life won't be worth living. Is that clear? Is that clear?" Mitch repeated.

"Yes" replied Isabel in a small voice. He rose and walked over to a drawer from which he removed two pairs of handcuffs and a length of light chain. He returned to the bed and closed a cuff around Isabel's right ankle. He looped the other cuff through a link on the chain and walked over to a ring set in the floor and repeated the procedure with the other pair of cuffs.

"Just a little insurance." he said with a smile. Mitch then lit two candles and turned off the storm lantern.

He picked up a bottle of oil and tossed it at her as he lay down on the bed. "Start with the right foot." he said. Isabel opened the oil and smelt the wonderful aroma of Sandalwood. It had always been her favorite. Was this coincidence or did he know? She began to have a sneaking suspicion that this hadn't been an accidental meeting in the woods. She poured a little oil into her palm and rubbed her hands together, then lifted the foot and began to massage his toes. She moved up to his heel, kneading it deeply and then running her thumb along his instep. "You do that really well." Mitch uttered quietly. "Go on to the other and then my calves. Isabel completed the left foot and lifted each foot onto her shoulders as she squeezed his calves in the palms of her hands.

"Now my hands please." asked Mitch, with courtesy that confused Isabel. She just wished he wouldn't be nice it made all this pretty confusing and right now she was having a hard time hating him as she knew she should. She stroked his fingers and kneaded his palms and without asking moved on to his face.

She gently stroked his face, running her finger along the ridge of his brow and down along his chin. She slipped her hands under his head and pressed her fingers against the bumps of tension at the base of his skull, moving them in circles. Mitch groaned in appreciation. Isabel's plan was in action. If she could get him to want and like her, then perhaps he wouldn't kill her and she could walk away from this mess.

She felt him take a hold of her hair and he pulled her head into his groin. "The cuff keys are downstairs so you better not get it into your tiny mind to bite me." was all he said before he let her go. Isabel began to stroke his thighs. She was thinking fast and decided that this might as well be the start of her "get him to like her" campaign since it was obvious that she was going to have to do it anyway. At least it would be on her terms and in her favor. This was going to be the best damn blow job ever.

Suddenly she was pulled over and toward him, He pulled her to his side and cradled her in his arm with her face against his chest lightly brushing her forehead with his lips. She was wracked with confusing emotion and tried not to let him see or feel her tears. She lay quietly in his arms, horribly upset. Why was he pretending to want these things and then suddenly stop? Despite her worries and fear, she fell into an exhausted sleep searching for answers.

CHAPTER THREE

East Hubbardton, Vermont, Saturday

As Mitch heard her breathing deepen he looked at his watch. It was almost time for him to check in. Sleep would have to wait. Mitch slipped his arm out from under Isabel and stood, before quietly descending the stairs. He grabbed a cup of coffee and opened the door to the closet beneath the stairs and stepped inside. Bending down, he opened a trapdoor and as he descended he pulled the closet door closed. Mitch walked over to the desk, sat down in front of his laptop, and put on a headset in anticipation of the satellite linkup that would allow him to receive the call.

At six-thirty a light flashed on the monitor and he pressed 'Receive'.

"Crazy Dog?" he heard,

"Yes," he replied, "howl at the moon."

"Hey Mitch old buddy, how did it go?

"Well! Mack, real well, she doesn't suspect a damn thing."

"Is it working?"

"You are a genius Mack, how on earth did you

come up with this approach, it's working like a charm. Two more days and I'll be her knight in shining armor. She should hate me but its going exactly as you predicted."

"Well, it's my job to profile people and predict their behavior chum. That's why I get to script it and you get to play it, you lucky devil. Anyway buddy, things didn't go quite according to plan. It appears her husband was keeping tighter tabs on her than we expected and the short fat bitch called him as soon as she woke up. The place was crawling with his goons within two hours. So far the infra-red heat seekers show them tracking you to the river. Now they are combing both ends of the gorge but it will only be a matter of time before they realize their folly and find the cave. We will monitor them and keep you informed but be ready for company."

"How soon can I start pumping her for info Macko?" Mitch asked his colleague.

"Slow down Mitch, she has to volunteer the info or she might smell a rat and our whole scheme falls apart. Don't go soft on her. Firstly she has to fear you more than her son of a bitch husband. Secondly, she must be past caring about him being able to hurt her, and lastly, she must figure it's safe to unload on you. So keep up the fear thing but make her want you. She needs that and this scenario gives her the excuse to enjoy it. Have you read her file yet?"

"No!"

"Oh for Christ sake Mitch, do your homework. This is one seriously fucked up chick. Read the goddamn file."

"OK, OK I'll read the file. Lay off the language

will you Macko you know how it bugs me."

"I'm the shrink Mitchel Hammer, and I just played you like a fiddle, now you'll read the file"

"Go to hell Mack"

"I love you too Mitch"

"Bye Mack"

"Bye Mitch"

Mitch tapped 'Disconnect' and sat and stared at the monitor. He made one quick cryptic call over Skype. "John, the von Trapp's OK?" he asked the man who answered.

" Yes sir, safely away." and the man wiped his nose and pulled his ear signaling all was well. Mitch disconnected without another word. Perhaps he had better read Isabel's file he thought. But he sure needed some sleep. Oh heck, he supposed he had better start reading it before he talked himself out of it. Mitch kicked the desk in frustration. When was he supposed to sleep?

He collected a second mug of coffee, leaving the dirty mug next to the pot. He pushed the menu bar and clicked on the folder "Isabel Lebedev". A password box popped up and Mitch entered "nutcracker". He hated all the corny code nonsense after all any hacker worth his salt could access files on a PC. He opened "Isabel Lebedev/Background" and he began to read.

Name: Isabel Caroline Lebedev, nee Mayfair
Father: Winston Harold Mayfair
Mother: Margaret Victoria Mayfair-Ferguson, nee Michaels
DOB: 02/06/81
Place of Birth: Charlotte, NC

Comments: Father was "spoiled brat, daredevil, abused alcohol and Margaret" according to Mrs. Michaels (grandmother). Mrs. Michaels also stated that after beating Margaret so badly that she was hospitalized, he disappeared and to the best of her knowledge lived in Korea and Japan until recently. However they did not know his whereabouts for many years. Margaret, Isabel, and newborn twin son, Justin and Jordan, went to live with Mrs. Michaels in North Carolina.

Soon after Isabel started school, Margaret met and married Liam Ferguson, and they moved to South Florida. Isabel went to live with them and was later in and out of boarding schools. Didn't always get along with her step-father. According to Mrs. Michaels, Isabel was a very good scholar but lacked self-esteem, something she could never understand because "the girl was always bright, slim and not bad looking" However she did say that Isabel was prone to serious depression and often called her in tears when she felt that her stepfather was being nasty. When asked if Isabel had mentioned any sexual abuse, Mrs. Michaels was shocked and stated that she and Isabel were close and that Isabel would never withhold something so terrible from her. She stated that she was not in favor of Isabel's involvement in her stepfather's racing stables and blames him for Isabel's marriage to 'that beast' Nikolai Lebedev. For a full transcript see file Isabel Lebedev/Mrs. Michaels.

Mrs Ferguson (mother) tells same story. Also denies sexual abuse history. However she says Isabel and stepfather had same interest in horses and got along just fine. Refuses to discuss Nikolai and denies belief that he has illegal dealings. Appears afraid and asked us to leave. See file Isabel Lebedev/Margaret Ferguson for full transcript.

The brothers Justin and Jordan tell different story. They say that Isabel was abused at ages four years, nine years, and twelve years, and then repeatedly by her husband. Justin mentioned that the abusers all died in 'accidents' since her marriage to Lebedev. Justin Mayfair used air quotes with the word accidents. They also say that they would like to help Isabel get away from her husband but don't know how. The brothers stated that they fear for her life as well as their own and are afraid to rock the boat in the event that it causes Isabel more harm than good. Both refuse to testify, or sign sworn statements, and will not speak to us again without a subpoena. Jordan Mayfair advised that we "Speak to her shrink". No transcript exists of the conversation with the brothers as they would only meet at a ball game if we were shirtless, in shorts, wearing paint. Meeting lasted less than ten minutes.

Liam Ferguson told us to leave when we approached him, and actually said, "I'll kill you if you cause that girl harm." He refused to speak to us at all and will need to be subpoenaed.

Well this is all a little boring and repetitive, thought Mitch. He skipped ahead looking at testimony from various friends and family. He decided to come back to it later, right now he was going to jump to the shrink's file. That might be a little more interesting. He closed "Isabel Lebedev/Background" and opened "Isabel

Lebedev/Psychiatrist/Dr. Green".

Mitch started reading the typed transcript of the conversations between Isabel and her therapist.

July 16, 2014

IL: Where do I start

DR: Well most people find it easiest to start at the very beginning, or at least where they believe it all began and describe how each incident made them feel. Later we discuss how it all ties together, and how you believe it has affected you, and what you plan to do to correct what you feel needs correcting"

IL : I think it all began when my father disappeared, although, I say that only because it happened before anything else. I can't remember how it made me feel at that time; but later it affected me so I have to say that's where it all started. When I was four we went to visit my Aunt Elizabeth and her family. She has four boys all much older than I am. They were teenagers and all I remember is a long passage leading from the lounge to the front door and a bathroom on the left about halfway down. My cousins were left to babysit me. I remember the oldest two going down to the bathroom. After a short time they called me and I went in to see what they wanted. They had their pants down and …..

Mitch shook his head in disbelief. He read further. ….but I do remember that afterward they told me that I couldn't tell my mother because what I had done was so terrible that my mother would send me away. I had already lost one parent and I was terrified of losing another so I said nothing.

After that, until I left they would threaten to tell my mother unless I did as they said. I tried not to be alone with them thereafter and as I grew older I blamed myself for being too stupid to see that they wouldn't tell anyone.

I didn't see those cousins again until I was nine. My mother had remarried and I was feeling very insecure about my position in the new family. This time it was the younger two cousins who used the same threat of exposure. They had obviously found out about the older two.

We were all at my grandmothers for Christmas and at Granny's house there is this old storage room that is very dark and scary. It had an ancient oriental grass wall-hanging, of a tiger ripping a man to shreds, against the far wall. We younger kids would never go in there because it was so dark and scary. Anyway, we were forbidden from entering. Donald and Grant grabbed me in the playroom and carried me in there with a hand over my mouth.....

Mitch hated reading this, and skipped ahead... Donald started swearing when Grant said something about him being a baby because he couldn't control himself. Next thing Donald hit Grant and said that at least he could get it up. They started arguing and I took the opportunity to get to get away. I ran out and went and hid in the big doll house in the garden.

Later I went to the mirror and checked to see that I still looked the same. I was sure that there must be some outward sign that would tell the grown-ups what I had done. I looked the same so I went looking for my cousin Alexandra, and never left her side until everyone went home after New Year. I

went home with renewed guilt. I was bad, very,
very, bad, and so men did bad things to me. And I
was so very afraid of my new step-father. Would he
see how bad I was and also do bad things to me?

Oh shit! thought Mitch. "I can't read this stuff
and do what I'm doing no matter how many people
her husband has murdered." He closed the file and
went up the steps and out of the closet. He quietly
climbed the steps to the loft room and lay down
next to the sleeping form. The sky was becoming
brighter as he fell asleep with an arm cradling Isabel
protectively.

CHAPTER FOUR

So you think you can ride

Isabel awoke and turned to look at Mitch. He was breathing deep and slow. He appeared so peaceful and sweet that she was overcome with dread when she realized what Nikolai was going to do to him when he found them. She desperately needed to pee so she had to wake him.

"Mitch, hey Mitch wake up!"

"Go back to sleep." he answered harshly.

"No, I need the bathroom now."

Mitch got up and fetched a tin and paper from a closet. "Use that. Now let me sleep."

"Are you crazy? I won't use that; and anyway there isn't time for you to sleep. My husband is going to find us soon and you are going to wish the cops got you first."

"Honey, nothing would happen if the cops find us and you are the one he will kill if he finds us." "What the hell are you talking about?" she demanded.

"You remember that translucent writing paper with the horse watermark? The paper you used to invite your friends on the camping trip."

"Christ! How do you know about that? Who the hell are you?"

"Well let me just say that I too have an invite on that paper. Your handwriting telling me how this would be a great cover for your 'kidnapping' and how we would get to spend time together. I even mailed it from your mailbox."

Isabel attacked him with arms flailing. "You bastard, you bastard, I'll never see my kids again, he'll kill us both. You miserable, perverted, son of a bitch. To think I actually imagined you might be a decent person despite all this."

"Oh calm down. You're being hysterical. Nobody is going to find either of us until I am good and ready and then both of us will have sufficient amnesia to protect the other. You scratch my back and I'll scratch yours."

"I'm glad you think it's that simple. You don't know Nikolai. He'll hunt you down and kill you just like he has before."

"Are you telling me that your nice attorney husband kills people?"

"Shut up will you, you have no idea. He isn't just an attorney. .....Oh God, why am I telling you this? I dare say at this stage you're going to die anyway so who cares what you know."

"Will you please stop telling me I'm going to die. Nobody in this room is going to die."

Just then an owl hooted twice and then again. Mitch froze.

"Oh oh!"

"What do you mean 'oh, oh'? Isabel asked, her

eyes wide with fear.

"Honey, we have company. We have to get out of here."

Isabel started sobbing hysterically, "He'll kill me, he'll kill me. Oh God, please help." Mitch slapped her hard.

"Shut up! Hold on, I'll get the key." He ran down the stairs and grabbed his jacket. Upstairs he threw the key at Isabel. "Take that crap off, grab your bag and meet me downstairs."

Mitch ran down to the closet under the stairs and pulled open the hatch to the basement. He leaped down, closed the laptop, and placed it in his back pack. The pack was otherwise ready with two spare batteries, a fold up satellite dish, and some other supplies. Isabel shrieked with fright as he appeared out of the closet. "Quit all the noise and let's get out of here."

"I'm not coming with you."

"OK, I'll mail him the letter and the photos"

"Jesus you are an absolute asshole!" she said as she followed him.

On the way out he grabbed two mugs of cold coffee, he downed one and offered the other to Isabel who shook her head. Mitch went out the door, and off the deck facing the lush field of grass. He led Isabel up a narrow path that wound across the small valley in front of the cabin.

"How did you know that they weren't waiting out here? "she asked.

"The sensor they tripped is a good two miles away. We should have a safe eight minutes lead because they are on foot. The only road in is pretty bad and crosses a bridge that has a different type of alarm for heavier stuff. Now we must hurry. I want us over the ridge in the next two minutes so that they don't hear us start up the ATV. They should still be at least a mile away."

Mitch and Isabel climbed in silence. She was thankful that she was in such good shape. Just over the rise Mitch walked to a pile of brush and uncovered a Suzuki four-wheeler.

"Get on, let's get out of here." Isabel jumped on behind him; she had to grab a hold of his waist, straining to reach around his pack, as he took off down the rutted track jostling her as they bounced in and out of muddy potholes on the trail.

Mitch's thoughts were not pleasant ones. He had been caught napping. Back up would be on its way. In fact, that alarm might have been the backup arriving first but he had to get Isabel out of there before she saw any friendlies. He had no doubt that the Lebedev's goon party would be in for a nasty reception, but he hadn't had time to find out which routes were secure. More Lebedev goons were undoubtedly in the area casting a net. They would have to be ultra-careful. He definitely couldn't just go to the nearest road.

Mitch tried to think of the local farmers and their general routine that he had got to know while preparing for this case. Many were dairy farmers, so they would be sneaking out of the area in a milk tanker. He would have to dump the four-wheeler since it had tracks an idiot could follow. He veered right at the next available trail and headed in the general direction of an outfitter's operation near the main road. At a stream he turned into the water and followed the stream for a few hundred yards. When the stream dropped over a rock into a pool he motioned Isabel off and pushed the Suzuki over the edge where it sank into the dark water.

"Why the hell did you do that, moron, now we have to walk." Isabel said bitterly.

"Please just shut up and follow me, I do have a plan."

"Yeah, great plan. So far it's getting us killed. Fucking rocket scientist you are. AND," she said emphasizing the 'and', "I really need to pee now."

"Well, do it in the water, I don't want you leaving such an obvious marker." Isabel gave him a look that would have stopped Hannibal at the Alps.

"Turn your back you rude ape." Mitch just ignored her and walked off down the stream, keeping to the rocks so as to leave no trail for their pursuers to track. Isabel followed his lead as soon as she could, taking care not to step on the sand.

After about half an hour, Mitch left the stream and walked up the steep shale incline to a rusty barbed wire fence.

"This guy is an outfitter; there should be a ton of horses in here somewhere. They will be heading to the home pasture anytime soon for lunch. They normally feed the horses an hour before the tourists are due. We'll hitch a ride with the herd and leave no tracks. We must jump off on the stony patch at the bottom of the grade or we will be seen as the horses shoot out of the trees."

"How come you know about this place?" Isabel inquired.

"Well I decided to try horse riding a while back when I was setting up camp."

"You mean you can't ride?"

"I have been twice."

"And you think that you can jump on a horse out here and ride it home, no saddle, no bridle?"

"And why not?"

"Oh boy, oh boy, oh boy, oh boy. Good luck pal."

They waited in silence until they heard the horses walking down the trail.

"Listen", said Isabel, "trust me on this, jump on the horse I tell you to jump on. I know about this stuff OK. Give me your pack, you won't manage to get on with it."

"Sure, OK" he said grinning at the look on her face.

Isabel pointed to a small, fat, almost white pony, with dirty brown spots on its butt. She stood slowly so as not to startle the horses; and vaulted onto a sensible looking draft type after tying the packs together and throwing them over its neck. She looked back just in time to see Mitch disappear right over the little appaloosa. He stood up and walked after the pony and tried again, this time he landed across the pony and managed to drag a leg over. Isabel was laughing so hard her sides hurt. Mitch was gripping the pony's short mane and was hunched over like a monkey. Isabel was glad she had judged the pony well. It hardly seemed to notice the pathetic antics on its back.

They rode down the trail until they reached a rocky spot. Isabel hoped it was the right one and jumped off, pulling the packs of with her. She was

ahead and didn't dare call out. Mitch slipped down
the pony's side and landed on one foot almost
falling over. Isabel clamped a hand over her mouth
as she laughed, and she made a cry baby face
gesticulating the tears, at the indignant Mitch. He
picked up his pack, beckoned to her, and she
followed him as he crept along the tree line away
from the outfitter's and toward his goal.

"Sit down, we'll rest here. The dairy farm is just
beyond these trees. The milk tanker comes
sometime during the evening but the milking shed is
on the other side of the road. We will have to crawl
down the drainage ditch on the far side of the house
and through the culvert. Once on the other side I
suggest we climb into the loft and rest well until the
tanker arrives," Mitch explained.

"Do you mind if I have a snack? I haven't eaten
since yesterday,' she asked.

"I'm sorry, go ahead, but be quick. There will be
lots of time for eating in the barn."

Isabel removed a Nutrageous candy bar from
her backpack and proceeded to eat it slowly
savoring every bite. When she was done she
replaced the wrapper in the back pack and stood up.
"OK, I'm ready."

"We have to follow the stream to the road, and
then use the concrete culvert to crawl under the
road. We are heading for that yellow barn," he said
pointing down the hill and across the valley. "We
can hide there to wait for the tanker." Isabel
shouldered her backpack that Mitch had untied from
his. She followed him to the stream and they slipped
over the bank and crouched low as they made their

way downstream hidden from view below the crest
of the bank. It was difficult to stay out of the icy
water. Isabel slipped on the slimy stream bed, hit
her elbow on a sharp rock, and swore under her
breath. She was extremely irritated by the amused
grin she received for her efforts. He was being
childish playing tit for tat with her discomfort. At
the edge of the road, they crawled on hands and
knees through the thirty-six inch pipe, slipping and
sliding in the icy water.

About fifty yards beyond the culvert, Mitch
stopped and pressed a finger to his lips. He
whispered into her ear,

"Just above us there is a wooden staircase
leading up to the loft of the barn. It faces away from
the road, and the house, so we should not be seen as
we go up, as long as no one comes around this side
or no vehicle approaches us from the north. We will
wait for no traffic sounds and then stand and walk
calmly toward the stairs so we don't draw attention
with sudden movement. Once we get there, get up
to the loft and hide as quickly and as quietly as you
can" Isabel just nodded.

"Go!" She stood and followed Mitch across the
short stretch of grass and up the steps. She tripped
banging her shin hard on the edge of the step.

"Shit!" she squealed.

"Shhhhh" Mitch gave her a harsh glare as he
opened the door quietly and peered about quickly
before they stepping inside. She followed, holding a
hand over her mouth as she tried to stifle her
laughter. Mitch looked at her confused. What on
earth was the silly bitch laughing about. He hoped

she was not about to get all hysterical on him.

"My Dad used to tease me about being clumsy. He called me an accident waiting to happen and the only person he knew who could fall up stairs," she explained in a very fake low pitched voice. Wow, thought Mitch, maybe she is tougher than I give her credit for.

They looked around the huge loft. It was filled with bales of sweet smelling hay.

"Most of the human action below takes place at the front of the barn", Mitch said, pointing to the left. "Move towards the back and climb up over there where the bales almost reach the roof." Isabel did as she was told and climbed the tall pile of hay. At the top, she discovered that the bales of hay had been arranged so that they formed a hidden space. She dropped down into the hollow and sat down leaning against the bales. Mitch sat down beside her.

"What now?" she asked, one delicately plucked eyebrow raised into a curve way above the other.

"How do you do that" Mitch asked, trying to wiggle his eyebrows. Isabel giggled at his efforts.

"My brothers could wiggle their eyebrows, and I was so jealous. It's genetic you know, the ability to do that. Anyway, I spent years holding my left eyebrow down and wiggling the right one. Eventually it worked. So now I can raise the one independently. I don't recommend the effort," she said.

Mitch nodded and said, "We have to hole up here until dark. There is a milk tanker that comes here every night to pick up the milk after the afternoon milking. They milk here twice-daily four am and four pm. Sometime after six pm, when the milking is over, the tanker arrives and they pump the milk into it. It takes about half an hour. During this time, we are going to have to sneak into the storage area under the truck. I'll tell you about it later." Isabel thought about this obviously preconceived plan and wondered again who exactly this man was.

"Why wouldn't I just make a noise and get us caught right now?" she asked. "I'll try and explain to Nikolai that you forged the letter. If he still kills me, well he's probably just going do it anyway." Mitch's face grew dark and hard. Back to being the bad guy he thought.

"Listen you stupid bitch, the sooner you realize that you are not going home to Nikolai until I say so, the sooner you will actually get home. Firstly, Nikolai won't believe you because I filled your computer with lots of emails that you have been saving over the months, chronicling our budding relationship. Also, all the saved drafts of your replies are there. I even password-protected the files with the name of your favorite old dog so it won't take in a minute to find them. Secondly, I have your kids." Mitch stopped as little fists hammered his head and chest. He laughed and caught her hands, holding them tight. "Stop now, you don't want to annoy me. Behave yourself and you and the kids will be just fine."

"No we won't be. If you already have Demyan and Yuri, Nikolai is going to find us and we are going to suffer before we die. I suppose either way I am going to die since you're not even trying to hide your face, which means you aren't worried about me telling the police."

"Christ almighty, shut up already. Stop with this damn dying. Nobody's going to die. I told you that already. Okay!! You keep saying Nikolai will kill us. Why would a highly respected defense attorney kill anyone?" Mitch didn't think she was ready to talk, despite the comments at the hunting cabin.

Isabel turned away and hugged her knees to her chest. If only she could tell him. Maybe if he knew how dangerous Nikolai was, he would let her go. This was going to be tough to explain to Nikolai if she lived long enough to explain. Would he even believe that she hadn't said anything? She didn't think Nikolai knew how much she knew; but he also knew she wasn't a complete dunce. Maybe he was even behind this kidnapping, testing her loyalty. Or maybe he just wanted her gone. Shit, this was confusing. It was just a lot safer to say nothing and to try and find out how much Mitch knew about her husband.

Mitch looked at the peachy skin of Isabel's neck peeking through the huge open curls. She had such long, soft hair. He reach over and stroked her neck. Isabel stiffened with a jerk.

"Please don't," she begged; but Mitch leaned forward and gently kissed the soft velvety nape.

"You're cold, your clothes are still wet. Take them off and hang them over the bales. We will be more comfortable later if we're dry."

" I'll get changed," she retorted.

"No, don't waste clean clothes. We will need them tomorrow. We must use these until we get a chance for a complete makeover. It's nice and warm up here so they'll dry fast."

Isabel ignored him and sat instead, staring into space. She didn't even bother to think. What was the point after all, her future looked bleak. Mitch put his arms around her and quietly unbuttoned her shirt and removed it. He gently lifted her to her knees and undid the button and unzipped her jeans. He slid them down over slim hips and wiggling them around her knees. He pulled of her sneakers and socks. Her feet were freezing so he rubbed them until some color returned. He slipped the jeans off, one leg at a time, then stood and hung the wet clothes on the bales, adding his own. The hay was painful and prickly when he sat back down. He started kneading Isabel's shoulders. She jerked and then pretended to ignore the strong fingers that squeezed at tense muscles. She was pretty sure she knew where this was going but just didn't have the strength to protest. Her muscles were so cramped and painful. Tension and exertion had turned them into hard cords and every circular motion of Mitch's thumbs caused intense, exquisite, waves of pain.

After a few minutes, the heat spread through her shoulders and she started leaning into each push. She could feel her muscles relaxing. Mitch worked on the deltoids and biceps and she groaned with pain, her muscles so tight. He worked his way down her back. Boy, he thought, she is a study in anatomy with every rib and muscle visible. She must have the least body fat of any woman I know.

Mitch buried his face in her hair. She smelled so sweet. He took her earlobe in his teeth and bit down until he heard a sharp intake of breath and then sucked hard on the soft, peachy lobe while massaging the scalp beneath it. As much as she hated to admit it, Isabel was enjoying this and she loathed herself for it. Damn but the body is fickle. By now it was obvious to her that she had to go along with anything he did, but she didn't have to like it, she thought and she hated herself for that too.

Suddenly he stopped and turned away. Isabel wasn't sure who she hated more, herself at that moment because she felt so incredibly cheap, or the handsome pig messing with her head. How dare the bastard just turn away, he could at least pretend to care. But no, he just rubbed her nose in her own stupidity. Here she was, maybe dead and she was experiencing some of the most serious lust for the man causing it all.

She realized that Mitch hadn't yet forced her to have sex. Why? Something didn't mesh. Maybe he's married she thought. Nah, can't be it. Nobody who kidnaps another human would really worry about that small inconvenience. Maybe he thinks that what he's done so far rates a lesser sentence if he gets caught. I'll just give up thinking she decided. She stood up, retrieved her damp clothes and put them back on. She lay down facing the bales and after a much shorter period than she would have thought possible, fell asleep absolutely exhausted.

Mitchell covered Isabel with his coat. She appeared to be sound asleep, her breathing slow and rhythmical. He took out his laptop and set up the satellite dish on the small deck at the top of the stairs, hoping that it would be facing a satellite. He booted up and logged on.

Mitch thought about the files he was supposed to read but he just couldn't face more of Dr. Green's notes so he opened the file on Isabel stepfather, Liam Ferguson. Born June 23, 1950 to a New York City cop of Scottish decent, and his Irish wife. While he was stationed in England during the war, the senior Ferguson had met his wife Siobhan working in a London pub off Trafalgar Square. They returned to New York after the war. Siobhan was the daughter of a Dublin doctor........

CHAPTER FIVE

Some roller-coasters aren't fun

Isabel awoke extremely hungry, and tried to sit up jerking against the handcuff that attached her to Mitch. Her movement woke him. She glared at him.

"I'm not going anywhere you jerk. I happen to want to see my kids again. I'm not going to do anything stupid." Mitch smiled.

"Sorry, maybe it won't happen again." He unlocked the cuffs and they both vigorously rubbed their wrists. Seeing the irony, they started laughing. "Considering your plight," he said, "you have a remarkable sense of humor. I just can't see how you ever ended up with that humorless husband of yours." She just gave him a look. Once again she got the distinct impression this man knew far too much about her and her family.

"I'm hungry," she complained as a huge rumble issued from her stomach. They both started laughing again. Mitch gave her a concerned look and pretended to take a pulse and feel her brow.

"You may be hysterical, perhaps you need a shot of something." Isabel was horrified for an instant before she saw the wicked grin. She raised her hand as if to hit him and he feigned ducking from the blow.

"I think I'll have the Snickers," she said.

"How about dinner instead?" he asked, digging into his backpack and holding up two MREs called Menu 14.

They ate the Ratatouille heated with the supplied heat pack followed by the dried fruit, pound cake, and peanut butter and crackers washed down with something called a dairy shake. Isabel took some candy from her backpack and placed it in her pockets for later.

"How come you have so much candy in your pack?" Mitch asked.

"I have low blood sugar and sometimes I just need a fix so I keep it handy. Anyway, I am thin enough to eat as much damn candy as I please."

"Wow a woman who doesn't think she's fat, it's a miracle!"

"Ha, ha, very funny. I'm a size two. Even I'm not stupid enough to think that's fat."

Mitch looked at his watch. "Almost time to go," he said. "Pack up and let's fly this coop. We will be going out the way we came in, but we'll go around the back of the barn and pass the calves. With all the noise they make during milking, no one will hear us. We will go down as soon as the milk tanker gets here. There is a large metal box under the front end of the tanker trailer. It is usually used for tools and extra storage only this time it happens to be empty. As soon as the driver connects the hoses to the holding tank and starts pumping, he goes into the office for a cup of coffee. This is when we will climb into the box. It's going to be a tight fit. Throw your pack in first and then get in and kneel bending over your pack and I will do the same." He bent and showed her what he meant. "I know this is going to be a horribly uncomfortable ride for over an hour but it is the best I could do at short notice. Luckily, this is the tanker's last stop before heading back to the dairy co-op" Isabel said nothing. Over the noise of the cows and the milking below, she could hear the rumble of the tanker pulling up.

They shouldered their backpacks. Mitch took her hand and they climbed over the hay and approached the door. He peered out.

"All clear!" They hurried down the stairs and around the back of the barn. "Wait here," Mitch commanded, and he crept to the edge of the calf enclosure and watched the tanker. He couldn't see the back end, but as soon as he heard the pump start, he turned and beckoned to Isabel. She ran over to him and they quickly slipped past the calves and pressed against the wall at the corner as Mitch looked around it. He saw the light from inside the barn dim as the large door was rolled closed.

"Now!" He pulled her towards the tanker. The box looked so small to Isabel. Mitch opened the side by swinging the door up. Isabel tossed in her pack and scrambled in after it. Mitch followed with his and pushed in alongside her holding the door down and securing it with two catches on the inside. We are going to suffocate in here Isabel thought in the pitch darkness that enveloped them.

She voiced her fears aloud.

"We won't suffocate," he replied, "there are air vents. But, we are going to get incredibly hot until the truck starts to move and then you are going to get really cold. The nights are chilly this time of year. "Why did you go camping so late in the year?"

"I had to wait until after the summer break so the kids would be back at school," she replied.

"Shhhhh!" They listened as the pump stopped. There was some talking as the driver rolled up the hose and secured it to the back of the tanker. There were some footsteps, a door slammed, and the truck started. They immediately realized this was going to be a very painful experience.

Both were quiet for a while as the truck swayed back and forth on the small country road. The tanker-truck slowed briefly and then Mitch was forced hard up against Isabel as the truck and trailer took the tight curve of the on-ramp onto the highway.

"Ow, move over, you're squashing me," she yelled over the noise of the accelerating rig. Mitch did his best to push himself away. Soon they straightening onto Route 4 and the tanker's engine quietened to a steady hum as it settled into its cruising speed.

"This will be the best part," Mitch explained. "Once we cross the state line and get onto the New York roads, the ride is going to get very bumpy in spots."

"Great," respond Isabel, "I've always loved roller coasters."

They rode in silence for a while and then she asked in a small voice, "Where are my children?

"They are on a ski trip."

"Rubbish, nowhere has snow in late August."

"Some countries do. We thought it would be safer if your kids disappeared overseas for a while and ski masks hide kids' faces well. This way you won't get the urge to run and find them and your husband won't be able to find them."

"That's what you think, but he has tentacles everywhere. You have no clue how dangerous he is."

"So you keep telling me, but you have to get to give me an example."

"Why have you kidnapped me, if you want Nikolai to pay then why did you make it appear as if I ran off?. This will only make him very, very, angry and want to kill both of us. It doesn't make sense. I can only think you want something from me or you want to make him angry and that just doesn't make sense."

"Isabel, I can't tell you anything, I'm just doing a job. I'm just doing a job I was paid to do. I was paid to kidnap you and send a bunch of pre-dated emails, and place some from you to me in your sent mail file, so that when Nikolai looks in the mail he believes that you have run off with me and have taken the children with you. Someone else has the kids and is keeping them safe, just as I'm supposed to keep you safe. Maybe Nikolai has enemies. I don't know."

"Shit, of course he has enemies, just none stupid enough to pull a stunt like this. Knowing my husband as well as I do, I'm having a very hard time imagining getting out of this alive."

Despite the difficulty of shouting over the noise, Mitch continued. "How did you meet him?"

"Nikolai?"

"Of course Nikolai."

"I suppose that knowledge can't hurt anyone. I was a junior at NYU getting a Batchelor of Science in biochemistry. In the morning I was galloping horses for my dad at Belmont Park Race Track. Nikolai had horses in training with Johnny Fish in the barn opposite ours. One morning he came to watch his horses working out and I must have caught his eye. He tried to get Dad to train for him but Dad refused. My dad likes to train clean and at his own pace. He steers clear of punters."

"Punters?"

"People who bet big money with bookies, bookmakers" she clarified.

"I thought bookies were illegal in the US"

"Duh, why would that stop Nikolai. He plays the books in the Cayman's, London, Vegas, Dubai, Hong Kong, Singapore to name a few. Anyway, my dad had heard too many shady stories so he declined. He told Nikolai that he was downsizing due to his health and would only be keeping his two oldest clients. Nikolai drove a very, very nice, shiny, silver Maserati and kept stopping by after my classes and offering me a ride home. I just couldn't say no. I was young and all of the money, I had never seen so much cash flashed around. Nikolai took me to the theater, to dinners with movie stars, then trips to events like the Oscar's. There was so much you just could never imagine. It was a life I had never imagined anyway. We had never been

rich. Dad did well, but having come from a tough
working family, he was, and still is for that matter,
rather frugal. My dad tried to warn me but I
wouldn't listen because Nikolai just seemed to have
so much to offer. I could still go to school, but I had
a chauffeur. College was fully paid, so I wouldn't
be burdened with loans. There were more trips to
Europe. We went racing at Epsom, Chantilly,
Longchamps, all in private boxes. I felt like royalty.
When I mentioned that I wanted to see China, he
hired a Chinese girl from NYU to take me on a tour.
It was amazing, Ling Mei showed me wonders that
I had only dreamed of. Anyway, long story short,
we got married. I think that was Nikolai's plan all
along. As soon as we were married, the walls came
down. He was instantly the jealous, suspicious,
paranoid, man my dad had warned me about. I was
taken to and from school, I never went anywhere
without my bodyguard. My prison guard in reality. I
entered grad school to stay sane and to make sure
that I had an education if I ever got my life back.

I wondered at the beginning why he let me stay
in school. I was studying genetics. I was interested
in recombinant techniques and the future it held in
curing genetic disorders."

"Recombinant techniques?"

"That's when you remove some genetic material
from one organism and replace it with genetic
material from another organism. For example, they
added the gene for spider silk protein to goats, so
now goats produce milk that contains the spider silk
protein. The silk can then be extracted and used. I'm
sure you've heard some of the grumbling about the

genetically engineered crops. Anyway some of my ramblings must have sparked an interest in Nikolai because next thing he bought a biotech company."

"What, he owes a biotech company?'

"Yes, it's called New Era Genetics and Biotechnology Corporation or N.E.G. Biotech. They even do DNA and mitochondrial DNA verification testing for the National Transportation Safety Board."

"Good grief, how can a government utilized company be owed by Lebedev and we didn't know.?"

"Who's we?"

"Never mind, go on, this is fascinating."

"I got to Intern at N.E.G. and when I got my PhD I went to work there. We do some amazing stuff. By this time, I had popped another kid and I could see absolutely no way out. I love my kids, and I love my job, I just hate my life. So there you have it."

"He must have some reason for wanting a lab. What is he up to?" Mitch queried.

"Sorry that information is dangerous to your health."

"Come on, I'm already going to die, you said so at least twenty times in the past day."

"Nope!"

"This trip is painful and the story is so interesting and makes time fly. Tell me about some of the things Nikolai and Fish were doing that your step-father didn't like."

"I didn't tell you that he is my step-father but since you manage to do all this hacking stuff I'm sure you know everything about me and my family.

I'm probably not telling you anything new.'

"Rubbish, I know the bare essentials this is all very entertaining."

Isabel was very angry. He knew more than he was letting on and it was pissing her off. "I'm tired, leave me alone" said Isabel and she stopped talking.

Isabel remained quiet as they swayed and bumped along. Occasionally, Mitch called out their location based on the stops and turns. Isabel wondered if he was just guessing because he knew where they were going. After another half an hour, the sounds of traffic grew." We are nearing the dairy co-op in Glens Falls. We'll have to wait until the milk is pumped and the tanker lines up for washing before we can bail," said Mitch.

Eventually, they turned into the co-op. The tanker beeped as it backed into the pump bay Isabel listened to the thump, thump, thump, of the pump and started to fall asleep. She bumped her head hard against the metal box as the tanker lurched forward as it was moved to the truck wash. Isabel rubbed her forehead and was starting to feel a little nauseous. This was two hard blows to the head in one day and the diesel smell was disgusting.

After a couple of minutes, Mitch opened the hatch a crack and peeped out. All was quiet. He pushed it all the way open and climbed out. Isabel tried to follow but was so stiff she stumbled and fell. Mitch, picked her up, pack and all, and carried her across the parking area and into the shadow of the warehouse wall. Isabel tried to stand, but pains shot through her knees. She flexed them open and closed a few times and the pain lessened.

"Sorry," she said. Mitch lead her around behind the warehouse. There were a lot of old trucks, trailers, campers, and machinery scattered across the lot. He moved toward a huge pile of scrap metal and lifted a tarp revealing a 250cc dirt bike.

Behind the bike was a bag with helmets and jackets. The bag; also contained two wigs, one with a long, dirty blond plait, and one with very long straight black hair. Mitch pulled on the blond wig and handed Isabel the black one, then he pulled on a helmet, handing her one. He got on the bike, pack facing forward, and Isabel climbed on behind him. Mitch started the bike and shot out of the lot like a demon possessed. He sped down the road taking random turns and turning to look behind them. Isabel looked back often and saw no one. He slowed, and rode into town.

As they passed a Denny's Isabel yelled for him to stop, "Can we get something to eat. It's very late, I'm sure no one will be looking for us in the Denny's. Nikolai doesn't do Denny's. Mitch parked in a shadow next to the dumpster that also happened to be near the back door.

They went inside and sat around a corner near the restrooms. The arch to the kitchen was behind them. Mitch placed Isabel facing away from the windows and sat across from her where he could keep an eye on the parking lot and entrance. A waitress came over and Mitch ordered them both a coke, steak, and fries. Quick and simple. Isabel found herself too weary to worry about the origins of the steak.

"There is a safe house near the southern end of

town. It's on a circle so any stranger is obvious.
Also, I can gain access from the street behind
through the neighbor's yard. I'm going to drive
down the road adjoining the circle. I can't go too
slow because that would be suspicious but I want
you to take note of anything either end of my circle
as we pass them. I'll squeeze your leg as we
approach the first entrance to the circle. Then we
will drive around and down the street with the
houses that back onto mine. If the house, four
houses down behind the safe-house, is clear, I will
pull into a garage and close the door. The people are
away on vacation. We can compare notes. If all
seems clear, I'll go through a few gardens and scout
the safe house from behind. Only after I'm sure
everything is OK will we go in. "Clear?" he asked.

"Sure," she said, nodding vigorously.

He went quiet as the cokes arrived. They drank
thirstily. The waitress would need to refill. Isabel
pointed at the toilet. Mitch nodded and she went in,
used the loo, washed her hands and face, and
checked her wig, She hardly recognized herself in
the long black wig.

When Isabel returned to the table she found her
steak and a new coke waiting. They both ate fast
and washed it down with more coke. The coke
tasted pretty good. She hadn't had one in so long she
had forgotten just how refreshing they could be.
She chose not to think about the chemicals she was
ingesting. Mitch got up before Isabel even had time
to wipe her mouth. He walked over to the cash
register, asked for the bill, paid, threw five dollars
on the table and pulled Isabel out after him as he put

on his backpack.

"Jeepers, talk about eat and run." she commented as she scrambled into hers. He hurried her over to the bike, started it and was pulling away as Isabel grabbed frantically for his waist.

They rode in silence for about ten minutes and Isabel felt him squeeze her leg. Ahead she could see a road to the right. She was about to look down the road as they passed it when she noticed a red glow in a dark van to her left. As the occupant sucked on the cigarette his face was faintly lit by the glow. Isabel buried her face in Mitch's pack and squeezed his sides as hard as she could. He showed no indication of noticing and kept going straight until he hit the main road.

"Hide!" he heard her scream as he slowed for the stop. Mitch turned right onto Route 9 and opened up the bike. He felt Isabel's fear and knew she had seen something that spooked her. He wasn't about to stop and find out what. When he was sure he wasn't being followed, he continued on Route 9 South and pulled in under some trees behind a motel near the interstate.

"You OK'?" he asked.

"No, did you see the man in the cable company van smoking a cigarette."

"Yes, that's why I kept on going. No need to panic."

"Oh yes there is. I recognized him."

"Rubbish, it was too dark."

"Don't talk to me that way. I know that man. I recognized him despite the dark. He works for Nikolai. He does jobs for Nikolai's security people.

I've seen him corning out of his office enough times. His name is Alexei Sergei Lashkov otherwise known as Sasha the Masher during the dinner table small talk. I have no proof he kills people but after meetings between Niki and Sasha, people have accidents that seem to benefit him. So don't tell me I don't know something when I do!"

"Sorry, I'm sorry. Damn, this is very bad news. All that checking was supposed to make you feel safe. No one should have known about that safe house. This is very, very, bad. Somehow your husband knows where we are going before we get there and that can only mean a mole. Damn, damn, damn. Thank God an entirely different division has the kids . My guys don't know anything about the kids. Damn. OK lets think, where to now? Son of a bitch! Sorry."

"Mitch, I know somewhere we can go for the night. Somewhere nobody would ever think of looking."

"Really, where?"

"'Saratoga. The season just ended but the horses stay until October. Some of Nikolai's horses are there, he would never think that we would have the guts to go there. Meantime you tell your guy that we are in Montreal. I have a very good old school friend who stays in the same old motel year after year. I haven't seen her in years because she lives in Louisville, but I know she's there. Just keep going south on Route 9 and then we can skirt around the center town. Actually you'll turn right at a Stewards and then another right onto Van Dam as the road makes a Y. Then just follow it as it changes to

Church all the way to the railroad track. At the railroad track, take a left and follow the tracks until I squeeze your leg. I'll show you a little dirt track that will take us into the motel from the corn fields."

"Lets go!" Mitch started the bike and they rode south for the next twenty minutes.

CHAPTER SIX

Saratoga, New York, Late Saturday Night

Mitch steered the bike slowly down the rutted road through a corn field. Isabel motioned for him to stop and turn off the bike:

"It's just about a hundred yards ahead on the left just across a road. Lets push the bike the rest of the way and hide it in the corn just across from the last cabin." He nodded and followed. They turned into a small grassy field and then followed a path through the long wet grass between more of the tall corn rows. When he saw the road up ahead, he stopped and they dismounted. Mitch pushed the bike into the corn until Isabel, in a stage whisper, told him she could no longer see the bike. They moved through the corn as close to the road as they could and then, with no one in sight, darted across the road into the tall reeds and bushes growing behind the row of tall trees that edged the back of property behind the cabins.

Mitch could see a neat row of cabins, with cream siding and dark green trim and narrow alleys between them. The parking area, visible between the cabins, was lit by one outdoor spotlight. Isabel explained that each cabin had a small porch in front.

"Cathy is usually in cabin forty-seven, the last one closest to West Avenue. We can check for her old Subaru Brat. Lets stay in the brush and go around the grass and into the bushes between the cabin and the street. That way the next cabin occupants wont wake up when we knock on the window and we get to stay out of the light. I'll tap on her window to get her attention so she can be ready to open the door and let us in. That way we don't have to go into the light until she has the door open."

Mitch nodded and followed Isabel through the brush behind the cabins. Small dogs started to bark in some of the cabins and a light went on. The dogs went quiet when a woman's voice told them to shut the fuck up. Two of them froze and sat quietly until the light went out. After that. Isabel and Mitch tried to move more quietly until they were under the window in the small gap between the bushes and the first cabin. There was a silver Subaru Brat parked in the closest parking spot to their left, so Isabel hoped that this confirmed that her friend was in her usual summer abode.

Isabel knocked quietly on the window. Nothing. Then a little harder. A dog growled. They heard,"shhh Dodger!" Isabel knocked again. The dog growled more fiercely,

"Cathy, Cathy," she called, again in a stage whisper.

"Who is it'?" came a voice from inside. They

could hear the strangled grumblings of a small dog whose mouth was being held closed.

"Cathy, it's Isabel, Isabel, your best bud from school." A face appeared at the window.

"Christ Isabel, do you know what time it is? Shit, do you know that Nikolai is going crazy. He tried to get you reported missing but based on the note you left with your friends in Vermont, they say you ran off. He is going nuts, threatening all kinds of crap. What are you doing here?"

"Shut up and let us in. Don't turn on the lights and be quick. I'll tell you inside." The face disappeared and they quickly moved through the light and onto the porch.

The door was opened by a thin, but very athletic looking blond, with piercing blue eyes and, huge dimples in her smiling face. They quickly slipped inside. The women embraced, hugging and dancing in a circle

"Wow. its been too long," Cathy said and she offered them a drink. Mitch and Isabel nodded and while Cathy opened the fridge and took out three Pepsi's. Isabel introduced Mitch.

"So, this is the man who is saving you from that pig of a husband." Cathy exclaimed. Mitch smiled as Isabel choked on a sip of soda.

"It's a long story and I can't explain tonight. I promise I will tell you everything as soon as I can; but in the mean time, it is very important that you don't let anyone know we are here. I'm sure Nikolai would kill us. We need somewhere to stay until we can find a ride to our next stop."

"Of course you can stay here." Cathy offered

immediately. "The landlord never comes in. He is sure Dodger will rip his throat out." Mitch looked at the tiny, writhing bundle of white curls. The small Maltese Terrier was still trying to get loose and protect Cathy from the strangers. Cathy saw his smile and explained. "I saved him from an abusive home and he is very, very aggressive toward men. He is likely to bite you and pee on your stuff before you leave. He always pees on anything belonging to men. We will have to store your back packs on top of that cabinet." she said pointing to a large, ugly, pale green chest of drawers that stood against the wall next to the bathroom.

"Why do you stay here?" asked Mitch as he looked around the small, studio like, space with the queen bed, harsh dark forest green carpet, sagging blinds, and cheap accessories.

"It's very reasonable for Saratoga if you book for five months and Dodger is welcome," she replied. "I have to be up in a couple of hours, so let's get some sleep and we'll talk when I get home around ten am. Issi and I will take the bed, you get the floor." She pulled the comforter off the bed and handed it to him.

Isabel woke as Cathy was getting ready for work. " Cathy, find out if any horse vans are leaving tonight or early tomorrow and where they are headed. Be very casual and discrete. Don't sound like you NEED the information. Just be interested." she directed her friend.

"OK, I'll be back as soon as I can legitimately blow the barn. I'll take Dodger so he does not eat Mitch. Later, gater!" and she was gone. Mitch got up off the floor, plopped himself on the bed and promptly fell back asleep. Isabel stared at him in disgust, wishing she could even remotely slow her brain down and fall asleep.

They awoke to the sound of the Brat pulling into the parking spot right across from the door. Cathy breezed in along with the smell of coffee and bacon.

"McMuffins and coffee, breakfast of kings," she announced after closing Dodger into the bathroom. While they all sat on the bed enjoying the food, Cathy told them that three Brook Ledge vans where due to ship horses out that night. One to Belmont, one Monmouth Park and one to Churchill Downs. The Belmont one is leaving at six pm, Monmouth departs around four am, and the one to Kentucky leaves this evening around ten, as soon as it is loaded." She stared at them as they chewed between sips of coffee until she could no longer hold it in. "So, tell me, what's going on?"

Mitch finished his sandwich, wiped his mouth, and shook his head. "Cathy, the less you know, the safer it is for you. I know we said we would tell you but I honestly think we should wait. From what I know of Nikolai, you must not let anyone know we were here or that you saw us otherwise you could be in grave danger. Don't look at me like that. Isabel will agree. She tells me he is not above killing you, after torturing you for information. Please, please take this very seriously and just pretend that we were never here. After it is over, we will tell you all about it. Absolutely every juicy detail. It is vital that you pretend to be impartial if Nikolai speaks to you, you can even empathize and voice your disappointment in Isabel's behavior. You will be much safer. You know you are saving Issi from a fate worth than death. Please be patient. OK?" Cathy looked over at Isabel who was nodding fiercely and she leaned over and gave her friend a very hard hug.

"Please Cat, listen to Mitch. I love you and I don't want you hurt. Cathy gave Isabel a reassuring smile.

"My lips are sealed. Now, which truck are you going to take, have you decided?" she asked. "and can I get you some supplies when I go out?"

"No, no, don't do that, don't do anything unusual. We are OK. We might raid your fridge before we leave though." He jumped up and headed for the bathroom. As he opened the door he was met with the sound and fury of a very angry little dog. He slammed it shut looking sheepish. "Sorry," he said, "We couldn't flush while you were gone." Isabel and Cathy laughed at his discomfort and Isabel got up to take care of the flushing.

Isabel and Mitch took turns taking a quick shower without turning the water off in between. Cathy made the bed and found a couple of packs of cards and they played rummy until lunch time. Isabel could see that Mitch was as anxious as she was to get moving again. Who knew where their pursuers were by now. Cathy got up to make sandwiches for lunch.

"Whoa, how many people are you planning to feed?" commented Mitch as he watched the pile grow, She made cheese, tomato, and onion, Ham and cheese, and peanut and jelly sandwiches and stacked them on a plate that she placed on the bed.

"What you don't finish, you take with you she said. Also take most of the fruit. I have apples, oranges and a couple of plums, oh, and some trail mix and as much Pepsi as you can carry."

"Wow. Thanks Cat," said Isabel between bites of her cheesy tomato sandwich.

"You don't happen to have any candy lying about, do you?" asked Isabel between chews.

" Crap, I nearly forgot, I know your love of the sweet stuff. She said as she opened her purse and tipped it over emptying a huge pile of chocolate bars onto the bed.

"Shit, I hope nobody saw you buy that lot, do you often buy candy?" asked Mitch.

"I'm sorry, I didn't realize the connection, I wasn't in super spy mode" Cathy replied with contrition.

"I didn't mean to snap, but we need to be really careful. It's unlikely anyone dangerous saw you but we had better leave a whole bunch of it here in full view and you can eat a some in public the next two days while you complain of PMS or something," he explained. Cathy nodded, looking pensive.

"Well guys, I have to go to the barn, so I must get ready." Cathy got up, collected her clothes and went into the bathroom.

As soon as she closed the door Mitch whispered, "We'll have to leave before she gets back. That will be safest for her. Can we get to the track without hitting the main roads?"

"Not really, I think we should take the bike back through the field and the woods, and back onto the railroad track. Then we can get onto Route 29 and follow that across behind the Oklahoma training area. There are a few woody lots on Fifth Avenue that border the back side of the training area. We can park the bike in the Elementary school parking, behind the school buildings, and then walk to one of the woody lots near the houses that back onto the stable area, and jump the fence. The houses along the barn area only have regular three and a half to four foot fences. Of course it all depends which truck you want to take as to where we park the bike. Personally I'd rather we didn't go to New York. I know Monmouth quite well, but Churchill would be best. Nikolai would never think of looking for me in Louisville AND, I have a crazy old aunt who lives there. She is absolutely NOT interested in horses and quite ignored by the family. Nobody would dream of me going there."

"Wow!" exclaimed Mitch. "You really are good at this kind of stuff. A few hours ago you wanted to kill me and now you're acting like an ally and super sleuth"

"Well, you have my kids, what the hell else can I do. I think that if I help you do whatever it is you need me to do, then perhaps I get them back sooner, rather than later. Also, it is quite a relief to know that they are safely away from Niki. I could never leave him because of them. Now, for the first time I have the opportunity, to get away from him and keep my kids. Of course, We might both land up dead, but, well, I resigned myself to that when you showed me the emails. I can never go back alive. Niki hates to be humiliated, NOBODY does it to him and survives unscathed."The bathroom door opened.

"I see you love birds whispering," said Cathy, "I am so glad you're getting Isabel away from that creep, I sure hope you let her friends come over. Well, I must be off. See you at six-thirtyish. Ooooh, I nearly forgot, I have news, Nikolai is due in town tomorrow." Isabel gasped in horror. "Don't worry," Cathy said, "He is just coming to see his colt that won the Hopeful last week. His filly made quite a stir when it won the week before. He made such a fuss about his other colts not getting to run, but quite honestly, they haven't shown much yet. You'd swear it was vital for all of them to compete against each other." She saw the horrified look on Isabel's face. "What, holy crap, what'?" she asked. Mitch too, was looking extremely concerned. Isabel was as white as a sheet and looked quite ill. Cathy grabbed her, "What is going on Issi?"

"Oh, um nothing," she answered distractedly, "I'm just worried about Nikolai, Cathy promise you won't ask him why he wanted them to run together so badly. Just believe me when I say something bad is going on and you don't want to make Nik jumpy. He is up to something with those colts, and I can't tell you about it just yet because I can get in some serious trouble. Please promise you wont question him. He will know right away that I have said too much and many people could get hurt." Isabel stood still, staring at the floor and wringing her hands. Cathy hugged her.

"Sweetie, you are my very best friend in the whole world. There is nothing I wont do for you.

You know that. That idiot husband of yours has kept you away from me and gotten you mixed up in some bad shit, obviously, and I am here to help you find your way out of it. You can count on me. OK. I just don't want to be the last to hear about the big scandal so be sure to give a gal a heads up before then.'" Isabel looked relieved, she hugged her friend hard as she could and said that she would do just that. Cathy grabbed Dodger and headed out to the barn. "Later Issi ,"she whispered , blowing a kiss as she pulled the door closed behind her.

Mitch looked at Isabel with interest. Nikolai Lebedev's trainer. Daniel John Georgio, the revered, seventy-four year old, hall of fame trainer, winner of numerous classics had died recently in a stable accident. Apparently he was killed by a horse in its stall. Back at 'ranch' they had briefly speculated about Nikolai Lebedev's involvement but could not find any logical connection and figured it was just coincidence that Georgio trained for Lebedev. Now he was wondering otherwise. The Lebedev horses had stayed on with Georgio's assistant Alistair Brown who had taken over training all the horses that had not been moved to new trainers. Isabel just shook her head when he looked at her quizzically.

"Sorry. anything I say could be bad for your health," she said with a grimace.

"So you keep telling me. One of these days you will realize that I am dead anyway so you may as well tell me all the juicy stuff. It might make my painful death more bearable," he countered with a big smile.

"Don't joke. This is not funny. I just wish you

had a teeny, tiny inkling of how dangerous Niki is."

"Well perhaps you will get around to enlightening me sometime." came his quick retort

Isabel looked at her watch and switched the TV channel to CBS. She sat and watched reruns of Days of our Lives.

"I can't believe you watch that crap," said Mitch.

"Shhh" He sat and watched her. At three she changed channel again and sat through Dr. Phil. He remained quiet even when she started watching Ellen DeGeneres. He was amused. She was trying to irritate him into commenting again on her choices. He played her game and watched quietly. Halfway through Ellen, she snapped. "SO? What, when, where. how, etc'" Mitch smiled.

"We need to leave here before Cathy gets back so we'll need to get moving in the next few minutes. I'm going to fire up my computer and send an email to my group telling them we're in Canada. Then we're going to try find a safe time to sneak out of here. I want you to sit near the front window and keep tabs on anyone you can see. We need to duck out when you think the coast is clear."

Isabel sat near the window, she didn't touch the blinds but tried to peer out around the edges. Luckily the blinds were as old as the carpet and sagged just enough to leave good gaps for peeping Toms. She could hear him tapping on the keyboard behind her. She saw no cars near the cabins. Maybe everyone worked at the track. Nothing moved outside. After about thirty minutes, the back door of the main house opened.

A man came out, followed by two skinny

teenage girls. The girls were pushing each other and smiling. The man disappeared into the garage and a dark green Ford Torus backed out. The playful girls jumped into the car and it moved away down the drive.

CHAPTER SEVEN

Saratoga, New York, Sunday

"Time to go!" She jumped up, pulled her wig on, grabbed her backpack heavy with the sandwiches, candy, soda, and fruit and moved to the door. Mitch joined her, hastily replacing the laptop in his pack. He had a wash cloth in his hand and wiped the doorknob as he closed the door behind them. They moved with feigned carelessness to the end of the cabins and then hurried to cross the road and blend into the corn near the motor bike. "I hope nobody notices that Cathy's door is unlocked; I feel bad we couldn't even leave a note. What were you doing back there? she asked.

"I wiped down the cabin so our prints weren't left behind. Just being careful'. I did my best to disable the GPS on my computer as soon as I fired up, and I logged on using IPVanish, my TOR software, and my email account on a French server. That way they don't trace this IP address. Even if they somehow do, they wouldn't know exactly who logged on because none of the computers here will match but we can't be too careful. No more using the satellite link up." "IPVanish?" she queried, "and a satellite dish, who the hell are you? What is IPVanish and TOR?"

"TOR is software that keeps you anonymous by encrypting everything you send, and a VPN or Virtual Private Network, ensures your privacy. You use them to make yourself anonymous online. If you use a VPN, it kinda links to other secure networks in series, and makes it very, very hard to track the original Internet connection. Very handy when you are watching for example the Olympics and NBC has the US blacked out. You log on with IPVanish, the Olympic site sees you as European and you get to watch what you want to watch and not the crap NBC thinks you should be watching, another one used a lot is a service called Tunnel Bear. Cool huh."

"What about the satellite link?"

"Not important except that if I use it now they will find us in a heartbeat thanks to our little mole. I warned the guys in Europe with your kids that they must not communicate with the US group until we figure out who it is. Let's get going, we'll talk later." said Mitch. They pushed the bike through the tall corn to the dirt track and down the track for a few hundred yards. "OK, hop on and lets get out of here." Isabel hopped on behind him and gripping his pack. She used leg squeezing and pointing to get him onto route 29 and then down through the residential area to the elementary school a couple of blocks north of the Oklahoma Track training complex of Saratoga Racetrack. They parked the bike on the school premises out of site of the road;

and then walked like casual hikers down the street to Fifth Avenue. On Fifth they went east and ducked onto an empty lot, creeping deep into the thick undergrowth of the small wooded area. Mitch pointed to the ground and they both sat down and waited for the sun to set.

"The mosquitoes are going to chew us up." Isabel said.

Mitch nodded, and said, "From now on no phones, and only Tunnel Bear or IPVanish whenever we can access someone's open WIFI. Keep the wig on until we can sort something else out. Why don't you tell me about some of the stuff your husband and Fish got up to and how come Fish doesn't train the horses Cathy was talking about?"

"All I can tell you about the ex Georgio, now Brown, trained horses is that Niki wanted the most famous trainer in the country to train the five horses in his experiment. And no. I can't tell you about the experiment. As for Fish, well. where do I start? Fish is dishonest and unethical just like Nik. He is willing to do anything to make money. His horses never win at short prices. His horses run 'no good' until the odds drift and the conditions are favorable.

Oh, don't look at me like that. No good means they are not trying to win and conditions are the eligibility requirements like age, sex, number of wins, and amount of money they have already won, etcetera. You know, like age and weight divisions in the wrestling you told Cathy about over cards."

Isabel continued to explain the divisions of horse racing to Mitch. "For example, all horses start as maidens. A maiden has never won a race. Now, he can either run in a maiden special weight against other potentially good horses or he can run in a maiden claiming race for a tag.

A tag is the price at which you are willing to sell the horse. Maiden claiming can start at one hundred thousand dollars at Saratoga and other major race tracks and go all the way down to claiming two thousand dollars or even less at cheaper tracks and fair grounds. You can run your horse against other horses of similar value. This makes it easier to win a race since the cheaper the claiming price, the slower the horses. Unfortunately, all horses in a claiming race are for sale and can be claimed out of the race. That is the risk you take if you run in a claiming race." Isabel stopped to take a few deep breaths and look around.

Her eyes returned to Mitch and she went on, "Now, when they win a maiden, they can run in allowance races. These races have conditions, that means that they have entry criteria. You can run in non winners of a race other than a maiden or claiming race. So basically the maiden race and most claiming races don't count against your conditions. `Then non winners of two other than, then three other than, etc. Sometimes they are written as non winners of three other than or non winners of four life time.

When they write the lifetime thing it can put a spanner in the works if your horse has won a few claiming races. Anyway the tracks offer tons of claiming races, maiden races, and races for non winners of one or two. After that it gets harder and harder to find races for your horse. Non winners of three other than, are tough; and non winners of four other than, are rarer than hens teeth. If you have a four time winner who isn't quite good enough for stake races it can be almost impossible to find him a race. Then you have to take a chance and run him in claiming races. At the higher claiming levels, unless he is very well bred, chances are no one will claim him.

Then for the cheaper claimers they offer such races as starter allowances and handicaps. These are non claiming races for horses that have previously run for a specific claiming amount in the past. There are also optional claiming races where some of the horses are up for grabs.

Then there are listed races and overnight handicaps witch are like mini stake races and at the very top are the stakes races like the Kentucky Derby. I'm sure even you have heard about that race. Those come in a variety of grades depending on the class of horse they wish to attract. Its been a while since I was on the track and I never was interested in the racing, just the riding, so I may have screwed that up a bit"

Isabel stopped for another breather, and to look around again. She could hear voices off in the distance but they never seemed to be getting any closer so she continued her explanation.

"Fish would run a horse no good for a few races and then win for a long price. They have a ton of ways of making a horse run poorly. In the old days the trainers would withhold water for a day or two and then give the horse water just before it went over to run. They would also train them hard on race day. Fish trains them on race day and doesn't give them water. Then he gives them oral electrolytes, this makes them thirsty so when they are offered water they drink the whole bucket or more. They'd have to be super horse to win after that: He can get a horse to have pretty bad form before they prep him correctly for a run in a race against inferior horses. Unless the horse stumbles out of the starting gate he has a pretty good shot of winning. Niki doesn't mind if they don't all win when they are supposed to, that would be expecting too much. As long as the win rate is better than fifty percent when he goes for the punt, he is making excellent money at the long odds."

"How do you prove that this happens?" Mitch asked.

"You can't really, can you? That's the beauty of the scam."

"Interesting, so do they pull scams you can prove?" Isabel looked pensive.

"I suppose they do if you put in the effort because they also pull insurance scams. Nikolai would claim a horse that had deliberately been entered above the horses' value, then insure the horse for the claimed price. Fish would break the horse down and Niki would collect the insurance. In reality, the horse had already been negotiated for at a lower price from the previous owner who is happy to go along since he is getting a better return on his useless horse than he realistically would have. Nik would get the claim money back and split the insurance with the previous owner. He finds no shortage of willing sellers for that scam."

She paused, "Nikolai also breeds horses which Fish gets his owners to buy for ridiculous prices. This way he can launder money he has from some of his other businesses. The buyers don't actually pay much more than the stud fee. That's the amount he paid for the stallion to breed the mare that produced the horse they sold.

Again it's a win win situation for Nikolai and the buyers. The buyers pay Nikolai, who in turn gives them most of it back as cash. The buyers get to hide some cash from the IRS, they can write off some of the purchase price if they have a breeding concern, and Nikolai gets 'legal' money in his account." Isabel stopped. Mitch was ecstatic. Here she was calmly discussing the stuff he hadn't even known he wanted.

"Wow are all of his criminal activities related to horses. I thought he was an attorney, with a large stock portfolio and some business interests," he said, feigning ignorance. Isabel started to laugh so hard that Mitch put his hand over her mouth.

"Shhh!"

"Well don't you have a lot to learn. What now?" she asked looking at her watch. "The truck to Louisville will only leave around nine so we can try take a nap until dark."

"I'll set my watch to wake us at eight." Mitch set his watch and lay back on his pack. Isabel looked at him. She figured he'd fall asleep instantly. She briefly considered running away but she knew she wouldn't. Somehow she would have to see this through. In some strange perverted way God had answered her prayers. She remembered the country western song.. Be Careful What You Wish For. Boy, did it have meaning now. She lay back against him and closed her eyes. She listened to his heart beat and snuggled closer when his arm closed around her.

CHAPTER EIGHT

In plain sight

Isabel awoke finding herself handcuffed to a branch. She swore and felt her stomach twist in knots of fear. What if he wasn't coming back? What if he was caught? Where the hell was he any way? She concentrated on slowing her breathing and trying to relax. Stupid, she could just break the branch she thought. He probably went to check out the surroundings.

She wondered how much he already knew about Nik. Quite a lot she supposed. He was way too relaxed about things pertaining to her husband, this could only mean he didn't know him at all, or knew a lot more than he was letting on. She suspected it was the latter. The bushes rustled nearby and she heard approaching footsteps. Mitch appeared through the trees. He bent down and uncuffed her before she could say a word. "I've been looking around the barn area. There are so many people everywhere. Groups having barbecues, people watering horses, security personnel walking around. How are we going to get on the truck unseen'?" he asked."We wont be unseen," she answered. " We will have to pretend to be part of the group that is leaving. If we help load the equipment, the grooms will think we are with the trucking company and the drivers will think we are grooms."

"Jesus. that's one hell of a risk. What if someone asks us who we are?" he queried.

"They never do. If we speak Spanish in front of the drivers they wont ask us anything, and in the truck we just ignore the grooms and they'll ignore us."

"I hope you're right, he muttered darkly.

"They will load the equipment first. We just step up and start loading the grooms beds, refrigerators, etc. We could take that opportunity to create a space for ourselves up at the front with the equipment. We store our things in there and while others go for more stuff, climb into our space and close up the gap. They'll continue to fill up all the way to the door and close us in. Once we are moving, that front section wont be opened again until we get to Churchill Downs. The grooms will ride with the horses. If all goes well, nobody will even know we are on board. They'll all presume we left when the equipment was stored."

"OK, I guess you've thought this through pretty thoroughly," he agreed. " I just hope your friend doesn't stay for the packing up.

" She wont. It is not her barn and anyway she worked all afternoon, she'll be home by now."

Isabel sat quietly for a short time and then suddenly jumped up. "I think we better go and hide closer to the truck ramp so we can enter the fray at the least suspicious time. I wasn't thinking when I said leave at nine because we have to help pack. We better hurry. We might have to leave the packs near the fence and then collect them with a barrow. No one will ask what we are doing with all the packing happening"

"Where should we hide?"

" In the first stall in Pete Zamboni's overflow barn a few feet away from where the Churchill truck is scheduled to stop. We can climb over the fence of the house closest to the back of his barn, walk over into the shadow of his barn and sneak around into the stall as soon as it is safe. You will need to crawl in under the webbing. Try not to spook the horse in the stall. I'll go first" Mitch led the way out of the woods and they wandered arm in arm along the street, like hikers in no hurry to be anywhere special.

At a suitable house, Isabel nudged him, and they turned and walked up the drive. The house was in darkness, either the occupants were asleep or away. It was far more likely they had already left for the season and the house was empty. "Probably the summer home of an owner," she commented.

Mitch prayed that no nosy neighbor would call the cops. They melted into the hedge along the drive and moved toward the back fence. With their backs against the garden shed they watched for movement in the stable area. A groom walked along the backside of the well lit Georgio-Brown barn. They could only see his legs below the awning except when he came into full view in the gaps. He looked into each stall and turned the corner at the end.

Mitch pulled on Isabel's arm and vaulted over the fence. Isabel passed him her pack and then followed. They ducked into the hedge opposite the Zamboni barn.

"OK, let's just stroll over to that barn, may as well bring the packs," she pointed." and if there is already gear being piled on the ramp we add our packs otherwise they come into the stall with us.

"Right, then just tell me when you decide its a good time for us to join the work force. Are you sure they won't recognize you?" Mitch asked. Isabel nodded.

"That's why I used so much of Cathy's makeup. Lots of tan base, heavy eyeliner and mascara along with the black wig and soon to be added dirt and I am just another tranny Mexican hot-walker." Mitch looked confused, so she explained. "The race track is a favorite work place for Mexican, and Guatemalan, gays and transvestites. In the morning they all stick to their birth gender until the work is done and then they change into their favored persona. The makeup is outrageous, as are the heels and mini dresses. It is such a normal part of life on the backstretch even the hard core redneck trainers and riders don't notice any more."

She walked off across the grass with him in pursuit. Isabel was glad it was such a dreary night with lots of cloud cover and no sign of the moon yet. She led Mitch to the corner of the barn and peeped around the edge. She could see people out in the grassy area across the road, grouped around a picnic table under a spot light playing cards or dice or something. There was evidence of drinking, and she reckoned a post win party was well under way. Zamboni must have had a winner at Belmont today. She got down on her hands and knees and crawled around the corner and in under the webbing of the first stall only to find it empty. Handy she thought and motioned for Mitch to join her.

The plan worked a charm, once the grooms from the departing barn started stacking their gear, the two waited until the huge white truck and trailer with Brook Ledge emblazoned in big blue letters pulled up, and then just joined the fray. They positioned themselves up front and took charge of the packing.

Very soon they were squirreled away in a cave of bed-frames and mattresses. They settled in listening to the hustle and bustle of the packing and then the loading of the horses. They even had a water bucket to use as a toilet although Isabel was hoping that once on the road she may just be able to get her bum over the partition and pee behind a horse. She had no intention of peeing in a bucket in front of this man. She'd have to see.

Eventually, they heard the big doors being secured and the rig rumbling to life. Soon they were swaying across the bumpy dirt road out of the Oklahoma complex and out onto the main road. In less than ten minutes and they were humming south toward Albany.

Isabel tapped Mitch.

"What?" he queried.

"Are you sure Demmy and Yuri are OK."

"Yes, we were very careful. They were safely on

a plane out of the country within two hours of being taken from the park."

"What happened to their bodyguard and nanny?"

"They all had ice-cream from the vendor and were asleep in minutes. It was easy really. We left him lying in the park and took her so that the kids would stay calm."

"Isabel sat up grabbing his shirt and shaking. "She is still with them?"

"Yes, why not, seemed like a good idea"

"Oh Jesus, she's been sleeping with Nikolai for months. She will try and contact him and then he will know that I don't have them. I don't know what I will do if he gets them back. I'll never see them again."

"Would have been handy to know a little sooner but we actually suspected it based on some surveillance footage. So we are erring on the side of caution and she thinks that she is hiding the children from you for him. The trick is to prevent contact, and we are doing our best. Try not to worry, even if she does contact him and find out it is a lie, we should be able to neutralize the threat."

"What do you mean, neutralize?" Isabel demanded.

"We cannot allow a foreign national to kidnap American children on vacation, now can we. Efforts to take your children are authorized to be met with extreme prejudice. Yes it is dicey, but try and have faith. You know she won't hurt them."

"I suppose you are right. She will do everything in her power to protect them."

They lay quietly, absorbed in their thoughts.

Isabel figured Mitch would fall asleep and be out
for hours while she imagined Riana contacting
Nikolai and spiriting her children away in the dead
of night. She didn't think there would be much sleep
for her. She was startled when he spoke.

"What did Nikolai do in Russia before he
immigrated? He is a lot older than you."

"Nikolai was thirty-five when we married. He
trained as a medical doctor in Vladivostok and was
a fertility specialist. When he came here, he found
he would have to go through residency and
fellowship training so at least five or six years of
grind, or he could do two years of law school. He
chose that instead. Learned all about how to screw
the system. He had only been practicing two years
when we met but already he was rich and had
horses so I suspect he had other means of making
money. Actually, now I know he had other means."

"Such as?"

"I've told you too much already."

"What? A little gambling, some money
laundering, that doesn't sound like the terribly
dangerous psychopath you keep telling me he is.
Tell me why you think this Sasha person is a
killer?" Isabel hedged, not yet ready to tell all.

"I have no real proof. I suppose it might be my
over active imagination but a few times over the last
twelve years people have conveniently disappeared
just when it seemed they would cause my husband
trouble with a case, or a deal. I just think it is
strange that Alexei Lashkov is the common
denominator." Yes, thought Mitch. That's what good
ol' Uncle Sam thinks too and that is exactly why we

are here.

Mitch tallied his gains, they now knew how Lebedev was money laundering, and that some of the money came from insurance fraud and gambling, and he had the confirmation of witness tampering, and possibly murder, definitely Daniel John Georgio's death was starting to look less and less like an accident. Then, there was this bio-tech company big into genetics, with Lebedev a fertility specialist, and some horse experiment that just had to be connected.

This was getting seriously interesting. He supposed that he could read more of Isabel's psych file but he didn't see the point anymore. She deserved her privacy and he was pretty sure he could accomplish his goal without that creepy tale of abuse. Mitch drifted off to sleep after taking her hand in his and giving her a reassuring squeeze.

Isabel lay thinking about her two little boys, Demmy and Yuri. Demmy was eleven and was a dark haired, dark eyed child, who people often commented looked exactly like a blended version of Nikolai and herself. Although he had many of his father's looks, and mannerisms for that matter, he was definitely his mother's child. He was a strong, but sensitive kid who really loved animals. He was not doing too well in school because he tended to be hyperactive, noisy and somewhat confrontational and defiant with his teachers. Dr. Green thought this was because of his father's bullying persona and its influence on the boy.

Yuri, well Yuri was a different kettle of fish, Isabel was not exactly sure how she produced this shy, quiet, book worm. At eight, he was already a grade ahead at school. He was never any trouble to anyone, and spent every waking hour reading or drawing his 'inventions' into a notebook that no one ever got to see. He also had yellow eyes and bright copper colored hair. Nikolai had actually insisted on a paternity test. Asshole.

She recalled stories told by her grandmother of her great-grandfather with the same coloring and figured that's where the odd genes came from. She wished she could be with them, even if just one more time. She wanted to see those faces and hug there warm little bodies.

Her phone popped into her head. The photos on her phone. She could look at them safely enough. It is not like she was going to make a call that could be traced. She would put the phone in airplane mode, that should make it safe. Now just to get the phone out of Mitch's pack. She knew it was zipped into the mesh pocket on the inside of the front compartment of the pack.

It was dark and very difficult to see. She gently felt along his pack and over the top, his head was lying on the pack that was placed horizontally at the top of the mattress. His head actually touched the lower edge of the pocket she needed to open. As slowly and gently as she could, she reached over Mitch and worked the zipper up the far side. As soon as she had an opening big enough for her hand, she slipped it in and felt for the mesh pocket. Damn the zipper was closed and the pull tab was right up against his head. She took the tip between two fingers and wiggled as gently as she could.

Millimeter by millimeter the zipper moved towards her. She worked until it was all the way across and then slowly delved into the pocket to find her phone. She grasped the phone between two fingers and drew it out. Damn, wrong phone. Back again for the second attempt. Luck was on her side and she tucked her iPhone under her shirt and turned it on. She scrolled through options looking for airplane mode and turned it on. At last she could look at the photos. She was paging through her collection when she heard Mitch curse. He grabbed the phone and pulled it apart, releasing the battery.

"What the hell are you up to. Are you out of your mind. What did I say about the damn phones?"

"I put it in airplane mode so that I could look at photos of my children. I didn't make a call, I promise," she stammered.

"That doesn't matter, you have the new iPhone, it logged your location as soon as it had a signal which is long before it finished loading your user interface. We are still relatively close to civilization so you probably had pretty good service. Oh well, I wonder how soon before we have someone on our tail. Your husband will realize we are traveling and correctly assume west. I'll have to start looking for a tail in about an hour. It wont take a rocket scientist to figure out we may be on this truck. No way of knowing how they will get on board. Either force a stop or wait for one."

Isabel was already cold with fear. "This company usually stops to water the horses just south of the New York - Pennsylvania state line. Nikolai will establish that with one call. Maybe he'll do it there.

Its near Erie. I'm so, so sorry. I didn't think of the Track my Phone ability. God I am stupid."

"Well there is nothing we can do until then. Now I just have to think." He put both phones back in his pack and took out his laptop and a cord. He had turned off the WIFI so that it did not automatically search for a connection. The screen lit up their little cave and Isabel looked at the cord. It had a USB connection of one end and a thickened opposite end with what looked like a lens.

"What's that?" she asked.

"That, my friend, is a camera. See how the cord is flexible but a little stiff, well it has an inner spiral lining and if you twist it clockwise it becomes stiffer, counter clockwise less so, so I can shape it. I am going to feed it out of the vent so I can watch the traffic. Good thing I have an extra battery and a quick charge backup because I may be staring at this for hours."

Mitch though about how to best handle the situation. Too many people could get hurt if the Lebedev henchmen entered the trailer, not to mention the chaos that could ensue if the horses were spooked. He figured he would need to get the hell out of the horse-van as soon as it stopped and engage any attackers away from the horses. He supposed he would also have to incapacitate their pursuers in such a way as to confuse them regarding where he and Isabel would go next. He would also have to make this happen in a hurry because he really wanted to be back on the horse-van before it continued..

Mitch scrambled out of the hidey-hole, after the

significant effort of getting some obstacles out of the way. He climbed over the piles of equipment to reach the sliding window that faced toward the center of the road. Mitch attached the camera to one of the cross bars and slid the window as closed as it could go. He fed the cord down the between the wall and the equipment and told Isabel to try and catch the end. As soon as she had hold of it he made his way back to the 'cave' and plugged the camera into the computer. Mitch wanted to make sure he could get a good view of vehicles approaching from behind.

Mitch looked at his watch, it was just after one-thirty and an hour since they may have been located. Probably about another three hours before the stop near Erie. He opened a Word file and made note of all vehicles passing both east and westbound. He asked Isabel for a sandwich and they ate in silence as he kept a sharp eye on the screen. He heard a can tab pop, and felt it being pushed into his empty hand as soon as he placed the last bite of his sandwich in his mouth. He drank thirstily. After downing the Pepsi, he realized that maybe he shouldn't have been so keen to drink. Soon he would need to pee and he didn't dare miss a passing vehicle.

At two-fifteen in the morning he was pretty sure they were being followed. About ten minutes before, a blue BMW had approached from behind and passed, keeping pace alongside for slightly longer than it should have, before speeding off. Several minutes later the same car went by going east before doing a U-turn in the distance and then settling in behind them. It was about an eighth of a mile or more back but he was pretty sure it was the same vehicle. The lights tracked them for mile after mile. After about half an hour, the car passed them again, this time racing by.

"I think we have been followed for the last half hour and that whoever is following us has established that this van is due for a truck stop. I think that they are off to wait for us in Erie. That, and the fact that, if it was me I'd still want to keep going to see if I pass anything else that could contain my target," he informed Isabel.

"We should be near the state line around four to four-thirty am. I think they will most probably strike at the truck stop, but they could stop the truck anywhere now that they are ahead. I am going to be ready to bail out of that small half door above the loading ramp doors, it's a damn good thing they left those upper doors open for ventilation. There obviously isn't any rain in the forecast. I'll have to decide which side I'm going to jump out of at the last minute, once I assess the surrounding. Then I'll go looking for the blue BMW with heavily tinted windows. I have the tag.

You will stay in here and keep going to Kentucky no matter what happens, even if I don't come back before the van gets moving again. Nikolai will be looking for his guys and I will try lead them away. I will catch up, I promise. Try to pile as much junk inside this hollow so you are well hidden, I'll toss some stuff in as I leave."

He dug deep into his pack and removed two small cheap phones. He handed her one.

"Turn it on." They each turned on a pre-paid cell phone and Mitch put them both on vibrate. He then called each phone to locate the specific number and put it on speed dial. "There," he said. I will call you and keep in touch. Don't call me unless you get into trouble. The phone is small enough to fit up your vagina in an emergency, so don't be too prudish to stick it up there if you get caught." Isabel had a strange look on her face and it made him laugh. "You can close your mouth," he said with a grin.

He continued to monitor the camera feed but didn't see any further suspicious activity. He hoped against hope that the van would not be stopped before reaching the big truck stop.

"Please don't use the phone unless you have to, I don't know if they are compromised thanks to the mole. I've been thinking, the mole is not directly in my team or he would have told your husband about the plan. No, this is someone in the organization who was asked to find out what is going on. Could be any computer geek in the place. By now my team is secretly running a tracer to see who accessed files and info they had no reason to be accessing."

Isabel touched Mitch's arm.

" Mitch, please be careful, it is quite likely Sasha is the one following us and he will kill you. I know I said before that I just suspect, he kills people, but that is not true. I know he does. There is one incident that I really am convinced he is involved with. We had a lab tech who was a grad student working for us part time. A very bright kid with a future, one day I found him looking at experiments that had nothing to do with his work, some days later I overheard the head of lab security telling Nikolai that the tracer software showed him looking at data related to the experiments. It wouldn't take a rocket scientist to figure out what we were doing. Next thing I know, we're going to dive some wreck, or other, in Lake Champlain and the guy drowned. Sasha tried 'saving' him and performed CPR. But I was pretty convinced that what I had witnessed in that murky water was Dave fighting for his life but I had no proof. The ME declared it an accidental drowning." Mitch just nodded and gave her the thumbs up.

They traveled in silence, the apprehension growing. It was becoming apparent that they were getting really close to Erie when they passed the state line. Mitch closed the computer and placed in in his pack. He told Isabel to move back as far as she could. He climbed out of their enclave and started shoving items into the gap.

Isabel took the opportunity to urinate in the bucket and then get comfortable in what little space remained. She was glad the bucket was the first thing he tossed back in.

Mitch made the opening appear well and truly packed tight. He wanted anyone searching not to bother with the obviously well packed front end. He placed a bunch of horse blankets on the chests that were facing towards the door, to make it look like somebody had been there but was now gone. He tossed some of their empty soda cans nearby and left papers lying scattered about. He hoped that anyone looking in the open window above the door, or the opposite one he might be jumping out of, would think that they had bolted. He pulled the camera loose and stuffed it down telling Isabel to pull it in. "It's time," he told her as the truck left the highway via the off-ramp to the truck-stop.

CHAPTER NINE

Erie, Pennsylvania, Monday

They pulled into a large parking area and Mitch immediately was scanning for the BMW. There was another big rig parked close to the left side so he opened the screen that spanned the gap and bailed out rolling in under the adjacent truck just as the driver climbed down and walked away around the front. He heard the doors on the other side opening and lots of noise as the grooms disembarked and started toting buckets over to the nearby faucet. He crawled through under a few trucks being careful to look around for anyone who might see him.

Mitch made sure to look up at mirrors to avoid drivers who might happen to look back and spot him. A few trucks over, he quickly stood up alongside a door and walked from the truck toward the McDonald as if he was a driver going for a meal. He went inside, and patted his pockets as if looking for his wallet, made a disgusted sound and walked back out. Outside he moved off toward the dumpster and out of the light. He blended into the shadows of the dumpster and scanned the parking area.

The blue BMW was parked in the front row of car slots nearest the exit for a quick getaway. He could see a man who quite easily could be the person in his photo file named Alexei Lashkov, and described by Isabel as Sasha the Masher. He looked around to see if he could find an accomplice or two but the man appeared to be working alone. He watched Lashkov approach the truck, talk to the driver and the two move toward the trailer. They peered in the open doors and then walked forward to open the front.

Mitch quickly texted Isabel to remain very quiet no matter what happened. He saw the man jump up to the deck of the trailer and peer over the equipment. He obviously saw the crumpled bedding and window open on the other side. He bent down and surveyed beneath the trailer. He ran around the front of the truck scanning the area and then did the same at the other end. Lashkov walked around the rig and then returned and climbed in to take a closer look. Mitch held his breath.

While Lashkov was in the horse van, Mitch quickly made his way to the BMW. Lashkov would bring Isabel back to the car if he found her and he would certainly return if he didn't. He knew he would not have time to put a gun to his head and chat. He would have to slug him hard, lock him in the trunk and move the car. He figured he had perhaps another twenty to thirty minutes, while the grooms got food after watering the horses, before the van would depart. He walked up to the battered yellow Honda parked next to the driver's door of the BMW and put his hand through the partially open window to unlock the door. He sat down leaving the door slightly ajar after turning off the overhead light and peered over toward the van. Mitch could not see the van from the car but he knew this was his best bet. The only downside would be showing his face to the enemy.

Mitch saw the man hurrying back toward the BMW. Lashkov arrived, one hand holding the phone up to his ear, the other holding the keys and electronic car opener that he was aiming and pressing as he approached. Rapid fire Russian spewed forth as the car beeped and the lights blinked. Lashkov gave the man getting out of the yellow car, and yelling for his honey to hurry the fuck up, a disgusted look and turned to open the BMW's door.

Mitch brought the forty caliber Glock down hard. He realized he might kill the man but he really wanted only one blow. Alexei Lashkov crumpled and was caught and dragged toward the trunk. Mitch popped the trunk and bundled the big man in as best he could. He did not bother to check for breathing. He closed and locked the trunk, wiped the inner and outer handles of the Honda with his shirt and picked up the phone, disconnected the call and turned the ringer volume off before jumping into the BMW. If anyone had seen the quick action that just went down there was no indication.

Mitch drove out of the Truck-stop, took the small

road diagonally opposite the exit, and within a couple hundred yards swerved off the road and gunned the car into the thick undergrowth under the trees. He jumped out after wiping away any potential fingerprints. Mitch locked the car, wiped the handle and walked back through the undergrowth attempting to pull the flattened bushes upright as he walked through. He looked back from the street and could not see the car.

Mitch jogged back toward the van. Once he was in sight of the truck-stop he walked casually back through the parked cars. He passed a state trooper's vehicle parked near the convenience store and with a quick glance around, took Lashkov's phone and tossed it through the partially open window and onto the floor behind the passenger seat.

He approached the big white and blue horse-van. The nearside door was once again closed and now the upper doors were also latched. He quickly went around to the less conspicuous side of the van and unlatched one of the small upper doors and swung it open. He called Isabel and told her to do her best to get the hell out of her prison and open the screen.

He could hear them shutting up on the other side. He quickly climbed up the side of the trailer and pulled himself on top of the roof. The driver appeared and climbed up into the cab. Mitch was peeping over the edge just waiting for the little screen to move. He saw it budge and looked toward the driver. If the driver glanced back he could be spotted.

Isabel pulled the screen open inside the truck. Mitch waited until the truck started moving so that the driver would be focused forward, then he dropped his legs over the edge and in through the window, He felt Isabel grab his legs and he let go of the roof and slid in on top of her. She wiggled her way out and jumped on him giving him a hug he really didn't feel he deserved but he hugged back anyway.

Relieved that they had, once again, miraculously escaped the clutches of Nikolai Lebedev. Mitch worked on closing the upper door before the truck was even out of the truck-stop. He secured the screen, and tied the door to the screen so it would not flap. He moved back to their refuge and went to task clearing their space for the next leg of their journey.

Once the area was a comfortable size, Mitch re-installed the camera and settled in for the long haul. He got Isabel up to speed on the events that had occurred and explained that, although it was likely that it would be presumed that they were no longer en-route to Louisville, they had to take all precautions to prevent being found. Mitch was not sure if it was the iPhone that had alerted Lebedev.

He explained to Isabel that he was starting to suspect a tracking device in her pack. He had her change into clean clothes but first he inspected each item carefully for any signs of tampering. She could keep nothing with heavy seams, just one sweater, some extra underwear, and a bra with no metal, all rolled up in one extra shirt . These, of course, in addition to the clothes she had changed into after they, too, had been carefully scrutinized.

Mitch placed all of Isabel's remaining clothes,

gear, and her iPhone, into the pack and squeezed it out through the bars of the sliding window where it was whipped away by the wind. He hoped it would be run over a good many times before daylight. He felt bad for her. "Don't worry," he said. "Your photos are safe in the Cloud." He asked her if she minded monitoring the camera for a couple of hours so he could sleep while the threat risk was low and to wake him if she needed to. Mitch rolled onto his side, face away from the glow and promptly fell asleep.

Isabel left him to sleep. Around seven am the traffic started getting too heavy for her to cope with monitoring the camera alone, so she shook Mitch's shoulder. He snapped awake,

"What's wrong?" he asked breathlessly, and she explained. He sat up and stared at the traffic flying by as he reached for one of the last two sandwiches and bit into it. Isabel grabbed the bag of candy bars, she sifted through and chose a Twix and an Almond Joy.

"You have the last sandwich, she told him. They both stared at the computer screen as the miles rumbled by. Exhaustion, however, soon took its hold and they both fell fast asleep.

Around Eleven, Mitch woke up startled and extremely pissed off with himself, That was reckless and dangerous he chided himself. He sat upright and tapped the space bar to wake the laptop but the battery was dead. He replaced the battery and fired it up. Isabel stirred and opened her eyes. In a fake child's voice she whined,

"Are we there yet?" Mitch grinned at her

resilience.

"Not so lucky. It is only just after eleven and I think you said we would get in around midday. We should be getting close to Louisville though. Do you have a plan for getting us out of this van unseen?

"Well these horses are trained by Houston McDonald and I have no idea where they are getting unloaded. The only barn I have spent much time in is Georgio's when Nikolai and I have checked in on our horses. My dad doesn't come to Louisville very often."

"Why not?"

"Why not what?"

"Why doesn't your dad come here?"

"He is a pretty small trainer, and with his love of horses and philosophy on drug use in racing, he has only a few dedicated owners who feel the same way. They are quite happy to stay in New York year round and just travel the occasional stakes horse for a big race. He used to go to Florida in the winter when he had a bigger string but not any more"

"You mentioned his stance earlier too, what do you mean?" asked Mitch

" My dad hates animal cruelty. He refuses to dope horses; that means use medications to mask pain or attempt to enhance performance. He insists on good food, and happy horses, so all his horses go out to play in the round pen daily and walk in the afternoons too. They also go out to a farm near Greenwich for R&R when they need it or if they need to recover from injuries. That is why he has sound older horses still racing. His runners last six or more years instead of six or more months.

In the United States twenty-four horses die on the tracks every week because they are training with masked pain. I could tell you stories that could make your hair curl. I read somewhere that we breed about sixty thousand Thoroughbred foals annually although most years only about half that number are registered. This year only about twenty thousand were registered, a sign of the economy I suppose. So the racing industry contributes greatly to the one hundred and thirty thousand horses slaughtered for European meat markets every year."

"I thought horse slaughter was banned." he said, looking disgusted.

"Oh, it is, but stupid horse lovers would rather close our slaughter houses than just ensure humane slaughter here, so now the poor animals are shipped thousands of miles just to die the same horrible death in Canada. Nothing was solved. We breed too many horses and we need to have a humane way to get rid of them. I digress, you asked about Dad. So he trains clean and runs against doped up lame horses, not really fair is it?"

They were approaching the city and the truck took the I-264. Isabel commented,

"We will be there in about ten minutes, then another ten or so at the gate. We will just have to pray for a time without too much interference to get out mostly unnoticed. Shouldn't be too hard, they'll get the horses off then be busy watering, bedding down etc. and then likely want to grab some food before they start unloading."

"I sure hope so," Mitch replied. He removed the

camera, and packed up all their stuff. With most the food eaten, and only the addition of Isabel's few clothes, his pack was smaller and lighter than ever.

Eventually, after many jolting twists and turns coming off the highway and negotiating the narrow Louisville streets, the huge horse van came to a stop at the gate. After a few more minutes they were driving very slowly through the 'backside' of Churchill downs. After two or three more turns, they came to a final rest. Isabel peeped out. She could see barn Thirty-three and laughed.

"What's up?" asked Mitch.

"Of all the barns at Churchill Downs we park across from Georgio's old barn. A sign maybe. I see from the webbings that his assistant, Alistair, inherited it. Well, if we hide out up in his hay loft at least we can listen to the private grooms that my husband hires and see if we hear anything suspicious and figure out where to go next." she explained to him.

"Yes, I am pretty sure they will check the area for signs of us possibly coming this way." Mitch replied.

"It will be busy all afternoon with horses going to, and coming from, the races; but there is no way to walk over to the front-side without being seen. Our only way out is through the main barn gate and I'd watch that if I was looking for us. We should probably stick around until tomorrow night and then try going out the back gate with a crowd and with your backpack in a feed bag or something. They'd never hang out for that long," she told him.

"I hope you are right," Mitch said. "We certainly

don't have many choices until I figure out who I can trust." They stopped whispering as all the doors were opened and the noise of the whinnying horses and general excitement filled the air.

A short older man, with a tanned face and a road map of wrinkles climbed up into the truck, threw out all the extra water buckets, and jumped back down. Isabel leaned over and whispered,

"This might be the perfect time to leave, just jump down turn and pick up a few bags, carry them into the barn, drop them and walk right out the other side."

"OK, lets go." he said. They scrambled out of their recess and approached the door.

"Let me just make sure that neither driver is outside." She peeped through the partition and could see both Brook Ledge men moving partitions inside the van and helping grooms move the horses out of the stalls.

Isabel nodded, jumped out, grabbed two suitcases and walked boldly into the shed-row, dropped them and walked out the other side. She kept walking around the outside of the barn and headed toward the track. Near the track she turned left and walked over to another barn where she entered the barn and walked down the shed-row inside the awning. The barn was devoid of people, so she was unhurried, looking at the heads poking out of the stalls staring back at her. At the end of the shed-row, she turned left again, walked across the open yard, into the bottom end of barn thirty-three and immediately climbed the ladder up onto the deck above the stalls. Only once she was on top did she look down and watch Mitch finish the climb behind her.

"Smooth move, you are a natural at this stealth in broad daylight thing. I'm impressed," he said as he followed her across to the stack of hay and straw.

They scrambled up to the top, and immediately moved bales in the center of the pile to form a hole much like the one in the cow barn in Vermont. It almost felt like home. Isabel said she'd be right back and climbed back down to the deck where she went over to a large white trunk, and on opening it, retrieved two horse blankets, She closed the trunk and returned to the newly made hollow. She tossed the blankets in and Mitch covered the floor of the hollow that was only two bales deep, two wide, lengthwise, and six long, width-wise. Enough place to lie comfortably and, when seated, still have a profile unseen by someone on the deck.

"It is going to be a long day. Horses are going over for the first race and once the grooms come back in for the afternoon there is likely to be activity down below until well into the evening," she informed him. "If you need to pee just pee on the coarse yellow bales, not on the sweet smelling green ones. OK," Mitch grinned at her.

"Yes ma'am, you're the boss." She punched his arm.

"We are going to be so hungry, we only have candy bars and trail mix. If you want to take a chance, you can walk around and find vending machines. I'm thirsty so I'm going to take a stiff drink out of a water bucket." Mitch looked alarmed.

"Don't be careless you could be seen"

"I'll be careful and quick." He followed her to the edge of the deck and watched her climb down, slip around into the stall to the right, and drink straight out of the bucket as a large brown horse sniffed her neck. She turned, gave the inquisitive horse, called Dr. Phoose according to the brass plate on the halter hanging by his stall, a quick pat and was up the ladder in a flash.

Mitch took out his laptop and tried to find an open WIFI connection but nobody was being stupid today. He felt so disconnected from his team. He could hear the announcer's voice loud and clear, discussing the runners in the upcoming race.

"There's a giant TV screen out there, " Isabel informed him. "It is the size of four basketball courts." Mitch looked amazed.

"Why?"

"This is the home of the Kentucky Derby and no one here on that day gets to miss a thing." she informed him.

"Impressive, I'll have to come back and take a look sometime," he stated before he lay back, head on his pack, and closed his eyes. He was about to tack a nap when he obviously decided he had something to do first. He cut the strings from a couple of bales and tied Isabel's ankle to his own, separated by about eight to ten feet of the tough blue twine. She gave him a filthy look.

"I could chew through that," she snapped. He ignored her and resumed his napping pose. Isabel followed suite out of boredom. They were lulled by the track and barn sounds and slept long and hard in their extreme fatigue brought on by the last three days of intense physical and emotional stress.

CHAPTER TEN

Louisville Kentucky, Tuesday

Isabel lay, in what she now thought of as the straw fort, and listened to the familiar sounds of a racing barn during morning training. She heard the sound of a vehicle on gravel as it puled up to the barn. Two doors slammed and she went stiff as a rod when she heard the Russian voices in the aisle near the office.

She quickly climbed out of the well and squirmed across the top of the bales, remaining as flat as possible so that grooms collecting hay and straw would not notice her. She forgot the baling twine around her ankle and squeaked softly as it suddenly burned into her ankle. She peered back over her shoulder to see Mitch dragging on the line and beckoning for her to return. She redundantly put a finger to her lips and turned wiggling back towards him.

Once safely back in the well formed by the stacks of bales around her, she placed her lips close to his ears and informed him of the presence of the Russian men in the barn.

"I must see who they are. I know the one voice. I am sure it is Vasili Gruzdev." he works for Nikolai, but is also his cousin. If he is here it is because they know we are here."

"Shoot, I thought your phone and backpack were the last connection. You don't have a hidden tracking device implanted somewhere inside do you?" he asked.

"Christ, get real, this is not the movies. Even Nikolai would not do that. We need to leave right now. They will find us up here. We will be trapped," she snapped.

"Shit, you think I don't know that," he retorted angrily. "They might send someone up to search the barn so we could be in trouble. I wonder if they know we are here or are just checking the area?"

"We will have to drop into a stall without spooking a horse and run like hell, she said in a frightened voice, the pitch rising with each word.

"No, we drop into the stall and wait, they are sure to have someone watching both sides of the barn if they actually suspect we are here, Mitch said in a calm voice.

"It's called a shed-row." she snapped at him. Mitch gave her a dirty look before replying,

"Yes, lets waste time on barn lingo why don't we." He cut the bailing twine from her ankle, grabbed his pack and climbed out of the hollow. Isabel followed.

They moved closer to the office. Isabel could hear Vasili talking to the Assistant Trainer, an Englishman called Gavin, whose last name escaped her. Gavin was denying her visiting and telling

Vasili that the trainer, Alistair Brown was still in
Saratoga and would not be back until next Monday.
Vasili asked to see Nikolai's horses and Gavin
escorted him to a nearby stall. As the visitors stood
below them in front of the stall, Isabel could hear
Vasili discussing the searching of this barn and all
the others close to where the truck had unloaded the
day before. Her Russian was not very good but,
after twelve years of marriage to Nikolai, it was
certainly good enough for her to know that they had
to get out of the barn fast.

She motioned to Mitch and quickly moved to the
opposite side of the barn, facing away from the
track and the Russians. She whispered to him that
they really did need to get out fast because they
were going to start the search right now. She peered
cautiously off the edge of the bales, and seeing no
one, scrambled down to the wooden deck that made
up the ceiling of the stalls and the floor of the hay
and straw storage.

She peered down into one stall after another
through the small openings that allow one to drop a
bale straight into the stall. She stopped, and putting
a finger to her lips she stuck her head into the stall
and made a tiny sound.

The groom looked up startled, she waved
frantically pointing to her lips and making the
universal zipper motion. Jaime Eduardo's face broke
into a huge grin,

"Seňora Issi!" he said.

"Shhhhhh, nessitamos tu ajuda. Por favor ocultar
nosotros rápida." She dropped into the stall. Isabel
lay down with her body up against the wall and dug

herself down into the straw while covering herself with more straw. Mitch needed no explanation. He dropped into the stall and saw the smile widen on Jaime's face. With his head toward the corner were Isabel's head lay buried, he too wiggled under the straw after burying his pack at his feet.

Jaime quickly fluffed up his new bale of straw banking mounds of it against the two walls, covering them both very well. He moved the soiled straw to the middle. Jaime dragged his muck barrow into the doorway, effectively blocking it and stood there expectantly saying nothing.

Instinct was kicking in. Señora Issi was with a sexy hombre and her husband was a very jealous person. Say no more. Edwardo had known Isabel since she was a teenager, helping in her stepfather's barn. She had married a bad man and he was going to help her be free to run off with her lover. He hated that cruel man who also owned horses in this barn, but hired his own grooms. They were mean men who spoke funny. Ha. Fuck you Señor Nik, he thought, fuck you.

Jaime could hear the Russian grooms calling down from the deck, but did not know what they were saying. He was pretty sure they were telling the two men, who often came to see Señor Nick's horses, that no one was up there. He slowly mucked his stall as they looked down from above.

"Hey Jaime, you see a woman up here or in the shed-row?" one called to him. Jaime was surprised that Piotr had even bothered to learn his name.

"I see woman, yes," he replied in heavily accented English. "Angéla Maria she take my dirty bandages."

"Not Angéla you fool, a strange woman, or maybe an owner or wife."

"Lo siento, Piotr, I see nada."

The men moved on and climbed off the upper deck. Jaime quickly tipped his muck cart over, and dragged Isabel from the floor, almost throwing her into the cart and quickly covering her with urine soaked straw and horse manure. Mitch realized what Jaime was doing and before he even had time to react. Jaime bent close and whispered,

" Señor, I come quick." Jaime pushed the cart out of the nearest end of the shed-row, closest to the end of the barn that housed the office and to where he could see a strange man standing. He wheeled it right past the man, around the back of the muck heap and tipped it out spilling Isabel onto the ground. He handed her a key. "Numero cinco de arriba," he said pointing at the dormitory building behind them. "Vamanos." he was flapping his hand at her and looking very concerned.

Isabel stayed on the ground and wormed her way over to the corner of the muck heap keeping a eye on the man who was standing looking into the barn. Jaime bumped the dirty muck barrow past the man and 'accidentally' wiped against the Russian's pressed khaki pants as he went into the barn. The Russian man swore a blue streak and started yelling at Jaime.

Before anyone had time to appear, Isabel sprinted in behind the dormitory building and around the back to stairs at the corner. She scurried up the stairs keeping her face looking away from

barn thirty-three a she ascended and entered the
building. She had never prayed so hard in her life
that she would not be seen. Isabel hoped that Jaime
would be as successful in getting the much heavier
Mitch out of the barn. She let herself into room five
and waited. About ten really, really long minutes
later, she heard him whispering at the door and let
him in.

"Oh dear God, we stink!" were the first words he
uttered. He dropped his feces stained backpack, and
locked the door. "How do you know a trustworthy,
blond haired, blue eyed Mexican in Louisville,
KY?" he asked her incredulously.

"You really are so damn ignorant. Jaime is
Guatemalan. I have known him for years. He has
worked for my stepfather periodically. Jaime has a
pretty colorful ancestry. His grandfather was
German and moved to Guatemala after several
years of wandering around South America. He
arrived shortly after WWII. It was never proven, but
the family believe he was SS because of his fear of
authority and questions about his past. They lived
deep in the hills and Jaime is named for the old
man. Jakob Edvard a.k.a Jaime Eduardo whose last
name was unknown as he must have dropped it
when he Latinized it. Did he say anything to you?"
she asked.

"Yes, after he came back, he first took my pack
and buried it in the muck heap, and then came back
for me. We had to wait until nobody was watching
too carefully because my weight was making the
canvas rub hard against the wheel. Anyway, after he
dumped me out he said, 'Nombre' and showed me

five fingers, and pointed to the building saying 'arriba' while gesticulating upwards with his thumb. He also said something like, 'Jew lob gher, jew tek keer ghove gher good. Si?'" Isabel burst into laughter at his pathetic imitation of Jaime's accented English.

"Now we wait," Mitch said. "After dark we can get cleaned up and see if Jaime can take us to a hotel up near Kentucky Kingdom. It should not be too hard to get a room even with minimal identification across from a theme park" He looked around the small room, just a cot, a couple of suitcases spilling clothes, a large blue plastic cooler and a hot plate surrounded by a couple of pots, a large dirty knife, a few bowls, and a small cardboard box with a variety of utensils. He stared at the walls covered in posters and photos of Doberman Pinschers. "What's up with the dogs?" he asked. "

I'm not sure," she told him, "but Jaime loves them, he has a beautiful red Dobey named Rex. He is huge. Dogs are not allowed at Churchill so when he is here, Rex stays with Debbie, the exercise rider who rides a lot of the good horses in this barn. Jaime will use the old communal van that they normally use for things like getting the bandages and saddle clothes to the laundry, to take Rex to the dog park later.

Mitch was quiet for a few minutes. Isabel watched him from her perch on Jaime's bed. She had placed a ragged Spanish dog magazine on the bed in a vain attempt to keep the horse urine and feces off his blankets. Mitch had plopped down on the floor next to the door so that he would be behind it if someone kicked it open, or opened it to look inside. They were both careful to stay away from the window overlooking the barn despite their curiosity about the men below.

"Why did you just help us get out of that predicament when you could have screamed and told that Vasili fella that I kidnapped you?" Mitch asked Isabel.

"You know why, you have my kids." she answered angrily.

"Nope, I don't think that's it. You have repeatedly told me that he will find you and the kids and thus far we have only just managed not to be found, twice now thanks to you."

"I have helped you so that I get my kids back on my terms but to be quite honest, I am far more afraid of Vasili and Anatoli than I am of you." Mitch pretended that he did not know the men to whom she referred. "Who are they?" he asked.

Isabel stared at him for a long time, the silence getting heavier and heavier. Mitch saw her expression change, she seemed to have come to a decision. He got the feeling this was the time to turn on the tiny voice recorder he had stashed in the small pocket sewn into his boxers. He pretended to scratch his balls and Isabel looked away as he knew she would. He moved the little slide to the 'on' position and waited.

"I've already crossed the line, I told you about the horses. I'm a dead woman walking. I don't know why I was so stupid. I don't know what Nikolai is thinking. I know he does not need me in the lab anymore. He hasn't for a while. His private lab has been running without my input for at least two years. I am afraid of what he has told Vasili and Anatoli to do if they find me. He will want the children home unharmed because he can easily control them and their thinking; especially if they can no longer see my family. Me though, I just don't know. If he even remotely believes that I have left of my own free will, I have no chance at all to convince him otherwise." Mitch knew all about Vasili Gruzdev and Anatoli Dubnovsky. He had read their files and seen their photos, along with those of Alexei Lashkov, but he remained quiet.

She began, "Both men worked for Nik long before we were married. Vasili is Niki's cousin. He is a small, cruel man who hates himself and his ugliness. He had bad acne as a teen and later had a chunk bitten out of his nose in a fight. The only women he can get are paid, and afraid because he is into vicious, violent, sadistic stuff. Afraid of what he will do, yet more afraid to say no. In general, Vasili likes to watch pain inflicted, but he does not himself inflict pain except on women during sex.

He has a ' security team'," Isabel used two fingers on each hand to make air quotes around 'security team'. "They are his little pack of hyenas who do his dirty work. I have heard rumors about some of his exploits but the only one I think I know for sure is a young gun shop owner from South Carolina. He had this Pro Russia video blog and somehow he got involved in fronting the movement of weapons for Nik and Vasili. Unfortunately, he got a little greedy and made a subtle comment in a blog as a threat.

I happened to be planting seedlings in the beds beneath Niki's office when I heard him shouting about it, and telling Vasili to take care of it. Some months later, I heard about the unsolved crime on Dateline, the poor man had been tortured in his establishment. There was blood everywhere. They allegedly castrated him, and skinned him alive, before cutting out his tongue. I knew right away that it was Vasili and his 'team'. Anatoli, however, is just Niki's personal bodyguard.

Mitch knew the case. They had no clues in the case, and no idea the young store owner had been involved in illegal gun sales or with Nikolai Lebedev or Vasili Gruzdev. He would have to pass that on. Perhaps they could find a link. Before he could think of a way to bring the conversation around to some of the criminal exploits the FBI was convinced were linked to Nikolai Lebedev, they heard the outer door close and footsteps in the hall.

"Seňora?" Isabel jumped up off the cot and let Jaime into the small, and now crowded room. She gave him a big hug and thanked him profusely for his help. The modest groom shook his head. He explained to the fugitives that the Russian men had searched all the nearby barns and were spreading further afield. He offered to take them out that evening when he went to see his beloved dog, Rex. Mitch asked if he happened to take Crittenden Drive and Jaime stated that he could do so if he stopped at the Kroger by the rail road tracks to get some dog food because that would then naturally make Crittenden the shortest way to Rex.

The subject changed to lunch and Jaime generously made some incredible tacos out of ingredients taken from his cooler. They washed the tacos down with pineapple flavored Topo Sabores, a popular sweet Mexican soda. Much to Mitch's disgust, Isabel and Jaime seemed to have lots of mutual acquaintances to gossip about, and lots of catching up to do, all conducted in Spanish. Now if they were talking Arabic, Farsi, or even Pashto, Azeri, or Kurdish, he'd have a shot, but the little high school Spanish he had bothered with was long forgotten. He opened his laptop and worked briefly before he closed his eyes and sat quietly, resting against the wall next to the door.

CHAPTER ELEVEN

Off Track

Jaime returned after the horses had received their evening feed, and he was done for the day. He had parked the van close to the bottom of the stairs; and reported that all the cars parked near barn thirty-three had left for the evening but that the same white rental car was parked in the Harthill Co parking lot opposite the main gate. The group descended the stairs, and Jaime opened the back of the van facing them. Around the vast stable area people were going about their business and nobody paid attention to just another bunch of stable hands doing their own thing. Isabel and Mitch climbed into the van and Jaime covered them with bandages, saddle clothes and sweat sheets. They were all freshly laundered, thank god. He had obviously gone to the laundry and returned as a trial run. Smart groom, thought Mitch. He wondered if the man was an illegal worker as so many of the backstretch workers allegedly were. He wondered aloud what the man had done in his native land. Isabel informed him that Jaime had been an accountant. Strange how so many immigrants were willing to do menial labor for the opportunity to work in the United States.

Mitch was impressed with Jaime. The groom surely knew how to draw attention to himself in order to allay suspicion. He had the windows down in the van, a loud Caribbean beat playing on the radio, and was bopping his head and singing along as he stopped at the main gate to check for traffic. He slowly pulled forward giving the occupants of the white rental Ford SUV plenty of time to peruse the scene. He then drove off toward Central Ave and made his way to Kroger's. It only took him a few minutes to pick up some dog food and they were back on the road past Cardinal Stadium, home to the University of Louisville football team.

Jaime turned right into the Arby's on the corner of Crittenden Drive as instructed by Mitch and pulled up to the dumpster, backing into the spot. Mitch told him to go and buy himself something to eat and handed him a pile of ten dollar bills. He did not tell the groom where they would be staying but told him to stay in Arby's for at least ten minutes. Isabel thanked him for his help and expressed her desire to help him when she next could. Jaime continued to pretend to sing along to the music on the radio. He said goodbye and good luck and pushed a small box of hair color back through the pile of cloth. Mitch was not happy to see the Clairol Nice and Easy and chastised the man for compromising himself.

"No worry senor," he soothed, I tek it no pay, nobody see."

"Jaime, my new friend, you are a brave man, thank you for everything, now go." Jaime got out of the van walked around checking the doors and quietly unlatching the back before walking off without looking back. Jaime was good at following directions.

Mitch and Isabel slid out of the van and quietly closed the door taking one of the square white cotton saddle cloths with them. They rolled behind the dumpster and looked around. Mitch fashioned the saddle cloth into a nice head covering for Isabel that effectively covered her hair and face when she looked down. He told her to stare at her feet until further notice.

Mitch gestured toward the gap in the fence and they slipped through and then walked nonchalantly toward the Holiday Inn, across the hotel parking lot that backed onto the Arby's. Mitch was grateful for Isabel's intimate knowledge of the area. She had told him all about the small shotgun home on New High Street that her aunt had lived in for more than forty years; and who had been bought out in 2006 by the Holiday Inn company who promptly razed the small home to make way for a new hotel. He left her standing by a side door with the dirty pack. He had changed into clean clothes and hoped that he did not smell too obviously disgusting.

Mitch collected the key to the room he had rented in the name of Forester Black, on the third floor, at the back of the south end of the building. This location made it almost impossible to be attacked from outside but gave them an escape through the window onto the roof of the utility building one floor below. He collected Isabel at the side entrance and they took the stairs up to the room. It was very much just your standard, run of the mill, hotel room. Entrance with 'kitchen' nook on one side, and bathroom on the other, looking straight through the long narrow room with two queen beds to the windows that overlooked the parking lot of another hotel behind this one. Despite the relative newness of the hotel, it was already well worn with the occasional carpet stain and well used furniture.

Inside, Isabel took off the makeshift shawl, and the hot black wig and took herself into the bathroom to run a bath. "While, I soak this stench off, I think you are making a trip down to the laundry," she informed him.

"May as well wash all our clothes and that disgusting pack." Mitch agreed wholeheartedly, he was tired of the thick smell of ammonia and horseshit. He opened a large drawer under the TV and tipped half the contents of his pack into it and the other half into the bottom drawer. He pocketed all the phones and removed the cord from the land line to the wall. Isabel gave him a withering look.

"I'm done making mistakes, if I am going to survive this, I can't do it alone; so I suppose it is you or nothing and so far you've done a pretty OK job, not great, but OK." Mitch smiled and shook his head.

"I want to believe you, but trust is earned so I'll keep the cord." he said as he pitched all the dirty stuff into the bag. "Now get in there and throw your clothes out." Isabel complied, and held the door open, just a crack, as she tossed all her clothes out including her thong. It's not like he hadn't seen it and a whole lot more already. She heard him leaving the room as she slipped down into the deliciously steaming water. She washed her hair and wished she had a razor to shave but no such luck. She would have to make a list of necessities. She had no intention of going blond, there was no point, she'd have dark roots in two days. They'd have to think of something else.

Isabel had a wonderful soak and was wrapped in two large towels watching TV when Mitch returned with her clothes. He ordered room service and they settled in to strategize.

"I think there is only one course of action," he said. "You are going to have to tell me everything. I hope you realize that I can't help you get away from your husband if I don't know what I am dealing with."

Isabel sat thinking for a while. She was already past the point of no return. Nik thought she had run off with another man, taken his kids, and successfully avoided his attempts at rescue or capture, and by now it must be obvious that she was hardly an unwilling captive.

"OK, where do I start?"

"From what you've told me, the thing you are most involved in and thus most familiar with is the biotech company, so how about we start there," he prompted. Thus, Isabel began her tale.

"As I said, I started at N.E.G. Biotech. when I

was working on my PhD in biochemistry. I was actually doing my thesis on synthetic hemoglobin, and specifically on its incorporation onto carbon nanosphere frames. My focus is trying to refine a completely synthetic blood replacement product.

Anyway, as soon as I graduated, I continued my research in the labs at N.E.G. My husband, it turns out, had invested in a biotech company for only one reason; he was interested in cloning technology. Nik imported a couple of Koreans, a Jap, and five Russian scientists all working on cloning. Of course, this was in addition to covering the DNA analysis work for the FBI and NTSB that worked as the cover for the company.

The company also does other legit research. In addition to my work, we have projects underway using a growth stimulant that is a derivative of the Russian Comfrey plant in the presence of hyperbaric oxygen to induce regeneration of cellular tissue, and we are using hepatocytes on a synthetic collagen frame to grow new livers for patients needing liver transplant. Livers actually can regenerate, well not exactly regenerate but significantly hypertrophy in a functional manner so we can theoretically grow a whole new liver on a frame.

The trick we haven't quite figured out is getting the forming bile ducts to coalesce into an attachable bile duct. As soon as we figure out a means to channel the secreted bile we have that one in the bag. We have already succeeded by growing the new liver inside the capsule from a cadaver donor when about a half centimeter of tissue and the major ducts are left intact. Using sheep livers that is. We just need to find the missing link in the first method"

"Anyway, back to the cloning, she continued. "I'm sure you know that cloning of horses, sheep, dogs, cats etc, that's all pretty commonplace already. We have no problem getting a few clones to live birth and normal appearing maturity. Nikolai wanted to not only clone horses, but famous racehorses. This is not a problem to do practically; however, it is illegal to clone Thoroughbreds and then attempt to race these clones.

Nik thought he could get around that by passing the clones off as the progeny of other horses. The only problem with that is that all Thoroughbreds are DNA typed prior to running. The proof of parentage is required. The way this is done is to take hair with an intact root bulb, from the foal, and test the DNA contained in the root at twelve specific locations. These locations are found by looking for gene markers, called micro-satellites. At each of the known micro-satellite locations there is a pair of alleles, one from each parent. An allele is a form of a gene. There are two alleles at each locus, which is the genetic term for location, one, as I said, from each parent. The two alleles of the foal are then compared with those from both parents at all these known loci. All twelve have to be possible combinations from the specified parents. The test is deemed ninety-nine point nine percent accurate. Like paternity suits in court. Are you following?" She asked.

"Sure, this is all very interesting so carry on,"

"Well, you inform the Thoroughbred governing body, called the Jockey Club, of the birth of a foal, and after a few months they send you a test kit. You take photos of the foal from both sides, and front and back, and then close up of the face. You pull out about fifty hairs from the foals mane, and affix them to the form with the foals complete description of every single mark and whorl. Whorls are those little circles of hair, like cowlicks that some people have in front causing their hair to stick up. All people have one on the crown of their head. Then you submit the form with photos, and hair, and the Jockey Club does the genetic testing.

Nik realized that with current recombinant technology we could insert the desired alleles into the DNA of the clones and pass them off as the progeny of the fake parents. Pretty easy actually. The kicker is that none of the loci are involved with the actual functional genes of the animals so it should have negligible effect on the clone. Anyway, his team went about cloning the horses he could get genetic material for, and switching out the markers. They then implanted the cloned embryos and eventually after much trial and error he had eleven live foals in the first viable crop. Of these, only five with suitable markers have survived to enter training. He has two fillies and three colts." Isabel stopped to take a drink of water before continuing.

"The fillies are both clones of a mare called Zenyatta, two colts are clones of Secretariat, and one is a John Henry clone. The Secretariat clones were tough because the DNA came from a tooth that was dug up. It took a lot of work to find a few relatively intact sets of chromosomes with relatively intact DNA. A lot of mixing and matching and placing into cells for repair mechanisms to be effective. The resultant cells very closely match Secretariat's sequence but are not quite identical. Both those are already winners, with one winning the Hopeful at Saratoga just last week. Nik was very angry that the other colt did not run in the same race. Prior to Georgio's death I overheard them arguing about the two a lot.

The brown colt, who was the one in the barn yesterday where Vasili was talking to the groom, he's the John Henry. He is bred to be a Turf horse and also for longer distance so he has not run yet. The fillies have both run already but they are not the same at all. The one is more robust and has run twice, for a second and a win, the other just seems to be needing more time and placed fourth in her only start. She may be somewhat defective because she just isn't thriving. That can be an issue with clones. The one filly and both chestnut colts are aimed at the Kentucky Derby. So there, you have it."

"None of this is legal?" he asked.

"Good grief no, you can't even use artificial insemination with Thoroughbreds. With Thoroughbreds the daddy horse has to actually DO mommy horse," she told him. Mitch laughed at her expression.

"Very interesting stuff. I suppose any of this coming to light would give him some problems." Mitch mused.

"Are you kidding? If this came out, he stands to

be barred from racing for life, disbarred as a lawyer, lose all his envisaged fame and fortune if these horses perform up to his expectations, get sued for all the prize money, and probably get charged with a bazillion counts of conspiracy to commit fraud. N.E.G. Biotech. would tank on the stock market. Oh, his life as he knows it will be over. I'm not sure how he could finagle his way out of serious prison time."

"So why didn't you go to the FBI and tell them all this?" he asked

"Yeah, and land up feeding fishes way out in the Atlantic, no thanks," she snapped. "I have my kids to worry about."

It was getting late. Mitch decided he could get more info in the morning. He told Isabel that she should take the bed farthest from the door and immediately roll toward the window and onto the floor if anything happened such as people flying through the door. He tossed her his biggest t-shirt to sleep in.

Mitch went into the bathroom, took the hair color and emptied the contents down the toilet after mixing it and dirtying the gloves. He stuffed the empty container, soiled gloves, and crumpled instructions back into the box and took it with him when he ran down to the concierge to pick up a toothbrush and a razor. He had his own toothbrush but Isabel needed one since he had tossed all her belongings so unceremoniously out the van window. He took a little detour to drop off the Nice 'n Easy box before returning.

Back in the room, they readied for bed. Isabel

felt clean and comfortable in her hotel bed after the strange places she had spent the last few nights. Mitch was pretty confident that he no longer had to worry about her leaving. She has passed over to the far side, he thought with a smile as he lay in the dark room. He racked the slide chambering a round in the Glock and slipped it under his pillow before falling asleep. Isabel heard the loud ratcheting sound and jolted awake, then relaxed, and drifted off to sleep thinking of her children and imagining them having fun in the snow.

Early the following morning, Isabel heard Mitch up and about. She could smell the coffee. She opened her eyes to see him dressed and ready.

"Are you going somewhere?" she asked.

"Good morning to you too," he answered with a smile. "Yes, I am going to buy a couple of things we need. I won't be gone long. Please don't leave the room, I don't want you appearing on the security cameras more than necessary. If I don't come back, I want you to stay right here and call this number." He handed her a card. "This is the US Marshal service. You tell them you are in the witness protection program and you are on the run because you have been identified. Refuse any further details until they pick you up. Once in custody, ask to speak to the man on the card and then say nothing until he gets to you. Demand ID before you speak. He will know who you are and what to do. Is that clear?" Isabel nodded.

"Be careful and please come back," was all she said before he left the room.

The door was barely closed before she jumped

out of bed and got dressed in some of his clothing, cinching the pants with a belt. She wrapped her hair in a towel, and used the cardboard from the back of the small hotel notepad to prevent the door from locking behind her. Covering her face as she pretended to cough into a tissue, she slipped into the stairwell, and on exiting continued to cough into the tissue until she reached the business room with the row of computers for guest use.

She sat with her back to the camera, logged on and posted one quick message to her fake Facebook account. 'Enjoying the Green Mountains. No sore heads in this lovely fresh air.' She hoped her brothers would recognize their childhood code they had made up in the event of a kidnapping. Green mountains meant stop this is the truth; no sore head meant not speaking against free will; and lovely fresh air meant free. She hoped they would realize she was safe. She logged off and returned to the room, coughing all the way. She replaced Mitch's clothes in his bag and got back into bed turning on the TV to watch the morning show.

Mitch got back with his 'supplies'. He tossed them at her. He explained that he would be cutting her hair and that she would be straitening it and then coloring it darker to hide the fiery red highlights. Isabel didn't bother to argue. Mitch cut her hair very short, leaving about four inches for her to straighten and color. She disappeared into the bathroom to do her hair. No point being horrified, it would grow back, she reasoned.

An hour later she emerged with the frightful, straw like, very dark brown, strands hanging around her gaunt, pale face. Mitch sat her down, conditioned her hair, and shaped it as best he could with some feathering on the sides. He was no hairdresser he realized. Isabel watched in the mirror and took over shaping the sides. Then she used the hotel drier to blow dry her hair. The result wasn't half as bad as she had expected.

Next she used the instant tan on her face, neck and exposed arms. She added a few layers until she was a nice deep olive complexioned, dark haired woman, and stuck on the false lashes. Mitch handed her two small pieces of molded silicon and told her to push them up into her cheeks to change the shape of her face. She tried it and was impressed with how different she looked already. Mitch was busy with his own transformation. He now sported a bald pate, and goatee. They looked very, very different from yesterday.

Once again, Mitch left for a short period. Returning within twenty minutes. He informed her that he had rented a car and parked it over in the Expo parking among all the visitors playing at Kentucky Kingdom. It was nine-twenty am and they settled in to eat a late breakfast from room service and plan their next move.

THE DARK SIDE

CHAPTER TWELVE

Manhattan, NY - The Saturday after Labor Day

In the Lebedev home, a four story townhouse on Eighty-Eighth Street, in Manhattan, Nikolai's cell rang. He reached over to his night stand and tipped the screen up. He could see the face of Isabel's bottle-blond haired sister-in-law that he had been fucking for the last eight months. His wife's brother had certainly married a stupid, slut of a woman; and he was using it to his advantage. It was six-thirty in the morning, and he wondered what the bloated cow wanted now. He answered and listened as Fran reported that Isabel had left to come home.

Nikolai thanked her for the information and immediately dialed his cousin and head of security for all the Lebedev operations, Vasili Gruzdev. Vasili informed him that Sasha was part of a three man team watching the parking area where the four women had left the Subaru wagon before hiking into the woods. He kept his boss on the line as he added Sasha to the call. Sasha immediately reported that Isabel had not approached the road via the

parking area. The men spoke only briefly before
disconnecting. Sasha led his men into the woods to
begin tracking their employer's missing wife.
Within half an hour it was apparent that she had left,
possibly unwillingly, by boat. A single set of man's
size ten foot prints marked the way to and from the
camp site and the river bank.

Sasha called Vasili to report the findings, and
within the hour they had established the extent of
the river that could have been navigated in a small
inflatable. It covered a few miles with very few
areas deep enough for even a tiny outboard engine.
They decided that the inflatable had likely just been
allowed to drift downstream aided by paddling.

Sasha dropped a man as close as possible to
each end of the barely navigable stretch of the
stream with instructions to radio any finds. Neither
man was happy with the task of wading in the cold
water but they knew better than to argue and set of
on the thankless task.

It was Marc, the dishonorably discharged
marine, who was fighting his way upstream, when
he came across the low cave and went in to check it
out. Inside, he found the bright yellow Selvylor
inflatable. He radioed his location and was soon
joined by the other two men. Together they
followed the obvious exit through the dark crack in
the earth and out behind the waterfall. From there it
was easy to follow the two sets of tracks for miles
through the woods.

They were going north, and then north east, as
they crossed a road and followed a small rutted
ATV track up through the fields of cows and back

into the woods on the other side. At times they had to climb through fences, with affixed signs denoting the trail as a snowmobile route. After another half a mile, they came to a narrow board bridge over a small steep sided gully and they crossed over it unknowingly setting of the alarm that sounded in the cabin to the east.

They noticed the cabin as soon as they rounded the corner after coming out of the trees into the valley over a small rise. The three men quickly ducked back behind the mound. They discussed the plan, and one man stayed behind covering the back of the cabin as the other two circled through the trees on either side. Once Marc was in place covering the front, Alexei 'Sasha' Lashkov approached the cabin from the windowless north side. He peered around the corner and onto the deck. He could not hear any sounds from within. It was almost fifteen minutes since they had crossed the narrow plank bridge. He crawled up onto the deck and across to the middle of three windows.

Lashkov turned on the camera on his cell phone and very slowly raised the phone over the sill watching the screen. It was dark inside the cabin that was lit only by the light coming in through the windows. He panned the room seeing no one, but noted the stairs near the door. He motioned for Marc to join him and they opened the unlocked cabin and, after carefully watching the top of the stairs, entered quickly and to the left out of direct line of fire from above. They hurriedly checked all the cupboards and then they waited, listening for sounds from above. After ten minutes of not a sound but the occasional creaking of old wooden floors, Sasha covered Marc as he climbed the stairs and again used a phone camera to peruse the upper floor. It also appeared empty. He waited in the stair well as Marc checked the cupboards and looked out onto the deck and up onto the roof. The cabin had no attic and was now deserted. Sasha was in a temper. He found the elaborate alarm system and immediately called Vasili to tell him that this was either the work of the Feds or a very sophisticated enemy.

It was obvious that somehow, somewhere in the last hour they had warned the occupants of the cabin of their arrival. Sasha mentioned the fresh coffee and four dirty mugs, one still full of cold coffee, leading him to presume that there must have been two people waiting for the man who had taken Isabel. Their quarry had between a half hour, and and hour, head start and had probably not come in their direction. He called to Rick, the man behind the cabin and the three set off across the grassy valley and up into the trees. Sasha's mood darkened when they found the ATV tracks and had to slog on, in pursuit of a motorized foe, on foot.

Almost two hours later they found the submerged ATV, and were unable to find a clue as to whether the group they were following had gone up stream or down. He presumed down as the former would lead deep into the hills and away from any roads. They set off downstream but never found any tracks, eventually arriving once again at the hardtop. Sasha updated Vasili, and the men started their long hike back to their car.

In Manhattan, Nikolai Lebedev and Vasili Gruzdev were making calls. Lebedev attempted to have his wife declared missing. Local police informed him that, in light of the note to the friends, and no evidence of foul play, the missing person report would not generate an immediate active investigation. Gruzdev called every informant they had on the payroll. He told them all that a twenty thousand dollar bonus was coming to the man with evidence as to the whereabouts of Mrs. Lebedev, or information regarding evidence of an investigation, of any kind, into Mr. Lebedev.

Within two hours Gruzdev had information from an IT specialist within the Department of Justice's Intra-agency Organized Crime Task Force. She had no specific knowledge of action against Lebedev, but she had come across a request from the OCTF to utilize a US Marshal Service safe house in Glens Falls, NY, which was relatively close to the abduction site. She recited the location of the safe house.

Vasili immediately relayed this information to the three man team, who then headed to Glens Falls. In Fort Ann they spotted a Time Warner Cable utility van parked outside a residence. The van was open, with windows rolled down, and nobody in sight. Marc climbed out of Sasha's dark blue BMW at the red traffic light and, after pulling his woolen cap down low and putting on a pair of very dark glasses, he nonchalantly walked up to the van, hopped into the driver's seat, and drove it straight out of town. He drove about eight miles over the speed limit and passed Route 149 West taking

Owens Rd. four miles further south. Then,
following small country roads, he made his way
toward Glens Falls.

Marc received a call from Sasha telling him to
look out for the BMW parked on Dean's Rd, just
north of town and to follow him down the dirt track
to the right. Once they were parked out of sight of
the road, Rick, the quiet man, who seldom added to
any conversation, replaced the plates on the van,
with ones taken from a vehicle in the local Time
Warner Cable lot. They tossed the stolen van's
plates into the bushes, covered the BMW with a
camouflage tarp, and drove toward their destination.

After perusing the location on Connor with one
drive by, they exited the half circle and parked
where both entrance and exit could be seen. Sasha
left the van and taking a long walk to the street
behind the safe-house, he approached the target
house. After the previous alarm system, he was
careful to watch from a distance. The house
appeared deserted with no cars in the drive, but it
was impossible to check the garage. He returned to
the van and they drove back into the circle and
pulled into the house directly across the street from
his target.

Sasha knocked on the door and, pretending that
he was at the correct address, asked if they were
ready for the cable. A very nice little old lady
explained that he, dear boy, had the wrong address
and that he was looking for the home across the
street. However, it was currently unoccupied as the
new owners had not yet moved in. She suggested
that perhaps he should try back tomorrow. Sasha

was reassured that the Feds had not yet arrived and returned to their vantage point on Pine Valley Rd and waited...

Back in Manhattan, Vasili was going through the emails on Isabel's computer. He had removed the hard drive and piggy backed it to his own computer to bypass her password. There were several pages of emails which chronicled a growing love affair over several months. Armed with this knowledge he approached his cousin with dread. Nikolai was going to come unglued like never before. Vasili explained what he had found and handed over copies of some of the emails to Lebedev.

Nikolai read them all, he was sweating profusely, and had become a terrible, dark, shade of red. Vasili was concerned that Nikolai may have a heart attack or stroke with his blood pressure that high. Lebedev drained the vodka in the tumbler on his desk and threw the heavy glass across the room. It smashed into the rock on the right side of the hearth and shattered into a million pieces.

"I will kill that bitch! He screamed. "I will kill her with my bare hands."

Nikolai Lebedev sat down, his head in his hands and said nothing while he breathed hard, in and out, in and out. He was counting to five with each stage of his breathing using the deep breathing to calm himself so that he could think straight.

"Glens Falls is near Saratoga. Tomorrow we will make plans, and the next day I will go to Saratoga to see my two-year-olds, and see if Isabel has contacted any of her old racing friends. I want you to get people watching her parents, her grandmother, and the other brother." By this Vasili knew he meant the brother whose wife Nikolai was not screwing. "Also, have those other two friends of hers watched. Maybe they actually know more than they say."

The two men continued to discuss the problem. It was confusing. Isabel had a lover, yet it appeared the Feds could be involved. If she appeared at the safe-house, then he was under investigation. Nikolai tried to think which of his criminal endeavors had been compromised. It never crossed his mind that he had merely drawn suspicion by being coincidentally just too damn lucky. In his arrogance, and with the experience of literally getting away with murder, he was oblivious to the odds of any one criminal defense attorney or entrepreneur being just that lucky. Finally he said,

"Don't forget to track her phone. You did install that App on her new phone, yes?" Vasili smiled, nodding.

"Niki, if she uses that phone, if she even turns it on, we have her."

Nikolai worked on making sure his covers were secure in the event that the Feds were involved. He spent the day making calls, talking to accountants, and having a third party investigative firm attempt to find the owners of his companies just to make sure there were no glitches that led back to him. Vasili monitored Isabel's phone, the Facebook account she thought they didn't know about in the name of Ali Benson, and kept lines of communication open with all the people he now had on stake outs.

Both men were busy when Andre Putin, the children's young, and usually vibrant, bodyguard stumbled into the house. He was disheveled and had a hospital emergency room band around one wrist. He entered the office and immediately started apologizing. Nikolai knew instantly what his presence meant and his rage bellowed forth renewed and unchecked. Vasili grabbed Nikolai as he tried to strangle Andre, shaking the desperate man violently. Andre realized his worst fear was valid. He knew it was why Riana was not answering her cell phone, she was gone and so were the children.

Together, he and Vasili moved Nikolai to his chair and sat him down. Andre was a far bigger man than either of the cousins but he feared, and respected his employer far too much to fight back.

Once Nikolai was seated with a fresh tumbler of Vodka in his hand. Andre described waking in the ER. He recalled a very colorful ice-cream cart, with balloons and stuffed toys and a special on today. The children had begged and the nice man in the three wheeled vehicle had said free ice-cream for all good moms and dads in the park on such a lovely day. He and Riana had laughed at the private joke as they accepted the treats.

That was the last thing he remembered before waking in the ER. As soon as he established that Riana and the children were not there, he had rushed back to the park despite his conviction that it was too late and that they would be gone. He had hoped against that hope they were home.

It appeared that Isabel had fled, taking his

children, possibly with the help of the Feds. Nikolai was starting to suspect that there was a chance his life was unraveling. There was much to do for damage control, and destroying his wife was just the beginning. He called and reported his children and nanny kidnapped.

Two detectives came to the house, and questioned Nikolai Lebedev for over an hour. They discussed the possibility that his wife and children had been kidnapped, or that she had left him and taken the children. They opened the missing person's case, issued an Amber Alert, and wanted to set up in the house to await a call. Nikolai declined stating that he would keep them informed of any information he received but that he did not have the room. The detectives questioned Andre, but he was unable to give them any new information. He again described the three wheeled ice-cream cart and the vendor, whose description quite frankly matched every sandy haired, bearded white male between 5'8" and 6'2" in the country. They requested Isabel's laptop. Vasili handed it over without mentioning the emails and the detectives left, promising to keep in touch.

Vasili's cell rang, his face paled as he listened to the report coming in. He turned to Nikolai.

"They are watching her family too. Every – single – God – damn – one – of - them - has - a - tail," he said emphasizing each word with force and a pause. " This is very, very definitely the Feds. I better get back to my contact in the DOJ, she needs to start earning her keep."

Night fell and no word came from Sasha as the

hours ticked by. No one showed up to the safe-house. Had they been made? Was it a false lead? Vasili and Nikolai were wound tighter than Swiss watches. Andre had taken two Naproxen to help with the headache from hell. All three watched computer screens just waiting for someone to activate a blip on the radar. The housekeeper, Mrs. Wessels, who spoke no Russian at all, could hear by the tone of the voices that these were dangerously angry men in her care tonight. She slipped in, and out, filling glasses, making fresh pots of coffee, and offering a selection of edibles as the night wore on.

She knew the children were gone, she knew Mrs Lebedev was gone, she knew the police did not believe they had been kidnapped, and deep in her heart she hoped they were safe and stayed that way. She did not want this man getting his hands on them when his heart was this black. She would be quietly supportive of her employer on the outside, but inside, but she hoped Miss Isabel was smart enough to never come back.

By Sunday morning, they were sure nobody was coming to the safe house. Lebedev told Sasha to return to, and search, the cabin for clues. Then to meet him in Saratoga. There was no activity on Isabel's phone, Facebook accounts, bank accounts, or credit cards. Neither did it appear that her family had been contacted. The detectives reported what the cousins already knew. The lack of financial activity convinced the cousins that this was a federally backed operation. Kidnapping for ransom was remote at this point as there had been no demands.

Isabel's step-father called as soon as the detectives left his house. He demanded to know what Lebedev was up to and accused him of being involved with Isabel's disappearance. Already Mr. Ferguson's allegations were making the police ask questions about his relationship. Lebedev was not sure if they had yet accessed the emails. He hedged his bets and told them that he thought they had a good marriage but that Isabel had been seeing her psychiatrist for depression related to childhood trauma, and that she had been somewhat remote emotionally for the past few months. He insisted that he was sure she would work things through and that as a couple they would survive stronger than ever. Vasili marveled at Nikolai's acting skills and ability to manufacture bullshit. No wonder he was such a good lawyer. Eventually Detectives Brown and Harris left and Vasili could get back to canvassing informants.

Sasha called in the late afternoon. They were on the way to Saratoga. The cabin revealed little new information. They traced an elaborate alarm system to both incoming trails, and additional sensors in trees throughout a a one mile circle around the cabin. They agreed that this meant the responsible party had sufficient advance notice of the camping trip. Vasili went back to his clone of Isabel's hard drive to establish a time line.

Sasha also told them about the ring in the floor and the abandoned cuffs. This new development was somewhat confusing. If Isabel was an unwilling participant, how was her lover involved? Was he a federal agent who had played her? If the Feds had his kids, were they using this to force Isabel to help them build a case. Nikolai was not only a suspicious man, but a suspicious criminal defense attorney. He knew just how much truth stretching and even outright lying police and prosecutors did to elicit a confession. He was suspecting, very strongly, that he was being set up. He thought about what Isabel knew first hand. He was almost sure her knowledge of his criminal pursuits was confined to his horse cloning endeavor. He wondered what he would have to do to make that case disappear.

Nikolai Lebedev called the lab on the encrypted line and spoke to his head of security, seasoned ex-military operative Brian Petersen. Petersen was to ensure that Dr. Hye, the only imported scientist aware of the entire project, took all the viable frozen embryos and stored them safely off site. In addition, he was to audit the individual research to make sure each project was maintaining its credibility as a standalone research effort with valid application.

Lebedev knew that he could trust Dr. Hye not to speak. The man was vested in his research, and its future, and was willing and able to return to the lab in Korea at a moment's notice. The research team had, since the inception of the project, worked well to cover any trace of the ultimate purpose. Lebedev was sure that he could cover up the entire operation but that would mean permanent destruction of the only living proof. He was not about to kill and incinerate his five magnificent, talented, two-year-olds, or the yearlings and weanlings on his small stud farm in Kentucky, unless he got proof that Isabel had sold him out to the Feds.

Just after six pm Vasili received a message from the woman at the DOJ saying that a secure message, bounced through a European server, had an agent and his target in Montreal, Canada and that the task force has a mole. Vasili discussed the need for her to be very careful now that the Feds would be looking for her. The bitchy little Chinese American informed him that she had that under control. Vasili and Nikolai discussed the validity of the new information. Considering that this informant's information on the safe house had been worthless, this too might not be related, but Montreal was not that far from Vermont or the safe house in Glens Falls New York, and the discovery of a mole would make sense if Sasha and his men had been observed in the vicinity of the safe house. There was not much to be done with the information until they knew more.

At ten pm Nikolai Lebedev retired to his master suite, and informed bodyguard/chauffeur Anatoli Dubnovsky, that he wanted to leave for Saratoga at six am. He was feeling frustrated, they had heard nothing from his informants, had no action on Isabel's accounts, had heard nothing from Riana, and had no other news of his sons. He needed, and wanted information to act on. Even his luck with his women had abandoned him. Isabel and Riana were missing and Fran was being watched by the police. He considered having Anatoli collect one of his girls from the strip club but thought better of it. That was surely one business no one could connect to him. The girls working the floor were all nice and legal, the girls for sale to the private members, them, not so much. What a time to be on a woman diet. He realized the irony.

Nikolai hoped that Riana was keeping her mouth shut. She was a weak link. He should never have allowed his feelings for a whore to cloud his judgment. He knew she was in love with him, or at least with his money, and she loved the children but she would be afraid of the government agents and what they could do if they realized that she was illegal. He prayed she would stick to her cover. She's a very smart girl, he thought, she knows what's good for her. Thinking about the tall, beautiful, slim, latte colored, girl, barely twenty three, with the slightly eastern eyes betraying her mixed South African heritage, made him hard. He had hurt her too sometimes, but she begged for more, she didn't whimper and cry like his stupid wife. Nikolai drifted off.

Sometime after midnight Vasili burst into his room shouting that he had a hit on the iPhone tracking App, and that the phone had registered only once at a location about an hour or two west of Albany, New York. The cousins discussed the coincidence of the location. The safe house was just off I-87, Montreal was north on I-87, and now the phone was a couple of hours west of I-87.

"Vasili, brother, I think your contact in the DOJ is on to something. They may have Isabel, but now, thanks to us, they can't trust their own handlers. I do believe that they have cut all ties to official equipment, which means they are not in government vehicles, or traveling to a sanctioned location. They are on the run, trying to hide her. Get Sasha on the road, NOW!" Vasili smiled and informed Nikolai that it was already done. It was the first thing he had done when the phone pinged the App. On a hunch, Vasili called and woke one of Nikolai's private grooms at Saratoga, because Saratoga was also right there on I-87 and right between the two locations. Maybe not such a coincidence. Bartoli had seen nothing unusual all day except one of the exercise riders walking around asking about horse vans leaving, and then this was not so unusual because stable staff often got rides on vans to their next track.

"Sorry boss, nothing." was his determination at the end of the call. Vasili and Nikolai conferred. Not likely that a bunch of agents and a captive woman would hitch a ride on a horse transporter. Nikolai called and woke his trainer. The irritated, sleepy Alistair Brown recalled a Brook Ledge van parked alongside an adjacent barn that evening but he did not know what time it left. However, he informed Nikolai that they usually tried to leave by ten pm.

Vasili called Sasha and told him about the horse-van. He was not pleased to hear that Sasha was alone because the other two men had not yet arrived after collecting the other vehicle in Vermont. They were about four hours behind him. Vasili returned to monitoring his computer and dozing in his chair with his head on the desk. Nikolai lay back hoping to get some sleep before Sasha called again.

Some time later a second call from Sasha confirmed the location of the truck exactly where it would be had the iPhone been activated from inside it. Another call to the confused trainer in Saratoga and they knew where the horse van would be stopping to water the horses. Sasha would await the truck in Erie.

CHAPTER THIRTEEN

Angry Russians

Sasha reported in just after five am. He had the Brook Ledge van in sight and was going over to see if he could find any signs of the targets. About twenty minutes later, Vasili received an irate call from Sasha who was yelling about blankets, food wrappers, and the open window. He could find no sign of Isabel or her captors and was returning to his car to watch the exit of the truck stop.

Suddenly there was a grunt, and the sound of the phone hitting the tarmac. Less than a minute later the phone went dead. Vasili tried calling him back but there was no reply. The Footprints app showed one location change but then reverted to the original location and remained stationary at the truck stop. He had no doubt Sasha had been both identified and disabled. Vasili immediately called Marc and Rick and told them to monitor their Footprint App and find Sasha's phone and with luck, the man himself.

Vasili walked slowly up stairs to wake Nikolai and inform him of the latest debacle. He found Nikolai dressing for his trip to Saratoga and brought him up to speed. He was surprised at how well his cousin took the news. Vasili was not sure what Nikolai was thinking but it appeared that the man was putting himself in his courtroom mode. Nikolai had the most uncanny ability to appear calm in court, however badly things were going. He said it convinced the jurors that he was unconcerned about the absolute rubbish the prosecution was spewing and therefore that the prosecution was making things up. The two men filed down to the kitchen for coffee before the car arrived.

En route to Saratoga, Vasili informed Nikolai that the DOJ informant reported that everyone on Team Four, the team receiving the messages she had intercepted, had returned to the temporary base camp at the FBI building in New York except one man. She did not yet have details on the man other than his gender.

So, Isabel was in the hands of a solitary agent who was no longer in contact with his team. That was good news. Nikolai arrived at the barn in Saratoga around ten am and his trainer Alistair Brown was all over him like a wet rag. They took a look at the two colts and the filly after discussing the upcoming plans. The horses would stay in Saratoga for about another few weeks and then ship directly to Gulfstream Park's outlying training center Palm Meadows.

When Alistair returned to his office, Nikolai asked Bartoli which rider had been asking about the departing horse vans. While it was unlikely to be related, he was not about to ignore the coincidence in the timing. Bartoli pointed across the barn area, indicating the stalls assigned to Mike Lee. "The lady rider, Cathy from Lee's barn." he stated. Nikolai recalled the Cathy who had worked for his father-in-law when he first met Isabel and he wondered if it was the same woman. One too many coincidences he thought for the umpteenth time.

Nikolai called Vasili, and tasked him with checking on Cathy. Nikolai was not about to go and spook the woman before he was sure. As soon as Vasili confirmed they were one and the same, he walked over to Lee's barn. He asked a groom where he would find her and stood in the tack room door until she noticed him. Cathy realized she was being watched and started. She saw who it was an every survival instinct kicked in.

"Nikolai, is that you?", she asked. He nodded and she rushed to him and putting her arms around him hugged him hard. Nikolai was startled and stepped back. "I heard about Isabel being missing," she explained. "Her dad called me to see if I knew anything and of course I couldn't help. What are you doing in Saratoga?" Nikolai explained that the police were looking for Isabel and that he had come to check on his horses and see if any of her friends had seen her.

He tried to catch her off guard by asking, very directly, why she had been asking about horse vans. Cathy looked at him as if she didn't understand the question but answered,

"I have a trunk of stuff that doesn't ever fit in my car, so I need to find a ride for it to Florida. I am on my way south as soon as Lee's horses ship, so I need to take care of my extra crap in the next few days." Now it was Nikolai's turn to hesitate. He had not expected her to actually have a reason. He had been sure she was helping his wife. He apologized and explained that the lack of sleep and worry was driving him nuts. Cathy gave him another hug.

"Issi and I have kinda lost touch since she graduated college and stopped riding. I'm sorry I couldn't help. Please let me know if there is anything I can do and if I hear anything I'll give you a call. Here, put your number in my phone." She handed him the cell, and he complied. He thanked her, and walked back over to his driver convinced that Cathy was actually telling the truth.

Back in the tack room, she was sweating. Never, in her entire life, had she been so grateful for high school theater camp. She looked at her watch. Even if Issi had taken the longest trip, the van to Churchill, she would almost be at her destination and Nikolai was here. Maybe Issi was safe, she sure hoped so. Not knowing was driving her nuts.

Nikolai climbed into the back of his limo, and settled in for the drive back to the city. Vasili called to tell him that Marc and Rick were in Erie and had located the phone. The phone had been checking in regularly but the pattern was unusual. It was was moving north to the NY state line and then south a few miles beyond the travel center. The two men had parked at the Welcome center near the state line marking vehicles and time. Eventually they had linked the time stamp to a white Ford Interceptor emblazoned with State Trooper. The two men had followed the trooper, staying as far back as they could and still see him. When the state trooper

turned into the Welcome Center, they had followed
him in, passing the stationary cop car and parking in
the last available bay nearest the exit. Marc got out,
and while the trooper was likely taking a piss, he
looked into the car. It only took a minute to spot the
phone lying on the floor behind the driver's seat. He
had returned to his car to call Vasili.

Nikolai, asked Vasili to go back over all the
locations from the dropped call until the phone
started its north-south loop. There were two
locations after Sasha stopped moving at the truck
stop. He told Vasili to have the guys check both
locations. Back in Erie, Marc returned to the truck
stop and used his Footprint to find the location in
the parking area. The BMW was not there, but, it
was obviously where he had been parked
overlooking the semi-truck and trailer parking.
They drove slowly out of the truck stop and to the
left, then turned right down the road into the trees.

They stopped and stared into the undergrowth,
which by now was showing the withered effects of
the broken branches. They parked just off the road
and walked into the undergrowth. Within ten feet
they could see the blue BMW and rushed over. The
vehicle was empty, but on a hunch, Marc went back
to his car and retrieved a screw driver which he
used to break the lock and pop the trunk. They
found the barely conscious Sasha curled in the fetal
position. Dried blood streaked his face. The two
men pulled him into a seated position and each
hitched their arms under the injured man's armpits
drawing him out of the trunk.

Rick looked at the head wound. Nine years ago

he was a medic in the army, and he knew a bad wound when he saw one. It was at least six hours since the blow to his head and Sasha was incoherent. He needed a CT and he needed it sooner rather than later. He was fairly certain that Vasili would tell them to bring the injured man back to New York. He was worried that a trip that long would probably kill Sasha. Rick mentioned this to Marc. They knew Vasili was going to be extremely pissed off if they even tried to get his permission to take the poor bastard to an ER, so they placed Sasha in the back of the SUV and drove him to Millcreek Community Hospital, which according to Siri was the hospital closest to I-90.

The men parked far enough away from the entrance to avoid having the SUV appear on the security camera and carried Sasha all the way past the senior center and around the building to the emergency department. They carried him in the door, and told the staff they had found him lying just off the road on the highway. Sasha was whisked away and before they could be questioned, Marc and Rick hurried back to their vehicle, and took off back to wards the highway.

Once they were on I-79 South, Marc called Vasili and detailed their find. He exaggerated Sasha's condition only in the sense that he said the man was unconscious, had lost a lot of blood, and was barely breathing. He expressed that Sasha would have died on the trip back to NY which is why they had rushed him to hospital before making the call. Exactly as predicted, Vasili went off on a screaming tirade, but fortunately directed at the fucking worthless federal agent and that slut, cunt, bitch of a woman, his cousin had married. Whatever the hell that meant. Marc and Rick exchanged a look that said it all. They had dodged a bullet.

Vasili didn't bother to call Nikolai, he knew his cousin was going to want to start killing people just to blow off steam. This was getting fucking pathetic and if he had something to kick right now he would kick its head in just for shits and giggles.

"Fuck" he exclaimed, "fuck, fuck, fuck!!" He wondered when they'd get a break They needed one, it was about goddamn time for a fucking break. He started the rounds again, calling informants, making threats, calling markers with acquaintances who owed Nikolai. He kept his laptop open on Facebook. The super cunt, as he was now calling her, would not have made the fake Facebook account and email if she hadn't intended to use them. Under our noses that bitch had her close friends and family 'Friended' to her fake account. All those sneaky ass wipes where thumbing their noses at Nikolai, well fuck them, he thought, you'll use this and we'll find you.

He had logged in to her account when he had her hard drive piggybacked and 'Friended' a quick fake account he had made. He doubted she would notice that she now had two friend accounts with the same name, she would think it was a glitch. He had uploaded the same woman's pictures, at first glance it would pass. He also had her not so secret email open so he could check for sent messages. He checked it now but there was nothing new.

When Nikolai called, he ran through the new

information, waited for his cousin to stop ranting and raving and then discussed their options. They did not have a clue which way the agent and Isabel were headed. Nikolai figured that the pair might have decided to continue to Louisville in the hope that he would conclude that they wouldn't go there. He told Vasili to take Anatoli and get the next available flight out to Kentucky. They were to get to Churchill Downs as fast as possible and make sure the pair had not remained on the horse van. In the meantime he would keep an eye on the computers monitoring Isabel's accounts and he would have the two men en route from Pennsylvania hole up in the nearest town to await further instructions.

The cousins decided that if Vasili found any sign of the pair on the run, Marc and Rick would also head to Louisville. Vasili left the computers running in his office, but also opened Isabel's accounts on the laptop that he was taking with him. He called Anatoli and told him to get his ass to Newark Airport for an eight pm flight to Louisville. He then called Marc and conveyed Nikolai's wishes. Vasili took the laptop and went home to collect his travel bag that was always ready with for last minute trips.

With a little time to spare, he took a long hot shower. He was feeling his age. He was only fifty-three but all this crazy work for Niki was aging him before his time. Too much stress, he thought. Time to work on a retirement plan. He washed is greasy black hair. He hated his hair, tomorrow it would be greasy again. Greasy skin, greasy hair. God he was cursed. He called a cab for the ride to the airport.

When Vasili and Anatoli got to Louisville they rented a car and attempted to go directly to the Churchill barn area. At the stable gate they were denied entry. There were no trainers in the area that late at night and no good excuse for urgently requiring entry. They were told to return in the morning when their trainer arrived for morning training at around five am.

The men parked across form the entrance and took turns staying awake to monitor all traffic in and out. Except for some drunken grooms trickling in until well after midnight, there was nothing to see until cars started arriving at four am. Vasili had called Nikolai and Nikolai had called the Churchill assistant to tell him that his representative was in town to check on the horses. At five-thirty the two drove up to the security gate and were allowed into the barn area. They followed the instructions and drove around to barn thirty-three.

The assistant trainer, Gavin Foster, appeared pleased to see them. He showed them the horses, and explained that the horses would be training soon if they wished to observe. He left them to talk to the grooms as he returned to his office to take a phone call. Vasili spoke to the grooms, inquiring about the horses and any unusual activity. Pyotr stated that nothing unusual had been apparent in the last day. Everything was as it usually is. Vasili explained that they had reason to believe that Mrs. Lebedev had been kidnapped by an enemy of Mr. Lebedev and that they may have come to Churchill Downs on a horse van the previous afternoon. He wanted the private grooms to search the surrounding barns and ask questions, starting with this barn. The grooms complied and within twenty minutes they had found the blankets in the hollow at the top of the hay bales. There was no way of knowing if the hollowed area was new, or the work of a couple of horny stable hands, so they continued the search further afield and came up empty handed.

Eventually, Vasili and Anatoli returned to their vantage point outside the gate. By midnight, after twenty-four hours of tedious, surveillance, they returned to the airport and booked into the Crowne Plaza. Little did they know that the couple they sought was exactly one mile away, sleeping peacefully.

Vasili and Anatoli were still in an exhausted sleep when Vasili's cell rang. It was a very excited Nikolai. Isabel's fake Facebook had a status update time stamped at six fifty-one am and it was now a little after eight am. Vasili tried to turn on his laptop but it was dead. He had not remembered to plug it in to charge. He hurried out to the car, collected the charger and plugged it in.

It took a few minutes to boot up and he wanted to smash the lap top against the wall when the screen read 'Windows is updating, do not turn off the computer, 2 of 7 updates installing.....' He waited impatiently as the computer completed its updates, walking in circles around the room while rubbing his hands together.

Anatoli ordered them breakfast while they waited. Vasili called Marc to make sure the men were gassed up and ready to roll. Once he was on the computer, he got Isabel's accounts up and open.

There, as big as day, was the message, which didn't make any sense, along with the lovely location update. Ha, the silly bitch didn't even notice that he had changed her settings and turned on the location service, added the App that automatically logged her ISP and added the Nearby Friends App.

When he checked Nearby Friends, he only saw log-on's in his vicinity and presumed they were variations on his own locations since his arrival in the area so he immediately got to work locating the IP address. He almost thought that the IP was also himself until he checked his own IP. He called Marc as soon as he verified that the IP was located in Louisville, and told him to get his ass to Louisville asap. Marc and Rick were about seven hours away in Grove City, Pennsylvania, but he figured getting them as backup was possibly worthwhile.

Vasili returned to the Nearby Friends App history. One of these was obviously not his own location. He knew that the locations were generally within a half mile of the actual location, and the little bubble indicating the log-on at six fifty am was more than a half mile from his location.

He opened Google maps and marked the location and drew a circle around it with diameter of a half mile. He stared at the circle. It encompass a whole lot of nothing in the form of the Kentucky Expo Center complex, Cardinal Stadium parking, railroad track, a small residential area, but close to the center lay five hotels. Hardly a coincidence he thought. Looking at the five he decided they would start with the hotel closest to Churchill Downs. Even though all five were within easy walking distance, why walk farther than necessary was his logic. Without wasting any further time, Vasili and Anatoli packed up and checked out.

They drove over to the Holiday Inn. It was only fractionally closer than the Four Points By Sheraton but as good a place to start as any. Vasili was not about to waste time with niceties or role playing. He marched straight up to the desk, took out a roll of hundred dollar bills and asked the woman behind the counter how much she wanted in exchange for a quick look at the previous day's new arrivals. The woman's name tag identified her as Stella.

Stella was only twenty-four, a single mother, and recent graduate of hospitality school. She took one look at the terrifyingly ugly man standing before her and knew that nothing she was taught had prepared her for this encounter. Instinct warned her that denying his request would be extremely bad for her health and, for that matter, so would refusing his money. She reasoned that this vicious looking man would be more inclined to accept that she would do, or say nothing, if she took his money.

"Two thousand," she blurted, my baby needs a procedure and I need a down payment of two thousand." She wondered from where, on God's green earth, she had pulled that complete lie, and prayed for forgiveness of her soul. She had considered herself a good Christian woman before this moment. The ugly, oily man with the horrible pock marks and disfigured nose seemed surprised. He counted off twenty bills and handed them to her.

Stella pulled up the log from the day before and Vasili looked at all the entries after midday. They would not have arrived earlier than that he surmised. Surprisingly, was only one entry without a vehicle registration, and no identification, and it belonged to a Mr. And Mrs. Chapman arriving early evening. They had purchased toiletries, and asked that their luggage be brought to their room as soon as it arrived from New York as they had lost theirs, hence the no ID or toiletries.

Vasili asked Stella if she knew anything about these guests. She informed him that she did not, but that the off going staff this morning had told her to expect the luggage, and that the husband had smelled like urine and had apologized to the night clerk that he had fallen into some horse manure at the barn prior to checking in.

Vasili and Anatoli locked eyes and nodded. Vasili told the girl that if she knew what was good for her, she would retire to the restroom for the next fifteen minutes and tell anyone who asked that she had diarrhea. The men then laughed, asked Stella for a master key, and the location of the security camera base. Stella looked at the door behind her. Vasili slipped through and pulled the plug on the array of equipment, instantly powering down the monitors and recording equipment. Then the two men walked off toward the elevators.

Stella did as she was told, pocketing the money as she she went in the woman's restroom. She let herself into the supply closet, pulled the door closed behind herself and dialed 911. She looked around and stuffed eighteen of the twenty bills down behind the huge box of toilet rolls. She needed some reward for her bravery she thought.

The two men exited the elevator and walked quietly down the hall toward the room. Outside the door, they pulled out the previously concealed, custom made pistols, and flanked the door. It was surprisingly easy to design a semiautomatic pistol manufactured from carbon fiber and steel that could be disassembled so completely, and the parts hidden in a can of fake shaving cream and a model train, or airplane set, all nicely wrapped complete with birthday card. Nobody checks checked baggage that closely.

They could hear the television playing in the room. Vasili checked his watch it was nine twenty am. There was a 'Do Not Disturb' sign hanging on the door knob. He pushed the key card into the slot and heard the slight whir as the light turned green. He turned the door knob and pushed the door open with force.

Anatoli hit the ground rolling into the room, and Vasili ducked into the bathroom. They waited to see if anyone would appear from behind the beds. Other than the overly loud noise from the morning show on the television, there was nothing to be heard in the room. Anatoli, from his position on the floor next to the first bed lifted the edge of the cover against the floor and peered through under the bed. He could see nothing. He reached up grabbed a pillow and tossed it over the bed and into the gap between the beds. Again nothing. He tried it again, tossing the next pillow against the window, dropping into the space beyond the second bed. Again nothing. He decided the room was empty and stood up walking around the beds gun at the ready.

The room was empty. They checked the closet and drawers. Except for the crumpled bedding on both beds, the used toiletries, and the discarded remains of a blond Nice 'n easy hair color kit, the room was devoid of any sign of human occupation. It was starting to feel like they were chasing ghosts. Then they heard the sirens and turned to get the hell out of there.

WEDNESDAY

CHAPTER FOURTEEN

Louisville, Kentucky

At nine twenty-one am Mitch's cell phone beeped. He leaped up, grabbed his pack, stuffed everything into it, ran into the bathroom, grabbed the toiletries, pulled a startled Isabel to her feet and dragged her to the window. He slid the window open, and peered out. Now or never, he thought. He motioned for Isabel to climb out. Mitch held her hands and lowered her to the roof of the utility building. He dropped the pack to her and climbed out backwards, hung from the window sill, and dropped.

"Come," he said and rushed to the edge. They repeated the drop, this time from the roof, landing behind the dumpster. Mitch shouldered his pack, grabbed her hand and ran around the end of the wooden fence separating the Holiday Inn from the Four Points By Sheraton.

On the side walk, they slowed and walked hand in hand, to Crittenden Drive. They darted across the traffic and hurried down into the Expo parking adjacent to Kentucky Kingdom amusement park listening to the increasing wail of police cars approaching. Mitch steered her to the Thrifty rental car, and within five minutes they were driving out the other side of the Expo grounds and onto Preston Drive. Within a couple more, they were on I-264 heading west. Mitch drove across the I-65 bridge into Indiana and decided to continue on I-65 north putting as much distance between them and Louisville as he could.

"What just happened?" asked Isabel. "How did you know the police were coming and why did we run from the police?"

"We are not running from the cops," he explained. "We are running away from the men who stormed into our room."

"What?" she stated, now totally confused.

" Yesterday, when you were chatting to Jaime, I made our reservation, choosing a room based upon the Google Earth photo. I booked the room as a single, older man, Forester Black . I also booked a room on the second floor, facing the front of the hotel, on the north side, for Mr. and Mrs. Chapman. When we arrived I got our room key.

Later, I went down after shift change, out the side door, back in the front and checked in as Mr. Chapman. I made a big deal of no car, no luggage, that we were awaiting new luggage from New York, and that I smelled bad and couldn't wait for a shower because I fell in the shit at the barn. Made a point of bitching that you were taking too long getting us some take outs from Arby's, bought toiletries and then went and set up that room. I even left the used blond hair color packaging in the waste basket. Then I set up a little gizmo we have at the FBI that we use for monitoring entrances. A break in the connection alerts your phone as long as you are within five hundred feet or so. Someone entered the room and we got the hell out of there. I don't know why all the cop cars but that does convince me that whomever entered the room was actively looking for us especially since I had the do not disturb sign hanging on the nob.

Isabel was impressed. She was starting to think that this man might just actually be her knight in shining armor. Her positive thoughts were crushed when Mitch pondered aloud,

"I wonder how on earth they found us? I have been using untraceable phones, a prepaid Verizon dongle for Internet and doing all online activities through the VPN. I have been so damn careful, even my boss doesn't know where we are. Are you very, very sure you don't have an implanted tracking device? Have you ever had surgery?" Isabel realized with horror that it was her fault. She had gone online. Somehow they had her, obviously not so secret, Facebook account information and had tracked her that way. With a heavy heart she said in a very small voice,

"It's my fault."

"What?"

"I said, it's my fault they found us."

"Do tell." he uttered sarcastically.

"When you went out this morning I went to the business center and logged on to a fake Facebook account that I made one day when I was worried about my life and my husband. I only told by mom, my brothers, and a couple of very, very close and discrete friends about it, and that I would use it to contact them in an emergency or if I needed to tell them something I couldn't do openly. I wrote only one sentence, it said I was in the Green Mountains and I wasn't having any head pain because the air was clear". Then she explained what that would mean to her brothers. "I logged off and went back to the room. I hid my hair and face the entire time."

Mitch was really angry. This woman was not very good at following directions and she was not making it easy to keep her safe. He hoped that she had learned her lesson and asked as much. Isabel just nodded meekly.

"I'm so, so sorry. I realize now that Nikolai, obviously, has ways and means of keeping tabs on me. I have never had surgery since meeting him so I really, really don't think I have any microchips or tracking devices of any kind inside of me. Is there any way to find out?"

"Yes, he said, but not without equipment that we just don't have access to right now.

They drove on, mile after mile without speaking again. Isabel's bladder became more and more uncomfortable. She needed to pee so badly but was too ashamed of her stupidity to ask. Eventually, just as she thought she was going to pop, Mitch pulled into a remote rest stop and they quickly used the facilities and were back on the road.

"Tell me about your kid's nanny," he said.

"Riana is South African. She is twenty-three and came to the US on vacation, or so I was told. I was not happy about Nikolai hiring her because it seemed so sudden and random after our previous nanny quit. Initially, I thought she was related to our housekeeper, Mrs Wessels because they talk to each other but Mrs Wessels is Dutch.

Anyway, I'm pretty sure she is working here illegally, and I overheard Vasili arguing with Nikolai about bringing a stripper into the house to look after the kids; so I think that he found her in a strip club. I have heard a few arguments about a strip club so maybe Nikolai has one of those too, although it is more like something his cousin Vasili would have.

She says she has two brothers, one is a farmer, the other works on the railroad, not sure what he does exactly. Her mother died when she was young, her father was a drinker and abusive to the kids so they lived with a aunt, her mother's sister, in some little town or other right at the tip of Africa, or so she would say.

That's about all I know. She wasn't very chatty. She turned out to be really great with the boys. They love her so I suppose I stopped minding that Nikolai brought a stripper to live in my house. Now I don't mind because that keeps him away from me and so long as they hide their adultery from my sons I am actually relieved." She stopped as if contemplating what she had just said, realizing that she was voicing what she hadn't really dared to admit before today.

Mitch drove on quietly, what could you say to a woman who was in a marriage so bad she was resigned to her husband fornicating under her own roof. He felt sorry for her but he did not want to insult her, or embarrass her by showing his pity. He would have to add the new knowledge to his list of potential Lebedev endeavors. He wished he could contact Mack. Mack needed this information so that he could start cross referencing unsolved cases, that may be related to these business dealings, that had nothing to do with his suspected crimes as an attorney. There had to be something. They needed to revisit Georgio's death, the gun shop owner in North Carolina, they needed DNA and fingerprints from Vasili, Anatoli, and the men in the woods in Vermont to match against any retrieved from those crime scenes of other unsolved cases that now might just be related. Mitch decided to come right out and ask the million dollar question.

"Isabel, do you believe you know of an incidence where your husband has killed a man or been directly responsible for his death, for which you have irrefutable proof?" Isabel's head spun around with such force she cried out in pain.

"Ow, my neck," she complained rubbing it fiercely. "Give me a little warning before you ask questions like that. I already told you I think he had the man in North Carolina killed, and the kid in the lab. But I don't think they are the only ones. We have a pretty remote summer home in Montauk, and a boat at the marina up there. I've always wondered why he and Vasili go up there. They fly up on business. I mean, what business could they possibly have in Montauk. I have actually wondered if they have bodies buried in the state park or dumped out in the Atlantic after a 'fishing' trip." She stopped. This was also the first time she had allowed herself to also voice this suspicion aloud. It made her realize how much she had denied what was going on around her in order to survive. This got her back to thinking about Demmy and Yuri. She wished with all her heart she could be with her children. "When will I see my kids?" She asked.

Mitch was thrown off track by the sudden change in the direction the conversation had taken. He was thinking about how he was going to tell his crew about all the new information he was getting and had totally forgotten about the children involved.

"As soon as we get settled somewhere safe, I'll make some calls. Right now they really are very safe and having a blast. Try to remember that. It is more important right now that we concentrate on staying one step ahead of your husband and figuring out how we can get him put away forever." Isabel suspected that he was right. There was no point it getting her boys back until Nikolai was safely out of the picture.

Safe, thought Mitch. Where the hell is safe? He threw it out there as if it were real. He drove on in silence, trying to come up with a reasonable place to go. He thought about the vast mid-west that lay in the direction they were headed. What was out there, and who did he know? The last time he was even remotely close to this area was his time in boot camp at Great Lakes where he met the girl, who was to become his wife for a couple of angry years, at the Pier during his first real liberty. Mitch laughed to himself as re realized where they were headed. Mandy's Nana's house in Milwaukee. That old bat spent most of her time in Florida but even if she was home, she would welcome them with open arms. Milwaukee here we come.

The pair stopped at a truck stop just north of Indianapolis, refueled, bought Subway's foot longs, Vegetarian with extra pepper-jack for Isabel and roast beef for Mitch. They also bought a cheap cooler, and filled it with ice, lots of bottled Starbucks coffee in the various foo-foo flavors as Mitch described them, along with a collection of caffeinated soda and orange juice. A nice healthy selection, Isabel joked.

While waiting in line they watched the news on the big screen TV up on the wall of the convenience store. Isabel made a squeaky sound and Mitch, who was watching, knew why. On the screen was a not too grainy and very obvious picture of a short, pock marked man sporting a disfigured nose, with the caption, 'Do you know this man?' They were running the story of the peculiar incidence at a Holiday Inn in Louisville.

Back in the car, they discussed the close call and the implication of the confirmation of their pursuers. Four times they had been one jump ahead by the skin of their teeth. This luck is just going to run out he thought, and we need to be ready when it does.

It took them almost five hours to get to the little house on Seventy-Third Street just around the corner from the park. There was a car in the drive, but Mitch explained that the car would be there whether or not Greta was in residence. He turned around in the drive of the neighboring house and

parked outside Mrs Gunderson's home. Through the
trees and garden overgrown with flowering plants
and tall ornamental grasses, Isabel could see a small
home nestled at the back of the property.

Mitch jumped out and approached the gate. It
was locked on the inside which meant Greta was
likely away. He wondered if the gate combination
still spelled dog, and gave it a try. Four for 'd', zero
for 'o', and seven for 'g', and the lock popped open.
Creature of habit the old bird was. He motioned for
Isabel to follow. She entered the yard and he closed
the gate.

It was almost five pm, too late to return the car
today. They'd do that in the morning. He left Isabel
standing at the front door and went over to the
garden shed. He stepped around behind it and come
back baring the key he had removed from the
magnetized hide-a-key affixed just under the
overhang of the roof.

He unlocked the door and stepped into the
sitting-room, quickly turning and silencing the
cheap alarm attached to the door. The place felt like
a furnace in the hot Milwaukee sun so he
immediately turned on the air conditioning unit in
the window facing the south side of the house. He
opened the curtains on the large front window
revealing a small room with hardwood floors, filled
with an ancient cracked , brown, leather couch and
chair and a nice modern thirty-two inch television
atop a fake fireplace. The room had large double
doors, as well as a large window into the dining
room behind.

The dining room was occupied by an old wooden

kitchen table surrounded by six chairs in various states of disrepair, and a large old dresser along the wall under the window to the sitting room. Off to the right was a small bathroom toward the front of the house and a bedroom toward the rear. Isabel could see a huge four poster bed that took up most of the room.

The back of the dining room led onto the kitchen, which looked like something out of the sixties crossed with garish modern. The counter along the right wall was new and contained a new sink, but the cabinetry was probably as old as the house. Heavy, and obviously hand made. The far wall sported the gas range and an old refrigerator that still had rounded edges. It was a Kelvinator. Wow, she thought, that's a testament to quality, if ever I saw one.

The near wall was wooden cabinetry of indeterminate age, whose paint had been removed and the original solid wood oiled. The floor was a heavy beige tile. The wall on the left had the only window looking south onto the neighbor's vegetable garden. Isabel looked out the window at the wildly out of control garden with tomatoes in all stages of ripeness, peppers in all colors, a variety of squashes intermingled with lots of flowers.

The kitchen led out onto a small walk-through bedroom, which in turn led around to the mudroom that contained the door to the back yard. In the mudroom were the stairs down into the basement. That was the whole house. It seemed small, old, and very lived in. Isabel didn't think she had ever seen such a tiny house. Well, not counting the actual latest fad of extremely ridiculously tiny houses that is.

After checking the refrigerator, which was nearly devoid of anything that would rot, and the cupboards that also contained very little worth eating except in an emergency, they returned to the sitting room and sat down to take stock of their needs.

"OK," Mitch said. "First things first. I will have to get hold of Greta and let her know we are staying here before a neighbor calls the cops. Then we have to go shopping. There is absolutely no way they know where we are unless you really do have an implanted tracking device. So, until we accidentally give up our location, which can't happen until we use a phone or go online, we have time on our side. I will go next door and get Greta's number before we go to the store. You can take a shower or whatever you want while I pop over there."

He looked over at her where she sat sunken in the huge soft armchair in front of the window. "Try to behave while I am gone. Don't touch the damn phone, please. We really need this time." Isabel just glared. She felt dumb enough already, wild horses couldn't get her to touch the stupid old land line.

Mitch left to go next door. They had seen a dark haired woman who appeared to be in her late twenties struggling up to the back door of the house to the south, groceries in hand, trailing twin girls of around four and a cute, dirty little toddler of indeterminate gender, although, based on the toys in the yard, likely a boy. Isabel went into the bathroom and thoroughly washed the old bathtub before closing the mildewy curtain.

The door to the bathroom had no lock and didn't even latch effectively. The towel she had retrieved from the narrow closet smelled clean. She took a very quick shower, washing her underwear and hanging it on the curtain rail above the window. So strange to take a shower and be able to look out the window. She looked across at the second story of the house to the north. She supposed that the angle was steep and the glass steamy enough for privacy. She was dressing in her old clothes when she heard Mitch return.

Isabel heard him call Greta from the land-line on the dresser in the dining room. From what she could hear, the elderly woman was away in Minnesota visiting her sister and would not be back until the end of the month and that they would be welcome to stay. She was back sitting in the comfy chair when he got off the phone.

"You heard that?" he asked. She nodded. Mitch continued, "She is telling the young couple next door that we are staying while I am here on business of unknown duration, Handy that. Let's go get food."

They locked up and drove the three blocks to the nearest supermarket. It was a Sentry, Isabel had never seen a Sentry. This one looked rather grim. She doubted there would be much in the way of organic produce in the place. Her fears were realized as they bought milk, bread, margarine, lettuce, onions, tomatoes, coffee, eggs, and an assortment of very cheap cheese and cold cuts. She had turned into a food snob she thought. Organic, pasture raised, grass fed were obviously not familiar words in this neighborhood. She wondered if she and the boys would be shopping at places like this after they lost everything to the government.

Back at the house, Mitch parked inside the yard and locked the gate. They took the groceries inside. While Isabel fixed coffee and sandwiches, Mitch got busy setting up the camera. He was bummed that he only had one. He would have to pick up a cheap home surveillance kit at Best Buy in the morning. He set the house alarms that Greta had installed on the front and back doors, and checked the windows. They too had the small magnets that squealed when pulled apart. Better than nothing he thought.

In the basement the small windows around the top were all nailed shut. At the far end of the basement was a door into what he realized was Greta's sewing room. It contained a chaise that appeared to be made up as a guest bed. The door to the steps outside was locked; he unlocked it and stared up the stairs. The stairwell was sealed by the heavy metal storm shutters and locked from the inside with the key in the lock. He returned to the upper floor to find the table set and the two of them sat down to eat.

"There is a bed in a room off the basement, the twin in the back room and the four-poster in Greta's room, which would you like?" he asked Isabel. She thought about that while they ate. The four-poster was close to the front entrance and the twin near the back. Neither felt safe. The basement, well she hadn't seen the basement but she was not sure she liked the thought of being trapped underground. There was another AC unit in the main bedroom so it would be pleasant in there. After a lot of thought she said,

"I think we should both sleep in the main bedroom, it will be safer that way don't you think?" As soon as she saw the look on his face she got mad. "Don't get any ideas you prick! I was being serious. I am afraid to be near either door by myself or alone in the basement." Mitch was having a great laugh at her expense.

He continued to chew and chuckle as she sat and huffed and puffed as she downed her coffee. He had known this woman for five days now and he really liked her. He liked her spunk, and her smile, and her smarts, and her really liked her body. Holy shit, he loved her body. Sleeping together was going to be a tough undertaking if he was to stay out of trouble.

Mitch finished his last sandwich and stood up taking his coffee with him to the sitting room where he turned on the TV to watch the news. Isabel cleared the table thinking that he was a dreadfully chauvinistic pig letting her do all the 'woman's work'. Soon she joined him and when he refused to change the channel, she retired to Greta's bedroom to watch TV in there. Greta must certainly like her television programming to have two big new TV sets in such a small house. Mitch came in and tossed her his big T-shirt again.

"Tomorrow we buy you new clothes." he said before going to take a shower. He returned in just his boxers and climbed into the huge bed next to her. While she watched CSI, he typed away on his laptop, and then, in order to avoid the mole at the DOJ, he logged on with the VPN, and sent an encrypted email from his French email address to his old boss at the FBI.

He had chronicled everything Isabel had told him to date, except the stuff about the horses and he included the location of the man in the BMW's trunk in Erie even though it was unlikely that Sasha was still there at the rate Lebedev was able to track people down. He warned Micheal Mandrake of the mole and suggested they keep the investigation in-house until further notice.

Without contacting his own team, he signed off. He left the computer turned on next to the bed showing the scene of the front yard visible by the porch and street lights. He had the camera plugged into a WiFi box on an electrical outlet next to the front door so that he was free to move around the house with the laptop.

Mitch fell asleep with his back to Isabel as she sat watching television too afraid to lie back and relax. After he was asleep, she turned off the television and snuggled down into the bed covers. The room was nice and cool so the feather comforter felt divine even though she could smell dog on it. She turned her back toward Mitch and fell asleep, it was not long before she rolled over and contacting the warm body instinctively wrapped her arm over him and spooned close.

CHAPTER FIFTEEN

Earlier back in Louisville

With the police approaching the hotel in Louisville, sirens blaring, Vasili and Anatoli raced out of the Arby's parking lot, and took off down Crittenden, then east on I-264; east again on I-64, and just kept on going. In Lexington, Vasili made the decision to go north to Cincinnati, where they turned in the rental car and booked the next flight back to New York. Vasili called Marc and Rick to tell them once again, to hole up in the next town they reached. The two were already just past Cincinnati en route to Louisville so they turned around.

The four men met at the airport, prior to the flight, to compare notes. Nobody knew how Sasha was doing because they had not wanted to call the hospital in Erie. Marc and Rick would stay in the area to await instruction. They speculated on whether or not the DOJ agent had known they were coming or whether they had left already to go somewhere specific. Most likely back to New York they surmised. Mrs. Lebedev was also likely now a blond. They were chasing a ghost and a blond woman in a country of three hundred and fifty million people, how hard could it be. The men agreed that they needed to go on the offensive. Vasili would talk to Nikolai and see what they could do to change their luck. There is no such thing as luck, Vasili bitched. We make our luck, so lets shake shit up and see what falls out the tree.

The two going to New York on the two-forty-five flight departed through security, leaving their weapons with Marc and Rick; who left to go and find an inexpensive, yet comfortable hotel on the outskirts of the city. Vasili had not bothered to call his cousin, and had not answered his calls. He was pissed off and not in the mood for Nikolai's tantrums.

On the flight to New York he was surly, and snapped at the flight attendant. He bought too much vodka and became more and more bad tempered as the flight progressed. Anatoli put in his ear plugs and watched a movie pretending not to notice. The big bald man was good at his job, protect and serve, and say nothing. He steered the drunk man through their connection in Chicago where another two vodkas chased those consumed in flight. Vasili passed out on the next leg, snoring loudly, annoying all those around him.

After arriving in New York just before seven pm, Anatoli hailed a cab, and delivered Vasili to his apartment on the East Side and then took himself home after agreeing to meet at Nikolai's house on Eighty-Eighth Avenue at eight am.

CHAPTER SIXTEEN

Orlando, Florida

Riana stood in the long line of people waiting for the Harry Potter ride at Universal Studios, Orlando. She and the boys were having an amazing time. She was deliriously happy that Nikolai trusted her with his children during his divorce from his wife.

Riana actually rather liked Isabel even though she had been very jealous of her prior to last Saturday. She went as far as feeling a little sorry for her losing her children but she was sure that Nikolai would let the boys see their mother once this was all settled, after all the boys were really close to their mother and would be devastated by the divorce.

She had had only one opportunity to try and contact Nikolai since then. She knew the men watching her and the boys said that Nikolai wanted no contact, but she also had her secret agreement with Nikolai and she had upheld that. Early yesterday, she managed to get a woman at Disney to take a photo of her and the boys and send it to the secret Snapchat account. She shuffled forward in the fake rock passage, and was wondering if Nikolai had seen the photo when someone bumped her from behind. She turned to see a vaguely familiar man with a finger to his lips.

Riana stared hard and realized that it was one of the investigators that Nikolai used in his legal firm. He was using a very good disguise she thought and she faced forward again as his finger motioned her to do. She heard him whispering from close behind.

"My name is Jackson Mason, I work for Mr. Lebedev. He sent me here to find you. Do not look back. How many men are with you?"

"Two," she replied, "They are watching the exit down in the gift shop. They used to come on all the rides but now they wait in the gift shop."

"Riana, I have to ask you to trust me. These men who kidnapped you and the kids, they don't work for Mr. Lebedev." She gasped and started to turn but he shoved her slightly to make her stumble forward. "Don't look at me, I don't want any possible camera or video feed showing us talking. Just listen. Those men are very bad men who want to hurt Nikolai. I am here to free you. I can't try that here in the park because they have a very good system in effect to prevent the kidnapping of children from the park. I have a tiny cell phone with the battery in backwards so the phone cannot work, just in case they are scanning you occasionally. Once you are back where they are keeping you, you can go to take a shower, turn on the water and start singing and splashing. While making this noise, replace the battery correctly and wait for me to send a text message. It will just say 'Love you princess'. This will mean that I have used the phone to locate the residence. Immediately take the battery out again. You cannot take a chance that the phone will be found, so either hide the phone in your vagina or flush it down the toilet. You might have to stick your hand into the bowl to push it over the hump. Put your hand over your mouth and cough three times if you understand? Riana coughed three times.

Mason repeated the instructions and told Riana to find a restroom as soon as possible and put the phone in her vagina. Until then she should put it under a breast inside her bra. He told her to pretend to stretch and reach around to rub her lower back and as she complied she felt the phone being placed in her hand. Riana's palm closed around the phone. She immediately brought her hand up to her neck as if to touch her throat and in a quick move placed her hand down inside her t-shirt and into her left bra cup.

When Riana next glanced behind herself, the man was gone. She readjusted a couple of times before boarding the ride. She certainly did not want to lose the cell phone before the end of the ride.

As soon as they disembarked and rejoined the two men who had been with them since Saturday, she requested a potty break on the grounds that they had had far too much Butter beer before the ride. Riana washed her hands before entering the small toilet stall. She pulled out the phone and found that was tightly sealed in a thin plastic vacuum pack with one small packet of surgical lubricant taped to it. She removed the Surgilube and hoped that the phone was not covered in germs as she ripped the packet open and rubbed the lubricant over the vacuum pack.

It was a tiny phone, she had never seen one so small, about two inches wide, three long and less than a half inch deep. It slipped quite easily into her vagina without too painful a stretch. Once inside she felt no pain but she was worried that getting it out would be far more difficult that getting it in.

She actually did need to pee, so with that accomplished, she washed her hands and rejoined the group.

The remainder of the day was filled with more childish fun and Riana could not remember a happier, and more enjoyable few days in all her life. The happiness was only now marred now by her new fear of the men escorting them from ride to ride. Riana tried very hard to control her urge to scan the people around them for familiar faces.

When it was time to leave Demmy and Yuri started whining and the man she knew as Bob yelled at them to shut up. The boys became very quiet as they followed Riana and the other man, whom they knew as John to the car. Riana had noticed that over the last few days the noise and activity generated by the two young boys was starting to get under the older man's skin. With the stiff, uncomfortable way that he interacted with the boys, she doubted he had children of his own. They drove back to the townhouse in a quiet neighborhood of Davenport, Florida in silence.

Mason stayed as far away from the group as he possibly could. He never followed them into any area that only had one entrance and exit. At these points he would fall back and sit somewhere, with a drink in hand waiting for them to reappear. Once it was apparent that they were heading home, he followed just until he saw them approaching a large white Lincoln Continental. Then he followed a group of tourists in the direction of his own vehicle and joined the throng of cars exiting the huge parking area.

It was easy to use the cover of the throng to follow the government car onto the I-4 southbound. He dropped further and further back until the car exited the highway. This was as far as he dare follow without making it obvious he was tailing them. He hoped that their final destination was not much further than another five minutes' drive.

Mason continued on I-4 South, and used the next exit to turn around and go back. This time he took the exit and pulled into the MacDonald's drive through. He ordered and burger, large fries, iced tea, and Mango smoothie to hold him over while he waited. He quickly filled up with gas, and parked in the Chilli's parking, to eat his food while he waited for Riana to turn on the phone.

The townhouse on Forest View Drive was a large, light gray, five bed, four and a half bath, condo available for rent by the day. It was very airy and bright compared to the brownstone in New York. The boys loved the huge pool, the Jacuzzi, and especially the games-room with the big air-hockey and pool tables. The place even had a jukebox for heaven's sake. Her room had an en-suite bath she was sure she would have no problem using the cell. Demmy and Yuri had the option of separate rooms but they chose to be together in the room with the two bunk beds so they could both have a top and a bottom bunk. Initially Riana was a mess of nerves watching them climb around, jumping, and swinging like monkey. Eventually they had calmed down and actually now slept on the bottom bunks because they soon had tired of the climb up and down.

Bob drove right into the huge garage and the door closed behind them before they even had time to get out of the car. Demmy complained of thirst, so Riana took the boys into the kitchen and poured them each a glass of orange juice. She added ice as requested and carried the drinks to the games room so that the boys wouldn't spill juice on ridiculously soft, pale cream, carpeting.

John settled into a comfy chair and switched on the television, tuning in to ESPN. Riana took the opportunity to say that she was tired and sweaty and would take a quick shower before fixing dinner for the kids.

Once in her room, she closed the door as she usually did, entered her bathroom and locked the door. She turned on the shower and quickly stripped naked. She squatted down and pushed against the phone whilst sliding a finger up and hooking it over the top edge and simultaneously drawing down. Her hymenal ring stretched tight and the phone caused some discomfort, but no real pain as it slipped out into her hand.

She rinsed the goop off the plastic with the hot water from the shower using a little body wash to get rid of the lubricant. Riana dried the small package and used her teeth to rip it open. She removed the back and turned the battery around pressing it firmly into place. The sound was off so the screen lit up and the phone fired up without even a buzz. She placed the phone in the window and proceeded to take a nice long shower while she sang some of the Afrikaans songs of her childhood. She ended with a favorite ,

"Oë ek het a perd, 'n blink vos perd," She thought that one was pretty apt and smiled to herself. Nik was coming for her, like a knight in shining armor via his investigator of course. She belted out the rest at the top of her voice, "met 'n splinter nuwe saal, en ek klim op my perd my blink vos perd en ek kom om jou to haal. Want jy het gesé as ek jou will hé dan moet ek jou kom haal, op my mooi ry perd my blink vos perd, met a splinter nuwe saal."

Jackson Mason was a talented investigator in all the ways Nikolai Lebedev appreciated. The man had a college degree in criminal justice and had been a police officer with a Newark police department until he was fired for beating a suspect.

Mason had previously been exonerated for unjustified use of deadly force when he had shot a man. His defense was that he thought the man was drawing a gun. The beating, eight months later was caught on video by a witness standing under a nearby tree. Mason had not seen the witness, and his lie about being attacked by the suspect was revealed on national television. It was only the expert legal help of a renown criminal defense attorney that kept him out of jail.

He had answered the ad for the position of

defense investigator with the firm of Lebedev, Cohen, And Sanders. after being unemployed for four months. It didn't take long to realize that the man interviewing him, the very one who had saved his skin the year before was treating his run in with the law as a 'pro' and not a 'con'. When Lebedev pointedly asked him, if there was anything he wouldn't do for the right price, Mason took a risk and said no. Nikolai Lebedev had smiled, stretched out his hand and welcomed him aboard.

To date he had 'fixed' twelve problems for his employer, making his body count a baker's dozen. Number thirteen had made him nervous. He was a superstitious man and had wondered if his luck would run out, and when it hadn't he felt invincible. Jackson Mason really liked to kill and, to him, nothing beat the thrill of killing a man and getting away with it.

Mason's phone on the console beside him beeped and he quickly turned on the App to find the location of the small cell phone he had given to the nanny. It appeared close on the screen but there was no direct route, he would have to drive around a large vacant area.

He started the car and made his way toward the house on Forest View Drive. He passed the house at a normal speed, careful not to look toward it as he passed. He allowed his GoPro taped to the passenger headrest under a straw hat to video tape the house instead. He turned right onto Lake Shore Parkway and parked under a tree as soon as he was out of sight of the houses.

Mason sent the text and was almost instantly

rewarded by the disappearance of the dot on his screen. Thank God that woman followed direction so well.

He loaded the video onto his lap top and studied the house. There did not appear to be any video surveillance but he did see small stakes in the ground at each end of the property where it bordered the sidewalk. He zoomed in and took a closer look. They appeared to be small, wireless infra-red sensors. He suspected there would be some in the rear of the property as well. These people had obviously not really expected to be found.

He made his way through the trees, and from a distance, zoomed in on the property and videotaped the back and sides of the house.

Back at his car, he uploaded the video and then drove back to the Chilli's for dinner. He sat in a corner booth and using earphones and a screen protector to prevent prying eyes from spying.

He located the infra-red sensors on both back corners of the property. They were actually very close to the house. He suspected the sensors were placed that close to minimize alerts caused by children playing in the field behind the house or perhaps the local wild life and occasional loose dog. He looked at the items around the screened pool area.

There was a small, stand-alone Tiki bar with two matching stools, a large gas grill, a round glass topped table surrounded by chairs that more or less matched the bar, and a few reclining deck chairs surrounding a decent sized pool and Jacuzzi.

He was confident that like most people, these guys would have a false sense of security resulting from the enclosed deck and pool. People would keep the front door locked but the sliding door out to the pool open as if mosquito netting was somehow impenetrable.

Jackson Mason polished off his rib-eye, skillet mashed potatoes and broccoli, Skillet Toffee Fudge Brownie desert and two glasses of iced tea before heading back to his spot under the trees on Lake Shore Parkway.

He pulled on a thin black hood made of a nylon pantyhose type fabric, and snug, ultra-thin, lambskin gloves. Dressed all in black, with night vision goggles, he had a nine mm Ruger with suppressor, a little Beretta Tomcat also with suppressor; four inch, needle pointed, double edged Kershaw Amphibian knife, a garrote, and a syringe with a hefty dose of Ketamine.

Mason moved quickly through the trees until he was opposite the gray house. He could see the lights blazing on the enclosed deck and from numerous rooms in the house. The home to the right was in darkness so he took advantage of the dark to do a slow leopard crawl across to it and move around, hugging the structure until he was adjacent to the covered porch where it attached to the house.

He used his goggles to check the location of the beam and stepped over it and hugged the wall. He pocketed the goggles and peeped around the corner to visualize the porch. Nobody was using the pool. The boys were playing some kind of game in the room out of sight through the open doors. A woman was telling them to wrap it up and get ready for bed. The kids begged for ten more minutes.

Mason used the cover of the noise and distracting children's behavior to slice the screen along the wood against the house and a few inches along the bottom edge, making a gap just big enough to slip through. Once through, he moved an inverted closed umbrella and leaned it over the corner to hide the tear, then moved in behind the Tiki bar. He could have peeked into the game's room but he was not about to blow his cover taking that chance on the very brightly lit deck.

Within a few minutes, Mason again heard Riana telling the boys to clean up. He heard a man say that he was going up to his room to make a call. A second male voice boomed, shouting at the children to listen to their nanny. Like magic, the kids were silent. The voice stated the man's intention to go for a smoke and his expectation that the kids be in bed by the time her returned.

With that, a large man, somewhat pudgy Mason thought for an FBI agent, and definitely on the wrong side of fifty stepped out onto the deck and walked away from the house while lighting a cigarette. The heavy man, with thinning hair, stood staring out through the screen into the darkness. The Jacuzzi bubbled about a foot away, to the man's left, as he stood in profile to Mason.

Mason quickly took advantage of the situation. He quietly removed the Tomcat from its holster against his chest and loaded the convenient little pop up barrel with one homemade round. The round was precision drilled from extremely dense rock salt mined on Avery Island. The result is a ninety-nine percent pure, translucent projectile without flaws. The tip is just barely rounded for aerodynamics.

The flabby man continued to smoke, oblivious to his surroundings when the salt slammed into his temple from less than twenty feet away. Bob's head jerked violently to the right and he staggered to compensate, tripping on the edge of the Jacuzzi, and fell, slamming his head on the opposite edge neatly obliterating the impact point. Mason was stunned; he could not have planned a move like that in a million years. Slowly the man slipped down into the Jacuzzi as he became water logged. Robert Sanders floated face down in the Jacuzzi and Mason left him to drown.

The game room was empty as he looked in the window. Riana had shepherded the boys up the stairs completely oblivious to the thunk and splash. Mason hoped that the other man's room did not overlook the screened porch. He slipped inside and started up the stairs.

He could hear Riana putting the boys to bed toward the back of the house. At the top of the stairs was a landing. The door to the left, which he presumed was the master suite, was closed. To the right he could see the room occupied by a woman based on the clothes lying on the bed. He presumed this was Riana's room.

He decided to use Riana to draw the man out because he was not sure that this other man was still unaware of his presence. He backed into her room. She entered about three minutes later and almost screamed in surprise when she saw him standing out of sight of the door. Mason put a finger to his lips and beckoned her over.

"I need you to get the man in that room to come to the door. I don't want him communicating with anyone when I disable him. Do you have a good excuse to draw him out?" Riana smiled and nodded. She knew the perfect excuse.

"I'll tell him I just started my period and I need him to take me out for tampons. But what if he tells me to ask Bob?" Mason realized that Bob must be the dead man.

"I already incapacitated Bob," he said. "Tell this guy that Bob said no." Riana walked over to the opposite door. Mason pushed himself flush against the wall to the right of the door because the man looking out from behind the inward opening door would be looking toward the left. Riana knocked and called

"John!"

"What?" asked the voice from behind the door.

""I'm sorry, this is very embarrassing, but I just started my period and I need to go to the gas station for some tampons before it closes."

"Go ask Bob, I'll watch the boys."

"Bob said no, he said he is already in his under pants and not about to get dressed again."

"Damn it, that guy is getting annoying," John grumbled. "OK, hold on, I'll be out in two."

They heard him finish a conversation and then footsteps approaching the door. Mason motioned Riana away. As soon as John stepped out of the room he saw Mason and the silenced gun pointed straight at his head.

"On the ground buddy if you want to see tomorrow." Mason ordered. "Keep your hands where I can see them and get down on your belly, legs crossed, hands above your head on the floor, you know the drill". John recognized standard cop directives and wondered what the hell was going on.

"I am FBI," he said as he complied, "My ID is in my room." Mason encouraged the confusion.

"Well, you just do as you are told and I'll check it. OK hands behind your back." As soon as John complied Mason straddled him and struck him on the back of the head with the butt of the gun. He cuffed the semi-conscious man and plunged the Ketamine into his thigh through his pants. He dragged John over to the bed and manhandled him onto it. Personally he didn't care where he left the agent but he was doing this to mollify the horrified woman who had just witness the rough treatment of an FBI agent. He motioned for her to follow.

"Quickly pack a bag with your essentials, and a change of clothes for yourself and the boys and let's get out of here. I'll explain as soon as we are safely away."

Riana ran into her room, grabbed the wheeled carry-on bag she had received after being taken from the park by the two men who she now knew were FBI agents. She threw in her toiletries, jeans, undies, two tee's and a sweater. She carried it down the hall and added similar items for both boys.

After three hard days of amusement park, both boys had passed out as soon as their heads hit the pillow. Mason whispered to her to carry the smaller boy and he gently lifted the bigger one in both arms and reached for the suitcase with fingers outstretched from the lower arm. They carried the children into the garage and placed them recumbent on the back seat of the Lincoln.

"Get in and I'll go find the keys," he said. "Who usually drove?"

"The big guy in the downstairs bedroom," she replied presuming that the horrid older man was equally unconscious in his room.

Mason went into the room but found no keys. He turned off the light to the screened porch as well as all the lights in the rooms adjacent to the screen porch. He did not want a nosy neighbor out for a stroll seeing him searching a dead man.

He pulled the corpse toward him and felt the keys in the man's right pant pocket. He reached in and retrieved the keys and stopped in the kitchen to dry his gloves a little before returning to the garage.

He switched off the garage light, and activated the remote for the garage door. As soon as it was open he started the car, and drove out closing the door remotely as they drove away. He was not sure who would be alerted by the alarm from the infra-red alarm system, other than the heavily sedated man, and had no plans to stick around long enough to find out.

Mason drove down the road and took the right toward his car. He pulled up behind it and while the road was dark made the switch. Yuri mumbled briefly but quieted with Riana's reassurance. He told her to wait with the lights out and to duck low if anyone drove by.

Then, he drove the large white car to the end of the green fence that lined this section of road. As he approached the houses up ahead he turned off the lights, and drove off the left side of the road and scraped through a bush to steer around the line of painted wooden posts that prevented vehicles from driving on the grassy park approaching the lake.

He followed the edge of the brush, and soon found the dirt track off to the left that he had seen on Google Earth earlier that evening. He followed the track to the end, jumped out, found a stick, put the car in drive, and with his foot jammed on the brake. Lodged the stick between the seat and the accelerator pedal. The car roared a little and he leapt away, the car leaping forward as his foot came off the brake. It drove straight into the lake and began to sink.

Mason jogged back to his car. He drove out of the neighborhood this time turning left on Ronald Reagan Parkway before taking the Old Tampa Highway through Kissimmee and heading toward Melbourne on the US-192.

En-route he made a call to tell a man that they would be about an hour. By midnight Wednesday, they were at the Melbourne Marina.

THURSDAY

CHAPTER SEVENTEEN

Melbourne, Florida

Jackson Mason told Riana that she was to pretend to be his girlfriend, and that they were taking her employer's children to meet up with the children's parents at a resort in the Bahama's where they had their yacht. The parents thought that a boat trip to the Bahama's would help the children develop their sea legs. He would go and find the hired charter boat captain and she must wake the boys and tell them of the adventure.

Mason left her to go and find the man, and Riana woke Yuri and Demyan. The boys, though sleepy, were very excited. This was an adventure that they could never imagine. Immediately they talked of seeing ginormous sharks, and whales that could swallow them. Yuri started to cry, and Riana reassured him that this was not true and no whale had ever swallowed a person.

The kids marveled at falling asleep in Orlando and waking at the sea. This had been a very exciting week for them. They chattered incessantly and Riana smiled at the gullibility and resilience of kids. It was so easy for them to accept these sudden and illogical changes day after day.

While she was horribly confused after being hoodwinked by the FBI, she was now very suspicious of Jackson Mason. Yes, she hoped he was telling her the truth because she was smitten with the lure of the life Nikolai could offer her. On the other hand, Nik was a somewhat violent man, and she was wondering why the government would want his children.

Mason returned, greeted the boys, and introduced himself to them as Jack, Riana's boyfriend. He grabbed the bags from the trunk, and they followed him around a building and onto the wharf. He led them to a very nice boat, a huge white fishing charter vessel. Riana guessed it to be about sixteen to eighteen meters long so about fifty to sixty feet she informed the boys when Yuri asked.

The boat was a charter out of Miami per her registration and called After Five. Of course Yuri asked why the boat was named After Five so Riana explained. Mason greeted the charter boat captain and introduced him as Eddie.

To Riana and the boys, Eddie looked exactly like a boat captain should look. He had a huge bushy beard, mustache, and eyebrows, huge smile with big white teeth in his leathery, sun tanned, weather beaten face.

Eddie welcomed them aboard, taking the two suitcases from Mason and leading them below deck into the nicest cabin they could have imagined. The boys oohed and aahed at the huge seating area and big flat screen television complete with Xbox and games per Eddie. He quickly went below and stowed the cases in the cabins before reappearing and suggesting that they all take some Dramamine. Riana though that was a terrific idea. She envisaged them all puking their guts out. Even Mason accepted a dose.

Eddie explained that they were traveling about three hundred miles so it would take at least ten to twelve hours to get there at a cruising speed of twenty-four knots. He suggested that they get some sleep until day break when they could enjoy some fishing after breakfast. He showed them the well-stocked refrigerator for beverages and snacks, and bid them goodnight as he went to prepare to cast off. Mason grinned at the boys.

"Fun stuff huh," he said. "Get something quickly and let's get to bed, there will be lots of fun tomorrow." Riana passed each of the boys a juice box and they followed her below. She had planned for the boys to share the one queen cabin with her but when they saw the bunk beds stacked in a closet sized cabin they were thrilled. This is how real sailors travel Yuri had informed her. Riana, tucked them back in, Demmy at the bottom Yuri on top, and turned the light off. She closed the cabin door and could hear the boys' continued discussion as she retreated to her cabin and secured her door.

Riana was very nervous about sleeping in a boat, surely under the water line, but she was exhausted. She climbed into bed marveling at the amount of money Nik could spend on vacations. As a child, her family vacations had consisted of a tightly packed car drive, through hours of blazing heat to the sea side, where they would spend two weeks camped near the beach, living on anything you could cook on an open fire. This was a whole new world that she would really like to be part of. Certainly a far cry from being a stripper in New York with grabbing hands and lap dances. Never again, she decided. Never again.

They all slept late on Thursday morning and Eddie called them up for breakfast around nine am. The boys, followed by Riana, scrambled up the narrow circular stairs and tucked into scrambled eggs, toast, cinnamon rolls, milk, juice, and coffee.

Eddie started breakfast with another round of Dramamine. He was good at keeping his passengers happy. He explained that he had cruised more slowly since they had not wanted to arrive too early. Currently, they were about three hours from their destination and that, if there was still no hurry, they could fish and snorkel once they were in the shallower waters close to the islands.

Eddie went above, and the big boat's engine rumbled to life. Mason sat at the table and watched as Riana set the boys up with the Xbox, and an age appropriate game, after several minutes of arguing about wanting to play one of the violent first person shooter games.

While the kids played, Riana went below to brush her teeth. She turned on the television in her cabin and was surprised to find all the regular Satellite offerings. She flipped through the channels, looking for FOX or CNN, and she found CNN. She was hoping that there might be news that could shine a light on what was really happening. She might only have a high school education, but she really did not think that she was stupid enough not to think that she just didn't know the truth.

Up on deck, Eddie also turned on the small TV set into the console above his wheel. He liked keeping up on world news so he too tuned into CNN and watched one story after another of rioting, police shootings, more ISIS, the expected hurricane season and more.

Just before noon, the topic changed and the news anchor warned of a breaking story out of Orlando. Two boys age eight and eleven, and their twenty-three year old nanny were missing, presumed kidnapped. The scene showed a gray house, surrounded by police, lots of yellow tape and many news trucks. One man had been drowned in the Jacuzzi, and although it appeared to be an accident, the police suspected foul play. Medical examiner had removed the body. Another occupant of the house was found handcuffed and beaten. There were reports that he had been drugged. He described the assailant as a male, about five feet ten inches, race unknown because he had been wearing a black mask and gloves. They went on to report the possibility that the nanny was involved.

Riana watched in horror, Jack had murdered Bob. She quickly changed the channel to one with a movie so that he would not realize that she knew. She hurried upstairs to see what he was doing. The boys continued to battle each other in the game, but Mason was not there.

She approached the hatch to see if he was up on deck and froze, sinking down to stay out of sight. Jack was dragging Eddie toward the back of the boat. She could not tell if he was dead or alive. Eddie must have been watching the same news coverage and Jack must have seen him. She peeped over the edge of the deck as Mason opened the bait well and tried to stuff Eddie inside.

When it became obvious that the man was not going to fit, he unceremoniously tipped him overboard off the back of the boat. Riana thought that she noticed the man flailing and hoped that this meant that he was still alive. She bolted back down below deck, and prayed that the poor man was a very, very good swimmer and that there were no hungry sharks around.

Riana rushed back to her cabin. The boys, thank God, were so engrossed in the stupid video game that they had missed everything. She doubted they had even noticed her moving through the room. In her cabin, with her door casually left ajar, she pretended to be engrossed in a rerun of 'The Whole Nine Yards.' It was one of her favorites and she knew it very well so she didn't have to watch while she frantically reviewed her options.

Riana had left South Africa to seek a safer life in the US. She had learned over the years that one must hide fear from all types of predators including the human ones. In her last eighteen months in South Africa she had lived through a violent attempted home invasion on the family farm. Her brother's family, and that of the immediate neighbor, had fought back with available weaponry for four hours before the gunmen with AK47 rifles had given up and left the area.

Prior to that she had survived a knife attack. The

knife attack had occurred when a man had attacked the Ndabele woman who rented the cottage at the entrance to the farm. Riana had grabbed her brother's nine mm Beretta and rushed to the woman's aid. The man with the twelve inch curved knife had immediately attacked her and she had had to shoot him as soon as she realized that he had no intention of stopping despite her warnings that she would shoot.

Shortly thereafter, the daughter of a neighboring farmer had been gang raped, sodomized with a glass bottle, and had her nipples bitten off before being gutted from xiphoid to pubis and left for dead.

This had been the last straw, and she had answered an advertisement for work in the US which had, unfortunately, been a illegal human smuggling operation that placed good looking foreign girls as strippers, hookers, and sex slaves as far as she could tell. She felt extremely lucky to have caught the attention of her ex boss, Vasili Gruzdev's cousin Nik. Now she prayed that this experience would help her act as naturally as possible in front of this killer until she could get the boys to safety.

Mason anchored about a mile from Nassau. He called to the boys to come and fish with him. Riana fought hard to remain calm. She asked if anyone was hungry and the boys begged for hot dogs with her special sauce. She tried to sound normal when she asked Mason if she should make some for him and Eddie.

Without blinking an eye, Mason lied, telling her that the captain was exhausted from piloting all night and morning and was taking his eight hours off. He had asked not to be disturbed and not to be woken before dinner if possible. Riana wondered just how many people this psychopath had killed.

She forced herself to leave the boys with Mason as she went below to fix lunch. She realized that they were probably quite safe with a man who worked for Nik since obviously this was the kind of work he did for her boss slash lover. She was starting to feel sick to her stomach at the thought that she had slept with a man capable of ordering death. It was clear the rumors were true. Nikolai Lebedev made problems disappear, and now she knew how.

She called out for everyone to come and eat, and when she got no reply she went on deck to entice the splashing males out of the bright blue ocean. Two wet boys, goggles still sucked onto their faces, life vests dripping, climbed up onto the deck and pulled towels around themselves before pushing the goggles up onto their foreheads.

They followed her down and crowded into the breakfast nook. The hot dogs smothered in the South African inspired stewed sweet and tangy tomato and onion went down well. The boys definitely ate too much and started complaining of having belly aches. Riana told them they would have to rest for an hour before swimming again so they headed back to the Xbox. Mason turned to her.

"Riana, a boat will be coming to pick up our passports to take to Nassau for entrance stamps. When he brings them back he will take us into Nassua and I will get you and the boys to the airport. I bought tickets in the name of three fake people to insure space for you on the flight.

When we get to the airport, I will get you all tickets to Panama City on standby. That way we can pay for them at the last minute. I don't want your name showing up on the flight manifest until it is too late to do anything about it. I will not be coming with you because I must get back to New York as soon as possible. I will be giving you a credit card so you can buy tickets on the next flight to São Paulo, Brazil. I also have a number for you to call when you have the flight information.

The person you are calling will pick you up at the airport and take you guys to a ranch where Nikolai will meet you. You will be staying at a lovely guest ranch with horses. The boys will love it there." Riana just nodded. She was not sure what she should or could say. She stood up and started clearing away the lunch mess.

As expected a boat came, went and came again. The boys were now bathed and changed, and really happy with their new bottle blond buzz cuts that matched Riana's new color. They were very excited about the next part of the adventure. This time she told them that mommy and daddy had flown to the next destination and they were following. A horse ranch, in the mountains, how cool. They could play cowboys and gunslingers. She didn't say cowboys and Indians; it seemed all the old stuff was now politically incorrect. They climbed across into the smaller boat and headed into the marina in Nassau.

Riana and the boys marveled at the huge hotels, especially the giant pink one that looked straight out of a fairy-tale, and the giant yachts, one even had a helicopter high up on the deck. The houses were all such pretty pastels. It looked like such a fun place.

At the dock a taxi was waiting and they all piled in, They drove for about a half hour through the streets of Nassau and out toward the airport. The boys loved that they were driving on the 'wrong' side of the road and squealed in delight around each traffic circle.

On the Tonique Williams Darling Highway they passed more and more open areas and then the green, desolate looking Lake Cunningham on John F. Kennedy Drive where a couple of people were kayaking way out on the lake.

After a few minutes of pure countryside, the taxi rounded a last circle and entered the airport. Mason told the driver to wait and grabbed the two carry-on bags. Riana, Demyan, and Yuri did not follow him into the airport. Instead, as directed, she had them wait until another family arrived and she casually struck up a conversation with the mother as they all approached the entrance.

Inside Mason had approached the counter, and placed them on standby for the Copa flight that he knew would have three available spaces when time came to board. The flight was due out at five forty-five pm but he was in a hurry to return to the After Five and head back to Melbourne and his car. It was now almost five 'o clock and Mason was getting antsy.

He handed Riana the manila envelope he had been clutching since they left the After Five containing the passports, a notarized letter naming

Riana as the children's cousin and authorized accompanying adult for the two minor children, instructions for contacting the man in Brazil who was to collect them at the airport in São Paulo, a credit card with her name on it with the PIN written on a piece of tape attached to it, and one thousand dollars in cash. He suggested that she hide the money in her bra. With that, he wished her luck and hurried out of the airport.

Riana wondered when all this stuff had been put together, she was quick to notice the last name in the boys' British passports, Yosef Levin and Derrick Martin Levin. She was stunned by her own, Anna-Leah Levin. Clever! Lots of South African's had British passports these days.

Did Nikolai have an escape plan already in place, she wondered, or had this been a last minute reaction to the kidnapping? She doubted the latter. Nobody could get British passports in five or six days, not even fake ones. The conversation months ago regarding the strange Snapchat method of contact made so much more sense and so she suspected the former.

Nikolai must have feared a kidnapping by somebody. Maybe that is why he hired her. Maybe he suspected that anyone taking the boys would not feel threatened by a very young nanny and take her too in order to keep them from panicking. Smooth move.

Riana waited until Mason's taxi was out of sight, and then rushed over and paid for the tickets so that they could go through security. She lined the underside of each breast with half the cash.

Once they were settled near the departure gate, she left the boys playing with the toy planes they had purchased in the duty free shop and, keeping them in sight, went over to the telephone mounted on the wall and dialed 911. She prayed that they used 911 in the Bahamas and was rewarded with an accented English voice asking the nature of her emergency. She read her script that she had written on the back of the receipt.

"I am calling to report a murder. An American citizen called Jackson Mason, threw the unconscious captain of an American motor boat, called the After Five, overboard about twenty-five to thirty miles off shore in the direction of Melbourne Florida at about ten am this morning.

The captain's name is Eddie, and the boat is registered in Fort Lauderdale and left Melbourne at approximately one am last night. Mr. Mason also killed an FBI agent near Orlando yesterday and kidnapped a nanny and two boys. He delivered the boys to a man in Freeport.

Mr. Mason is headed back to the After Five which is anchored about a mile off Nassau in a northerly direction. He is returning to Melbourne to collect his car. He is armed and extremely dangerous. The car is parked at the main Melbourne Marina and is a dark maroon Audi sedan." She immediately disconnected.

They were calling for the Copa flight to Panama City. Riana hurried back to the boys, asked Demmy to bring one bag, and towing the other, they lined up to board the flight. They should be well on their way to Panama before any police came looking for the anonymous caller. She just prayed that they would take her call seriously.

Suddenly she thought of the dungeon at the Pole Vault. She wondered how that sweet, but oh so very stupid girl from Alabama was doing, the one she had shared a room with in the dungeon. Maybe she should have mentioned that. The police really needed to know. She would have to tell them, it just wasn't right how the girls were treated.

As soon as they landed in Panama City, Riana looked at flights to São Paulo. There was a TAM flight leaving at nine pm and there were seats available. She paid for three tickets and she took the children to get a good meal. Riana was very nervous and kept expecting official looking men to appear and arrest her.

With huge relief, she guided the now very sleepy boys aboard the flight and they settled in to their seats. The kids were asleep before the plane even leveled off at thirty-three thousand feet. She halfheartedly watched a movie while she considered her options.

There was no way in hell she was contacting the man in São Paulo. Immediately upon landing she would find another flight for them out of Brazil. She needed to get the boys to a country with good ties to the US where they spoke either English or a Dutch dialect. She picked up the in-flight magazine to look at the map and assess her options. She was staring at the map when she fell asleep.

CHAPTER EIGHTEEN

New York, New York

On Thursday morning, the two men arrived within a minute of each other and nodded a greeting as they climbed the few steps to the Brownstone's entrance. Mrs. Wessels answered the door before Vasili could use his key, and promised them coffee in Mr. Lebedev's study in two minutes.

They filed upstairs to Nikolai's office where they found him seated behind his huge, antique desk. He had seen the short news brief on the Louisville hotel incident and wanted the details. Vasili filled him in.

As expected Nikolai got all loud, angrily ranting and raving about Isabel, the government, and the assholes that need to pay; but his outburst was less vigorous and unsustained. He had already quietened completely by the time Mrs. Wessels knocked and entered the room pushing a large tea trolley with coffee pot and cups, creamer, and sugar on top, and a selection of toast, waffles, and scrambled eggs on the bottom. The smell reminded all three men just how hungry they were.

Nikolai thanked Mrs. Wessels and told her to take the rest of the day off. When she protested, he insisted that she at least take the morning off, and return at lunch with something for them from anywhere nice. He handed her two hundred dollars to cover the lunch.

As soon as she had left they got down to business. They would need Marc and Rick back in town, so the men were summoned and told to swing by Saratoga and pick up Cathy Miller, Isabel's obviously lying friend. It would take them all day to get back to Saratoga. That meant they would snatch Cathy that night and have her in New York by the early hours of tomorrow morning.

"Be careful, and discrete, and don't get seen." they were told.

Vasili called the DOJ informant and asked her if she could establish who was most likely to know the details of the operation. The woman said she would review the members of task force team four and get back to him. They had decided the time had come to make this whole thing go away. There was too much to lose.

Obviously, the feds thought they had something on him, but not enough for an indictment, and thought that by taking his wife and kids they could coerce her into saying something incriminating. It would have to be more than her testimony because that would be inadmissible and he was confident he would have his kids back sooner rather than later. They would want concrete proof of illegal activity. He thought that the only illegal activity she was privy to was the cloning, and she was as guilty as he in the cloning enterprise. He supposed they would offer her immunity for her information.

Once again he worried that she knew more, he certainly hoped not. The clones were a problem though. Three of them were set to run in the Breeders Cup and he was not about to lose that. Not now, and not ever if he could help it. What seemed to be evident was that the man, with Isabel, was out of touch with his team. He would not have been able to pass on any information gleaned since the initial kidnapping, thanks to the mole. If he could get rid of the Fed, and Isabel, the DOJ would be back where it was before, full of suspicion and short on proof.

Vasili heard from his informant before noon and passed the information on to Nikolai. The New York team that appeared to have taken Isabel has a forensic psychologist or psychiatrist from the FBI profiling section at Quantico, working with them. He is also a personal friend of the man who appears to be the agent on the run.

The profiler is a man named Mackenzie Brewster, a twelve year FBI veteran. The field agent is an FBI Special Agent Paul Mitchel Hammer, no details other than he goes by Mitch. The informant had given him an address for the shrink who is staying at the Hampton Inn, near the seaport. Nikolai and Vasili sat in the office making plans.

Anatoli wandered off down to Vasili's office and played Call of Duty Advanced Warfare on the big screen. He was never consulted, just always ordered, and he was quite happy.

Upstairs the two discussed where to take Cathy

and this Brewster guy. They did not have time to go
out to Montauk. It would have to be here in the city.
Vasili thought their best bet was the hidden
basement that they referred to as the dungeon
located under the strip club. It was huge, and
already had the rooms that housed the illegal girls
when they first arrived. There was nobody down
there right now and it was about as sound proof as
they could hope for.

Nikolai decided to go to his office down town.
For the sake of appearances it would be important
for him to be seen at work, getting on with his life.
Vasili went downstairs, to his own office in
Nikolai's home, to research Brewster.

Once Vasili had a photo of the FBI profiler,
Mackenzie Brewster, he sent Anatoli out to canvass
the hotel and the various routes from the FBI
building to the hotel. Then at about four pm he was
to stake out the FBI building and try to follow
Brewster and get a sense of his habits.

He called the club to get a hold of his security
chief. Brent Farber would have to fill in for Sasha
and help with the stake out. Brent was a cruel man
and loved every opportunity he got to 'help' his boss
with more personal tasks. Lebedev had also
defended this man in a murder trial and after the
guilty man had walked free he had come to work for
Vasili.

Initially he had been strictly club security,
eventually working his way to chief after seven
years. After the first two or three years, the cops no
longer harassed him and for the past two years he
had been a special team member when Vasili

contracted to clean up a sticky problem.

Brent was more than happy to get the call. He was in Vasili's office in the Lebedev home within half an hour. Farber was tasked with fixing two rooms in the basement with extra locks, in addition to getting two chairs, with arms, fixed to the floor opposite each other by about eight feet. They must be close enough to see each other well, distant enough for working room. As soon as they were in place he was to secure the second basement and then join Anatoli to figure out the best place to snatch Dr. Brewster off the street.

Vasili got a call just after five pm telling him that the good doctor walks the little over half mile from the Federal building to his hotel. They figured he would probably change and then go out again to get dinner. It was unlikely that he ate in the hotel every night. They could grab him if he went back out.

Vasili called Brent telling him to use the club's plain black Ford van and to stop by Nikolai's house to pick up a syringe of Ketamine.

When Brent arrived, Nikolai was home from the office. He drew up twenty milliliters of Ketamine and told Brent to cause the target to trip and fall and then plunge the entire syringe of drug into the man's buttocks as he made the show of helping him up. They were then to walk away.

The drug would act within three to four minutes so they needed to follow and then casually 'help' their drunk friend into the van. Try and do this away from any obvious cameras on the street. Fucking cameras were everywhere these days. Brent took the syringe with needle safely capped, and went to collect Anatoli from his surveillance overlooking the hotel entrance.

Both men were a little nervous. This was the most hastily planned, potential disaster they had ever been part of. Nikolai and Vasili usually put a lot of time and effort into making these operations untraceable. Things must be pretty bad when the bosses take chances like this.

They found a parking space along the street a half a block away from the hotel and Brent, since he was not as obvious as the giant bald man, sat in the bus stop shelter across the street and watched the door.

When the target, Dr. Mackenzie Brewster, appeared, he did not hail a cab but turned left and walked to the corner and took a left onto Dover. Brent stood and crossed the road to follow. He had a do-rag covering his hair and a large baseball cap pulled low over his face. He was also wearing one of the handy masks you can now buy on the Internet to fool face recognition. Someone would have to get really close to see the edge of the mask around his lips and eyes. He followed the shrink down Dover, quietly relaying his route to Anatoli via the small Bluetooth device in his ear.

They had walked almost two blocks when the subject turned and entered a little Thai restaurant almost hidden in the ugly flat building. Brent continued to the corner and crossed Dover to walk up the other side of the street. He called Anatoli to bring the van down the one way street.

Anatoli drove up and parked next to Brent who climbed in; and they waited for Brewster to eat his

Thai meal. They hoped he wasn't just getting
takeout. Not likely or he would have had it
delivered.

While they waited, they discussed the only two
real options. Brewster would go back up the one-
way street, in which case Anatoli had less than four
minutes to get around the block before the man was
comatose.

Alternatively, and less likely, he would continue
around on South and walk back up to the hotel via
Peck Slip. That would be the easier from their point
of view because South Street ran under the
highway, and this discouraged anyone other than the
homeless from loitering in the area at night.

After almost an hour, Brewster appeared. He
turned right and Brent couldn't believe their luck.
He leapt out of the van ran around the corner
making sure he slammed into the departing man
bringing them both crashing to the sidewalk. Brent
buried the needle into the man's buttock depressing
the plunger and jumped up apologizing to the dazed
Brewster who was trying to sit up.

Brent glanced around, nobody appeared to be
paying attention a few vehicles passed as he offered
the man a hand and asked him if he was OK.
Brewster was already feeling a little off kilter. He
said he was fine, or at least he thought he did. He
walked off up the street rubbing his right buttock.

Brent let him get about fifty feet ahead before he
started following. When the man turned the corner,
Brent hurried to catch up, and as he rounded the
corner he saw Brewster stumble. He rushed to the
man's side and put an arm around him pulling

Brewster's arm up over his shoulder so they looked like friends.

Brent then called for Anatoli to hurry with the van. Brewster was starting to lean heavily against him. The drugged man tried pulling away, then tried to speak, but he was no longer managing to tell his body what to do. Brent talked loudly.

"Steady my friend, you've had way too much to drink," he commented for anyone within earshot. Anatoli pulled up and Brent opened the side door and climbed in pulling Brewster in with him as he made the loud comment that their ride had arrived, about damn time and all. He leaned across and closed the door and Anatoli drove away slowly.

At the club they went around back and into the private underground parking that was so handy for unloading the illegal girls. Anatoli hitched the unconscious man onto his shoulder and followed Brent to the locked door that was hidden behind the tool cabinet, in the south wall.

After swinging the tool cabinet way from the wall, and unlocking the door, they followed the long narrow hall into the second basement. The first basement had access directly to the back dock for unloading club supplies and was the storage area for the noisy club above.

They went to the first of the fortified rooms and lowered the man onto the cot, then pulled him onto his side just in case he puked. He was quite likely to puke when he started to wake up and they didn't want him drowning in his own vomit. He was also possibly going to hallucinate like crazy. The cot was a bare metal frame with a thin hard mattress.

Brent covered the man with a dirty gray woolen blanket, not unlike those so commonly used in prisons across the country. They did not bother to cuff the man; he could not get out of this room. In the corner was a five gallon bucket with the toilet seat accessory available from any camping supply outlet. This one had been purchased on Amazon.

They left the room and bolted the door, securely fastening the steel bar that would prevent the door from opening even if the bolts were somehow broken. Anatoli went home to sleep. After calling and informing Vasili that the cat was in the bag, Brent went to work, as usual, in the club upstairs.

Around the same time, Marc and Rick drove by the Cottage Motor Inn on West Street deciding to park just off the road under a tree near the south end of the property closest to the cabin their target had rented for the season. They knew the place probably had security cameras watching the parking so they would approach through the trees from behind and come through between the first two cottages and quickly onto her deck. Then it was a matter of knocking and entering as rapidly as possible.

Rick would wait in the gap between the cabins, and Marc would enter and subdue the small woman. They approached the cottage from behind and crept through the gap. Rick stopped, Marc continued, right hand holding the pistol shoved into his pants under his untucked t-shirt.

He knocked on the door and was greeted by the hysterical barking of a small dog. Cathy opened the door and was shoved violently backwards falling and hitting the carpeted floor with force that knocked the wind right out of her. She struggled to regain her breath as the man closed the door and kicked the tiny dog attacking his ankles.

Dodger yelped in pain and flew across the room, hitting the wall and falling to the floor, landing in a tiny white heap at the base of the wall next to the bathroom door. Cathy screamed and tried to get to him. The man shoved a gun in her face and told her to shut the fuck up or he'd stomp the fucking dog's head into the ground.

Cathy crawled over to Dodger. He was unconscious but breathing rhythmically without effort. She faced Marc and glared at him asking him what he wanted. Marc told her that they were going for a ride to see a man about a dog, and grinned at his own joke.

Cathy was terrified. This had to be Nikolai and if Isabel was telling the truth, she might not survive to see her poor injured dog. Cathy looked at the man and asked if they would be gone long. She knew if they left it was unlikely she would be returning but she didn't want this man to know that she knew. Marc looked at her. Stupid cow thought she'd be back. He nodded, and told her it would be a while.

Cathy begged him to allow her to leave food and water for Dodger when he woke up. Marc nodded. She rose and collected Dodger's bowls. She filled the water bowl and returned it to the small tray on the floor.

She moved slowly so as not to startle the man but also to relax him. She returned to the small table and bent over pulling the bag of dog food out from under it. She took the small metal bowl in her right hand and opened the bag with her left. Both hands disappeared into the bag. She straightened slowly bringing the bowl full of Fromm kibble into view, she hid her left hand in front of her body moving it across and under her right arm pit, and turning fired three shots from her tiny Ruger LCP, in rapid succession, and point blank range, into Marc's chest. He dropped, his pistol falling from his grasp.

Cathy, ducked behind the bed as she dialed 911 on her cell. Her door flew open, a second man appearing with a gun and she fired a shot into the door, not wanting to possibly hit an innocent responder.

Rick did not bother to return fire, he fled back to the Ford and got the hell out of Saratoga before the police arrived. He did not notice the cowering old man, walking his dog, hunkered down in the tall corn across the street.

Cathy then dialed the number that Mitch had placed in her cell to use if Nikolai ever came after her. She looked across at the man bleeding on the disgusting green cabin carpet and she wondered if they would make her pay for a new one.

It was just after ten-thirty pm when Rick called Vasili and told him that Cathy had shot and killed Marc during the attempted abduction. Vasili asked him if he had Marc's cell phone. They had strict instructions never to take any ID or electronics into a potential crime scene.

Rick pulled over and searched the car for ten minutes and couldn't find the cell. Vasili was furious. This was getting really bad. The cops would surely be at his door as soon as they started running the numbers on that fucking cell phone. It was his number they would find and not Nikolai's. Thank God he avoided texting.

Vasili got dressed and drove himself over to The Pole Vault. There was no more time to waste; he needed to get that piece of shit federal shrink to talk. No more fucking around, there would be cops raiding the place by morning. He was so angry that they did not have Cathy Miller. Torturing a woman in front of the Fed would certainly get him squawking.

He called Brent into his office and asked about the girl from Alabama who had been bitching to the other girls about conditions and threatening to go to the cops. Brent told him that Missy was working that evening and seemed to have settled down. "Doesn't matter," Vasili said. "I need her, and I need her in the basement, chained to a chair with a gag. She cannot be allowed to speak." Vasili called Anatoli and told the giant man to meet him in the dungeon.

Brent walked through the crowded club and told Missy he needed to see her in his office. She followed him out of the club and through the back into his office. He passed his office and she continued to follow him into the basement. Missy was accustomed to the men, with positions of power in the club, expecting favors. She was resigned to the blow job, or other sexual favor, she would now be expected to perform.

Brent told her to turn around, and when she complied, he handcuffed her and then placed a ball gag in her mouth and tightened it until she shook her head violently and moaned. Then he moved her through the basement to the far end where he opened the swinging wine rack to reveal in inner entrance to the dungeon. He took her inside, closing the door behind them.

Missy was led down the hall into a room containing two chairs opposite each other and strapped into one of the chairs. Each of her legs was strapped to a chair leg, and her hands were uncuffed, and each arm strapped down, with buckled leather straps, to the chair arms. Missy still thought this was a sex game.

Brent turned and left the room. He disappeared from view up the passage returning to his office and Missy was left tightly fastened to the chair in the cool basement. She was just a little confused. Maybe some rich guy was paying for a special service of some kind. Would have been nice to be warned she thought.

CHAPTER NINETEEN

The chase

Rick was racing down I-87 toward New York. He was trying to stay only ten miles per hour over the posted speed limit so that some idiot trooper didn't try to pull him over.

About forty-five minutes south of Albany he passed a trooper parked in the wide grassy median. This time the trooper did not stay put. This time the asshole pulled out of the cutting and was gaining on him. He slowed fractionally, hoping the trooper would fly on by but this cop just settled in behind him, probably running his tags. Don't panic he thought.

He called Vasili and informed him of the tail. Just then the trooper's blue lights began flashing and he heard the whoop, whoop of the siren. Rick had no intention of stopping with a vehicle full of very illegal weapons so he gunned the Expedition and tried to out run the trooper.

He had no idea how he could realistically get away. In fact he was no longer thinking much at all. He did not even disconnect the call to Vasili. The call was forgotten as Rick tried to outrun a life in prison.

On the other end of the call, Vasili could hear Rick's panicked cursing, and crying. He could hear the racing engine and the distant sound of the siren. He heard a bang and Rick screaming that the cop was trying to ram him. The sirens were louder and Vasili imagined more troopers in pursuit.

He grabbed the remote to his TV and flicked through the news stations as fast as he could. FOX had the coverage live via a feed from FOX 23 in Albany. The news helicopter could not get too close, held at bay by the presence of a police helicopter highlighting the chase below.

The zoom on the camera in the news helicopter was worth its cost because the action was up close and personal. Vasili was sure that, if there had not been glare from the spotlight reflecting off the windscreen, he would be able to see Rick's terrified face.

The news reporter was commenting that the suspect was fleeing the scene of a suspected kidnapping attempt where another suspect had been gunned down by the intended victim who was now in protective custody. The dead man had allegedly seriously injured the victim's dog who was expected to live.

The corner of the TV screen showed a separate image that changed as the reporter discussed the different elements of the breaking case. The scene now showed the limp body of a small white dog inside a veterinarian clinic hooked up to a bag of fluids.

Vasili's eyes returned to the chase. Mile after mile, the troopers followed Rick, at speeds up to one hundred and seventeen miles an hour per the reporter. Not exactly the world's fastest getaway car the idiot joked.

Vasili watched in rapt disbelief as a trooper edged alongside and swerved his car into the back corner of the Explorer. The Ford Explorer fish tailed wildly and Rick, in his efforts to correct, lost control of the SUV and spun sharply, losing traction and going into a roll.

The vehicle bounced first end over end and then slowed rolling side over side until coming to a stop in the middle of the highway. The spilled gasoline had been ignited by the sparks and the last three flips were lit with trailing flames. The stationary SUV was instantly engulfed in flames and the troopers backed away in anticipation of an explosion that never came.

The news crew continued to show the flaming vehicle and the arrival of the first firetruck. For the gore hungry news fans, the coverage continued until the last flames were out and the blackened shell of the SUV lay bathed in the ring of light from the police helicopter spot light.

Vasili had the decency to throw up. Two friends murdered in one night. That fucking Fed was going to be the first of many to pay. He called Nikolai and gave him the news.

Anatoli parked in the secure underground parking bay and closed the heavy metal doors to the street. Vasili joined him and they opened the hidden door to the dungeon and closed it behind themselves, sealing in all sound. The two angry men entered the underground room and saw the young woman strapped into the chair. She was younger than the girl she was impersonating and far too full of makeup.

Vasili told Anatoli to clean her up and get rid of the makeup and ridiculous strippers clothing. Anatoli opened one of the many cupboards lining the walls and found some suitable clothing. He chose jeans and a checkered button up shirt. He also found some very normal looking underwear.

He cleaned off her makeup as best he could without removing the gag. He brushed her hair and braided it into what he thought might be a normal country girl look. He rubbed a little grime from the floor onto her face in an attempt to make her look a little older. Undoing one strap at a time he stripped her and redressed her in the borrowed clothing. He threw all the old stuff into a metal trash can and replaced the lid.

Once Missy looked the part, the two approached the door of the cell holding Mackenzie Brewster. They unlocked the bar and let it swing down and then pulled the bolts back. Vasili pulled his gun from its holster and they stood back pulling the door open.

The man in the room sat on the side of the cot. He did not even try to rise. The room smelled of vomit and there were copious amounts of vomitus decorating the floor and cot. Anatoli approached Mack, took his arm and yanked him too his feet. Mack swayed precariously before stumbling to regain his balance.

Anatoli led him out into the big room and pushed him down into the chair. Mack attempted to resist but was no match for the giant, bald man who just back handed him across the jaw eliciting immediate waves of nausea and disorientation. He sat fighting the feeling as he was strapped tightly to the chair in the same manner as Missy.

Missy's eyes had widened in shock. She was just starting to suspect that this was no sex game and that she was in trouble. She started squirming and shrieking behind the gag. The huge man walked over and slapped her across the face with such force she was blinded by pain.

Mack noticed the girl and tried to see who she was. He could just see a slim, brown haired girl, with extravagant highlights, dressed in jeans and a green shirt. She was crying now, tears pouring down her face as she gasped for air around the red ball that gagged her mouth.

It didn't take a rocket scientist for him to realize that this must be related to the case he was working on. How? He didn't know how, but he suspected it would not be long before he found out. He had recognized the two men before him from the file on Lebedev. The small, extremely ugly, pock marked man was Vasili Gruzdev, Lebedev's cousin, and the other was Lebedev's bodyguard, Anatoli Dubnovsky.

Mack knew then that he was going to die in this room. These men were not hiding their identity; so that meant that they intended to kill him when they got what they wanted. Of course he didn't know what that might be, but whatever it was he would have to stall for as long as he possibly could, his life depended on it.

Vasili came and stood before Mack.

"Tell me about this investigation you are doing?" He said in a very faintly accented voice. Vasili had moved to the US as a teenager. Mack shook his head confusedly.

"I don't know what you mean," he replied. Vasili just nodded and walked over to the girl.

"Do you know who this is?" he asked. Mack shook his head. "This is Cathy Miller, know her?" Again Mack shook his head. Vasili explained that Cathy was the very best friend of Isabel Lebedev, and that she had lied to his boss about Isabel's whereabouts when they had spoken to her in Saratoga a couple of days ago. "Isabel was there with your friend and colleague Mitchel Hammer, starting to ring a bell?" Again Mack shook his head. "Well, maybe you will start to remember when we jog your memory a little."

Mack realized that Vasili intended to torture this woman to make him talk. As a forensic psychologist and FBI profiler, he understood far more than this psychopath in front of him realized. Mac would have to allow the torture in order to actually try to save both their lives. He just hoped that the poor woman would pass out sooner, rather than later. The longer he could keep them alive, the better their chances of being rescued. He was dismayed at the thought that this would be a very long time since it was very likely he would not be missed until after nine am.

He stared at the woman. Whoever she was, she

was not in their Lebedev file and she certainly was not Cathy Miller. The woman continued to cry, sobbing hysterically behind the gag. Vasili stood next to the woman, who Mack could now see was not more than a girl. She was definitely much, much, younger than Cathy. The ugly man looked straight at him and grabbed the woman's right hand.

"She needs these to do her job. Maybe we can do something about that. Anatoli pulled a small table across the room and placed it next to Vasili who had pulled up a stool. Vasili picked up a disposable scalpel from the table and slid back the plastic safety shield covering the blade.

The unfortunate girl fought hard against her restraints, thrashing her weight left and right trying in vain to loosen the hold. Vasili grabbed the hand again, holding onto it firmly, twisting it to bring the palm face up. He dug the scalpel into the pinkie finger just below the last joint, careful to avoid the arteries paralleling the sides, slipped it through under the flexor tendon and sliced upward, severing the tendon before withdrawing the scalpel through the entrance hole.

There was very little blood, but the woman was choking against her gag as she screamed in pain. Unopposed by the flexor, the little finger stood straight as the other fingers curled around the end of the armrest that she gripped in terror. Vasili walked over to Mack.

"Who has Mrs. Lebedev?" he asked

"I don't know, I don't know!" he shouted, trying to sound convincing. Lebedev just nodded and walked back across to the young woman who bucked wildly as he approached. He grabbed her hand again.

Mack closed his eyes. Instantly Anatoli was there to pull his lids open. He took two strips of duct tape and taped Mack's eyelids up. With extreme effort, he could still blink just enough to keep his eyes a little moist but he could not keep them closed. He tried turning away but Anatoli used the tape around his head and the chair to force him to look straight ahead.

When he was ready, Vasili deftly operated on the ring finger. Again eliciting new waves of muffled screaming as the woman was bathed in pain. The two fingers dripped a small amount of blood that pooled on the floor beneath her hand. She was staring in horror at her hand, the two fingers now sticking out when she flexed a fist around the chair arm.

She now had a trickle of blood coming from her mouth where she must have bitten her tongue or torn her lip on the gag. Tears streamed down her cheeks and mixed with the blood that dripped off her chin and onto the shirt. Vasili walked back over to Mack and repeated the question.

"Who took Mrs. Lebedev?" Vasili already knew the answer, he also knew that Mack knew the answer. He wondered how much pain this doctor would allow this woman to endure before he broke. After that the answers would come thick and fast. Again Mack denied knowledge.

Perhaps I must change the type of torture, he thought. He walked back over to Missy and ripped open the green plaid shirt. This was closer to what the unfortunate girl was accustomed to so she felt some relief. Vasili unhooked the bra and tucked the cups behind her. He grabbed one full breast and started to squeeze. The pain intensified and Missy struggled and fought, trying to free her breast from the vice grip of pain. Once again she was screaming against the gag, and choking from blood and saliva running down her throat.

Vasili walked around behind her and cupped the other breast, crushing it with the same force and blinding Missy with the pain so intense she prayed to die. She went limp and Vasili released her when he realized she had fainted.

"Ice water," he barked at Anatoli.

Again he approached Mack and repeated the question and again Mack denied the knowledge. He was stunned when the small man hit him hard across the face, splitting his lip. He tasted, and smelled the ferric content of his own blood. His head spun. He was still feeling woozy from whatever they had used to drug him and he started to dry heave. Anatoli returned with the ice water and the poor young woman was unceremoniously doused in the frigid water that brought rushing consciousness and pain back into her head.

Vasili said something that Mack could not hear. Anatoli disappeared for about ten minutes and reappeared with a battery and mini jumper cables of the type used to charge a motorbike battery.

He attached the clamps to Missy's nipples. The girl did not fight. Mack was not sure if she was semi-conscious, or past caring. Vasili looked straight at him as he touched the cables to the battery. The girl screamed and her body arched right out of the chair. She slumped unconscious again.

This time Vasili did not ask him the question. He walked over, undid Mack's belt, undid the button, unzipped, and attempted to pull down his pants. He was not successful, so Anatoli grabbed Mack from behind lifting his buttocks off of the chair so that Vasili could pull down the pants, and underwear.

Mack knew what was coming. Vasili collected the cables and attached them to Mack's scrotum, each small clamp pinched the skin next to a testicle. Vasili took one testicle in his hand and started squeezing the clamp into it.

Mack felt for Missy. He had seen her suffering but it is so different when you actually feel the pain yourself. The pain intensified. He was not sure when he started screaming. Suddenly the pressure was gone and slowly the pain subsided and he could breathe again. He wondered if his testicle was permanently crushed. Vasili asked again,

"Who took Mrs. Lebedev?" When Mack started to shake his head, the shock to his testicles blew his mind. He started a strangled scream before he passed out.

Vasili looked around in disgust. He told Anatoli to leave them to wake up fully. In the meantime he was going to go and get something to eat. Vasili was careful to wash up in the bathroom and check himself for specks of blood before he left the dungeon in search of food. Anatoli went to one of the better rooms and lay down on a cot to get some much needed sleep. It was almost three in the morning and it had been a very busy day.

CHAPTER TWENTY

Thursday Night in New York

At the police department in Saratoga, Cathy followed the advice of Mitch. She refused to speak to anyone until she had spoken to Michael Mandrake, the SAC he had told her to ask for.

Once they connected her to Mr. Mandrake, she told him all about Isabel and Mitch coming to her for help. She explained the three departing trucks and not knowing which one they had taken. She told him about Nikolai Lebedev coming to see her at the track and pretending not to know anything. Lastly she told him that Mitch had warned her that if pushed to desperation Mr. Lebedev might do something dangerous and try to get information out of her if he somehow suspected she knew anything. She said that she owned the small Ruger quite legally and had started carrying it quite illegally out of fear.

When the man had attacked her in her cottage, half killing her dog, she realized who he was and managed to get the opportunity to take the gun out of the bra holster as she retrieved dog food, by tipping it into the dog food and chambering a round while calling for her dog to respond. She had then drawn the man's attention to the bowl of dog food as she swung it out of the bag with her right hand and at the same time had shot him through under her armpit with the left.

Mandrake marveled at her quick thinking and asked her how she had come up with the plan. Strange thing, she told him. Her Uncle Robert was a Correctional Officer and he had taught her to play the 'what if' game. Whenever she was driving long distance or lying in bed, she would think of scenarios that could go wrong in her life. Say - what if this happens, then find the solution.

She explained that she had done it for years thinking of ways to get out of trouble if a bit broke on a horse, if a horse bolted, if a girth broke, if a horse reared up and went over backwards in the starting gate, or broke down in mid gallop. Rehearsing in her head had saved her life when some of those things happened. Since Issi's visit, she had been playing what if they came for her. Asking to feed her dog, or leave food for him, was in her plan.

Mandrake told her to ask for an attorney and not to make a statement until she had an attorney. That would give him time to get agents he knew he could trust to her location. He asked to speak to the detective in charge and informed the man that Ms. Miller was a witness in a federal case, and that she was to be held in protective custody until the FBI arrived.

The local man was certainly not happy when she

refused to give a statement until she had an attorney. They read her her Miranda Rights and booked her on a homicide charge. The detective knew the charge was bogus, this was a clear case of self-defense, but he needed to keep her locked up tight until the FBI arrived. Meanwhile the press was clamoring for statements outside. Well, they would get no comment just yet. Ha!

The detective who caught the case, Bruce Sloan, had been with the Saratoga PD for seventeen years. He liked the pace of law in this town. Seldom anything too freaky. He looked at the contents of the evidence bag. Inside where all items, other than clothing, recovered from the deceased man in the cabin.

It was obvious that Ms. Miller knew how to use a gun. It would be interesting to know why. The three small, but obviously powerful self-deference rounds were neatly clustered on his central torso. One just below the xiphoid, one three inches above that, and one two inches to the left of the second. There was no way of knowing the order, but he suspected any one of the shots could have been the lethal one.

The woman had buried a fourth shot in the floor to frighten off the second suspect rather than accidentally shoot an innocent man or someone outside behind him. That was a lot of thinking for a frightened woman to manage. Well, the corpse was at the morgue, tomorrow he would have some answers. The second corpse, the severely charred remains of the fleeing driver, had been taken to the Medical Examiner in Albany. That accident was outside his jurisdiction.

He opened the evidence bag and tipped the contents into a sterile tray. With gloved hands he looked through the wallet for identification. The New York Driver's license was issued to Marc Elliott, a thirty-one year old, Caucasian male from the Bronx. The photo on the ID certainly looked like the deceased.

He picked up his phone and called the Bronx PD. He identified himself and asked if someone could go to the house on record and inform the next of kin. He also asked them to find out who the dead man's employer was. Next he tried to check the phone, but it was locked. They needed the info off that phone immediately. He called down to the squad room and asked for an on duty officer to take possession of the phone and get it to the state crime lab in Albany, STAT!

In his house in Lorton, VA, Micheal Mandrake ran through the events of the evening, then the previous evening in Orlando, and reviewed the contents of the emails from Mitchel Hammer. He decided to call Mackenzie Brewster at his hotel. Bypass the mole and get him up to speed so that they could brainstorm. He already had the cyber division working on uncovering the mole.

He called the hotel reception and asked to be connected to Mr. Brewster. He was told that Mr. Brewster had not returned from dinner and could he leave a message. It was after midnight. Brewster should have been asleep. He identified himself as an FBI agent giving the man a number to call back to verify.

As soon as the call was patched through to him, he asked the concierge if this was normal for Mr. Brewster. No sir, he was informed. Mr. Brewster had told the concierge that during his absence he was expecting a very important call and that he would check in when he returned. He was going out for Thai but had not returned as expected.

Mandrake asked the man what time he had expected Mr. Brewster to return and was informed that Brewster usually returned to the hotel around five-thirty, changed, worked out in the hotel gym, and around seven 'o clock went out to one of the variety of local eateries for a quick dinner. He was seldom gone for much more than an hour. Until Mandrake called, the man had presumed that Brewster had returned unnoticed and was asleep in his room.

Mandrake thanked the man and disconnected the call. He looked up the nearest Thai restaurant on Google and tried the number. Much to his surprise a man answered. Mandrake asked the him if he was able to tell what time a customer left the establishment. The man said he could, but only by the stamp on the credit card receipts. If the customer had paid cash he wouldn't be able to help. Mandrake was fairly certain Brewster would have used his expense card so he gave the Thai man the name to search.

There was a long silence before the man returned to the phone to inform him that the time stamp on the credit card receipt was eight minutes past eight. Mandrake thanked him and hung up.

Brewster had been missing for over four hours.

Two people involved with the case faced with possible abduction on the same day; around the same time could not be a coincidence. He was now very angry. Thanks to the mole, it would be hard to get an investigation into Brewster's disappearance going without alerting the suspects. He considered the local police and wondered how fast their involvement would get back to Lebedev.

He rubbed his hands vigorously back and forth through his tightly cured hair. He kept it short, but it was a habit so he often found himself doing it and tugging the short curls in frustration. He worried that Lebedev would kill Brewster if he realized the feds were looking for him, on the other hand, knowing how little evidence they had ever been able to gather on the man's suspected dalliances with the law. Brewster was likely a doomed man anyway.

Mandrake made up his mind. Full bore investigation and search effort, hard and fast. He called the SAC in New York and informed him of the potential kidnapping. He suggested a dog as soon as possible to track Brewster's route before it was too stale. He left it to the New York office to roust the agents and local police.

At two am he received a call with the news that the dog had tracked Brewster to the Thai restaurant, then around onto South Street under the viaduct. Here it cast about, locating Brewster's phone knocked in under the edge of the curb. The bloodhound then followed a trail around the corner and back towards the hotel before losing the trail in the street about fifty yards from the corner. This was likely where he was placed in a vehicle. They were busy canvasing local business for camera footage.

By this time Mandrake was in his office at Quantico with his hastily assembled team. They were requisitioning phone records belonging to Lebedev and his known close contacts.

As these came in it, was apparent that there had been a fair amount of traffic between the major parties. Lebedev's cell location remained stationary at his house on Eighty-eighth. Gruzdev moved between the house on Eighty-eighth, his own apartment, and his club, The Pole Vault. Lebedev's bodyguard's cell showed the same locations in addition to his house in the Bronx, and a location in lower Manhattan close to the abduction scene.

There were numerous calls that also involved the club security chief, who somehow also found himself in the lower Manhattan area around eight pm, and two men with cell locations in Saratoga. One was the dead man Marc Elliot, and the other a Ricardo Santorini whose last cell tower hit was on I-87 just south of Albany. He suspected this was Mr. Crispy as they had named the unsub in the chase. He called the Albany office and shared the information.

Mandrake gathered his team, and told them that they were all headed to New York. They needed to take lead on this investigation because the lives of several federal agents were at stake. They would be raiding the strip club since it seemed the only logical place that Brewster was being held based upon the cell phone locations. The raid would start without them because they needed it to begin as soon as possible if Brewster was to survive.

Before heading out to the waiting Gulfstream Jet, he sent a quick email to Mitch at the strange French email address, lamourdemavie@france.pe updating him on the events in Saratoga and New York.

CHAPTER TWENTY-ONE

Earlier that morning in Milwaukee

On Thursday morning, Mitch had woken with his arms wrapped tightly around Isabel, hugging her close to his body, with an early morning erection so hard it hurt. He touched his lips to the soft skin on her shoulder and kissed his way toward her ear.

For a moment she groaned slightly and snuggled closer before she woke enough to realize what was happening. She dived out of bed, tripping on the bed cover and falling into the wall banging her elbow hard enough to make her get tears in her eyes. She turned and glared at his accusingly.

"Asshole!" she spat in his direction. Mitch just smiled.

"It wasn't just me you know. What do you expect from a healthy all American boy when you wiggle that delicious little butt against my dick?" She stormed out and tried to slam the bathroom door. "I'm just a normal man you know." he yelled after her.

He heard the shower running and imagined her tight, lean body naked under the cascading curtain of water. He chided himself and turned his thoughts to the day ahead. Take the car back, get new clothes, or better yet, old new ones from a thrift store, then hit Best Buy before returning to play house for a few days while the FBI followed new leads. He'd be her witness protection program until they arrested Lebedev, then he would have to turn her over to the US Marshal Service because she would never be safe while that man was alive, incarcerated or not. The thought of never seeing her once she disappeared into the witness protection program depressed him so he turned and picked up his laptop.

Isabel was still busy in the bathroom when Mitch checked his email. He was stunned and horrified to find that so much had happened overnight. Somehow, Lebedev had located the children. Somebody had kidnapped the boys and their nanny. In the process Bob Sanders had been killed, it appeared to be a drowning and whether an accident or not, it was likely as a direct result of the assailants, whomever they were.

John Hames had a severe concussion and a laceration on the scalp that required a number of stitches. He was hospitalized but expected to make a full recovery. The infra-red security alarm had sounded during the evening and the FBI had called the local police department to check on the house when neither man responded to calls.

Canvasing the neighbors revealed only that the agents' car had left the garage, obviously what tripped the alarm

The car had not yet been recovered although

using the tracking device it was located, submerged in a lake, a little over a mile away. No one seems to have seen or heard a thing.

Current whereabouts of the children unknown but all the airports were on alert in addition to the southern border with Mexico. An Amber Alert had been issued even though no car description was available yet.

The only positive in the email was that Lebedev and Gruzdev were currently under surveillance in New York. Although he did not like waiting for the cameras, Mitch felt reasonably sure that they would be OK for the next few hours. He wouldn't tell Isabel right way, he's wait to see if Mandrake got news to him first.

Mitch sat down at the dining room table where Isabel had placed a mug of coffee, and a pile of toast. She came in with his eggs and joined him. They ate in silence. Mitch finished his eggs then ate his way through all the toast. No food was going to waste on his watch. After breakfast, Isabel followed him in Greta's car and they returned the rental.

They hit the Salvation Army Store on the way back to the cottage picking up a good assortment of clothing for under one hundred dollars apiece.

At the Best Buy across from the Mayfair Mall, Mitch purchased a home security system with two cameras. Between the three cameras he figured he could cover most of the yard.

They stopped at The Outpost organic food co-op on State Street and Isabel stocked up on a nice selection of fruit, vegetables, and some pasture raised meat for the carnivore, before they headed back to the cottage.

Back at the small battleship-gray house, she set about packing the purchases away while Mitch hid one camera just under the eave above the front door with a full view of the front yard.

The second he set up under the eave at the corner of the small back deck so that he could see the back door to the left and most of the north side of the yard to the right.

His own small camera he attached to the fence at the back corner of the property on the south side. He snaked the cord through under the poison ivy that grew in the narrow strip of yard between the house and the back fence and through a small hole drilled in the nearest basement window frame. From there it was attached to the WiFi box at the electric outlet just inside. This way the back camera could see down the last two sides of the house where the house lay very close to both perimeters.

He fired up Greta's old PC and loaded the software he needed to use the camera feeds. He split the screen so all three feeds were visible. The front yard got half the screen because he wanted the biggest view of the street.

Next he went out back, and just out of sight of the back window of the tiny second bedroom, he hammered a few little planks horizontally across a section of the six foot wooden fence to form a crude ladder that could be used to escape into the property behind. He did not disrupt the creeper covering the fence but slipped each rung in behind the creeper to keep the ladder as hidden as possible.

Once he was done, he called Isabel and showed

her the ladder. If they came under attack, she could climb over the back fence and run to somewhere very public like the gas station on the corner of Burleigh and Seventy-sixth and call the police.

Mitch went back inside and studied the basement. Not really helpful, getting out up the basement steps still forced you past one or other of the doors and thus potentially in sight of potential attackers.

Back in the kitchen he noticed a hatch in the ceiling. Looking around he saw a long hook on a pole hanging almost unnoticed down the outer edge of the door frame. He used it to open the ceiling hatch and hook the attic ladder. Once the ladder was extended down into the kitchen, he climbed into the attic to take a look. The attic was small, with boxes and an old trunk on top of a very shaggy old yellow sixty's carpet. There was one dormer window overlooking the front yard. The wild garden looked quite nice from up here.

Mitch called Isabel to come up. He pulled the ladder up and told her to try pulling the hatch shut and latching it from up there. It was a struggle but once they retrieved the hook, she was able to use it to draw the hatch up to where she could grab the back of the latch and twist it into place on the frame.

"If we get trapped in the house, I want you to climb up here, with the hook, pull the ladder up and lock yourself in. You stay here until you are sure everyone is gone. They will try to trick you, so stay up here for at least half a day.

He emptied out the trunk putting all the contents

into other boxes. You can get in here just in case
someone actually bothers to climb up and manually
unlock the hatch and take a look. Practice it again"
Isabel ran through the whole routine from the
kitchen. It took her over two minutes. They would
practice again later.

Isabel felt sweaty and dirty, the attic was
disgusting so she took a nice cool shower while
Mitch went to check his email again to see if there
were any updates, still nothing on the whereabouts
of the children.

He went into the kitchen, and started making a
late lunch. Isabel soon joined him with hair still
damp and smelling wonderful. She gave him a
bright smile when she saw the big green salad with
chunky blue cheese dressing, hot rolls just out the
oven, the lump of real butter on the small plate, and
the bowel of fruit in the middle of the table. She sat
down, and Mitch poured her a glass of ice cold
milk. He felt terrible that he was deceiving her but
she looked so happy, and beautiful. He soon perked
up as they made small talk and she laughed at his
silly jokes.

After lunch he made her practice the attic escape
a few times until she was dropping the hatch, then
ladder, getting up and closing the hatch behind
herself in less than forty-five seconds. He yelled up
to her to be quieter once she was up there. This was
just a precaution since the thick old carpet muffled
any sounds from up there very well.

It was so hot up in the attic and Isabel was once
again sweaty with bits of insulation stuck to her wet
skin. Her cheeks were flushed bright red and Mitch

could hardly stand to look at her he found her so beautiful. Isabel caught his stare and poked her tongue out at him. He made a grab at her and she danced away laughing.

"Going to take another shower," she stated and disappeared into the bathroom closing the door as best she could behind her. Mitch stood at the door and commented that he had never met such a dirty stinky bitch that needed so much showering. He crowed with laughter at the stream of profanities that bubbled through the door. She really needed to work on that potty mouth.

After Isabel came out of the shower, Mitch had two beers open in the sitting room and was draped on the couch. He indicated her beer and she flopped into the big comfy chair. She commented that the leather chair was remarkably well made and did not mesh with the house or the neighborhood. Mitch called her a rich snob and she told him to go fuck himself.

"Wow, such fine language from a lady," he said and he went on to tell Isabel how Greta's furniture was all second hand, collected over the years on bulk pick up day along Lake Drive. "Greta likes the finer things in life but she sure as hell refuses to pay for them."

They spent the next hour talking about their childhoods, first serious dates, parents and high school experiences. Mitch realized how very different their lives had been. Isabel was a city girl, animal savvy but still a city girl. Very animal rights conscious to the point of being a vegetarian who only occasionally ate animal products from humanely raised and slaughtered animals. He pretended to be disgusted when, after he suggested that she eat roadkill, she actually agreed that this was a terrific source of humane protein.

When it was his turn, he told her all about growing up in far western Washington state, out on the Olympic Peninsula, in a tiny community called Beaver, population two hundred and ninety-one. In the summers he'd hike deep into the Olympic National Park to pan for gold.

He took just his tent, bedroll, fishing-tackle, a cooking pot, and his panning gear, living on trout, rabbits, Cama bulbs, Dandelions, Fiddle heads, Blueberries, Blackberries, Thimble berries, Salal berries, Bear berries, Huckleberries, mushrooms like the Hedgehog and Chanterelle and other fungi of the bracket persuasion, especially Chicken of the Woods. Isabel was enchanted by his tails of bears, cougar, mountain goats and the fluffy little marmots.

She was totally spellbound when he described his first encounter with a Polar bear. It never entered her mind that there are no polar bear in Washington. She sat on the edge of the chair, eyes wide as he narrated the tale.

"I was taking my younger cousin for his first ever camp out in the mountains. I took him to the Seven Lakes Basin. It is a magnificent hike. If you go counter clockwise you start with the Sol Duc Falls and then climb up to altitude almost immediately and then follow the ridge far above the Hoh River with vistas clear across to Mount Olympus but you descend into the valley for a very long flat hike home once you are tired.

I much prefer to do the long flat hike, then the five thousand foot climb past Heart Lake to camp in Cat Basin. You get the relatively boring part of the hike out of the way and the huge climb while still quite fresh. Anyway, the poor kid was crying all the way up the natural steps to Heart Lake about how his bum was burning. Too funny. We set up camp and I told him to walk around the tent and pee on the ground to keep the critters away at night." He stopped and took a sip of beer.

"After the fire died, we climbed into our sleeping bags and zipped them up around our heads because even though it is the height of summer, at that altitude it gets freezing cold at night. I had my knife and the bear spray inside the bag with me so I would find them in the dark if I suddenly needed them. We fell asleep quickly because we were pretty exhausted from the climb.

Well into the night, I hear snuffling sounds. I am instantly very wide awake, and I hear licking, something is licking the tent, and I can barely make out the tent dipping inward with each lick. The creature is obviously pretty big and my sixteen year old brain pretty much goes into panic mode.

I find the knife and the bear spray and try to get the zipper open on my sleeping bag, but it is stuck." Isabel's eyes have grown even wider. "I throw caution to the wind and fight wildly to get the bag open. My thrashing wakes the kid and I whisper for him to be very quiet. He, too, is now sitting up watching the tent dip.

As soon as I have my arms clear, I reached for

the zipper of the cover over the mosquito mesh window and very slowly draw it up so I can peep out. My God, I instantly froze with fear, my life flashing before me eyes, the whole window is obliterated with white fur." Mitch paused for effect; Isabel leaned right across the coffee table, hanging onto every word.

"Polar bear I said to my cousin, it's a polar bear." Mitch stopped for dramatic effect, and then continued "Then logic returned, and I remembered, there are no polar bears in Washington State."

"So what was it?" Isabel asked breathlessly.

" Well, it moved sideways, revealing the cutest little kid you have ever seen. It was a momma mountain goat and her kid. Stupid Paulie had peed on the tent and apparently the goats come to lick the salt. I think it took about an hour for our hearts to stop racing." Isabel was laughing now, tears running down her face. It was so good to see her this happy. He looked at his watch.

"What should we make for dinner?" he asked hoping that she would offer so that he could check his email for an update on the children. Isabel was quick to offer. She wanted to make him a 'great vegetarian dish'. He groaned inwardly, but outwardly he acted enthused and encouraged a nice big dinner as he was starving.

Isabel got up, picked up the empty bottles, there were now five, three that he had imbibed, two from her, and walked off toward the kitchen. Mitch checked his email. NOTHING.

In the house good smells were starting to emanate from the kitchen. Mitch decided not to tell

Isabel about the children at all, they had no idea where the hell the kids were, who had them, in fact they didn't even know what country they were in. He would tell her once he knew her boys were safe.

When he heard her setting up the dining table for dinner, he wandered out to help her. He went down to the basement and snagged a nice cool bottle of Greta's wine from her rustic home made wine cellar. He chose a nice crisp white to go with Isabel's vegi-surprise.

Back at the table, he poured them each a glass as Isabel dished up a divine smelling eggplant Parmesan. She passed him the basket of garlic bread and he settled in for a meal he would never have believed possible. He was not about to rethink meat, but this certainly was terrific anyway. After dinner he helped her clean up.

Mitch was determined to keep Isabel away from the news, he had been supremely lucky they missed any news of the children's kidnapping. He suggested they watch a movie in comfort. She looked at him suspiciously.

"I want to watch something funny to get my mind off this mess. Have you ever seen 'Down Periscope' with Kelsey Grammer?" he asked. She shook her head, still not convinced. "I promise I won't touch you." he declared. Isabel suddenly decided she had had enough secrecy. She looked at him with a new determination set on her face.

"Not until I get some answers. I want to know what the hell is really going on. Who are you, who do you work for, why am I here?"

"Fair enough," said Mitch. "Wine or beer?" he

asked and she pointed at the wine. He poured them each another glass and carried the glasses into the sitting room. Isabel, again, took the big comfy chair and he handed her a glass and sat down on the couch.

He explained to her exactly who he was and what he had been tasked to do. He apologized for his early inappropriate behavior. That was all Mack, he said. The profilers used your history to decide the best way to make you vulnerable and cooperative and that was it. I was following orders. I realize that that is a very poor excuse but your husband appears to have been instrumental in many deaths and needs to be brought to justice. Isabel glared at him.

"You assaulted me, I am sure that is against the law in any capacity what so ever," she snapped at him. Mitch felt horrible saying what he said next but he needed to be honest with Isabel.

"They have that covered he said. You will receive full immunity even if you don't testify, because we can't force a wife to testify against her husband, but only if you waive any right to pursue sexual assault or harassment charges against me. If you refuse, they will charge you as an accessory."

Isabel tossed the remains of her wine in his face and stormed out of the room. Mitch followed, still scared that she might turn on the news and hear about the kids.

"Isabel, I really am sorry, truly, truly sorry. I will make this up to you and your boys if I can. I am certainly going to try. I'll put on the movie and I promise it will make you laugh however angry you are now." She just glared at him so he turned on the television, and purchased the movie rental from Amazon.

Soon he was watching his favorite stupid comedy. It was only a few minutes before he heard the first giggle from next to him but he pretended not to hear her. Before long they were roaring with laughter and an hour and a half later, with good mood restored, they turned off the TV and settled down to sleep. Mitch did not check his email one last time.

FRIDAY

CHAPTER TWENTY-TWO

Back in New York

Vasili was sitting at the bar in The Pole Vault. It was close to closing time. He had eaten his club sandwiches and was nursing his third ice cold vodka. His personal stash was kept in the ice chest behind the bar. No fucking contaminated ice blocks for him. The bottle was kept below 0°C and on the glass condensation below the fluid line.

He was contemplating the next round of torture. That goddamned Fed was a callous bastard letting the girl suffer. Well, they would both suffer a lot worse fate when he got back down there.

His cell vibrated in his pocket. He hauled it out to see what idiot was calling him at almost four in the morning. It was his woman from the DOJ. What the fuck could she want this early? He answered the call as he walked back toward the offices to get away from the noise. He told the woman to wait.

Once he was behind closed doors he asked the woman who called herself Jenny Doe, but whose name Vasili knew was Kait Lin Ho, what she wanted. She told him that the FBI was investigating the disappearance of an agent called Mackenzie Brewster and were about to raid The Pole Vault looking for him.

Vasili felt the acid rise in his throat, he tasted the sour, bitter stomach acid in his mouth. Holy Mary mother of God they were fucked. How the hell did they know, or were they just guessing? He ran down to the dungeon, found Anatoli and woke him shouting at him to get his fucking sleepy ass out of bed.

He ordered Anatoli to leave via the garage and to put the retaining bolts into the tool shelving unit to secure it against opening. He would do the same in the outer basement so the wine rack could not move. No cell phones he said. They must be tracking the phones. Anatoli was to meet him at Lebedev's at five am. Vasili told him to bring whatever he wanted to keep because this was it, they were bailing, mostly likely to Brazil.

Vasili wanted to shoot the two in the basement but he figured that if the feds didn't find the dungeon, this prick would starve to death down here sitting in his own filth. Good riddance to the callous fucker...

On the way through the room with the chairs, Anatoli took the ball gag out of Missy's mouth, he felt sorry for her, she was most probably going to starve to death right there in that chair. She was awake and staring at him with terror renewed. She and Brewster had no idea what was happening.

They just silently watched the one man come in and the two men leave. The woman was opening and closing her mouth. It hurt like hell after being forced open for so many hours. She made slow chewing motions as she worked the stiffness out of her jaw. Mack watched, not saying a word. At least not until he was sure the men were gone. He had no plan to be part of their next sick game.

Vasili raced home, picked up the bag he had packed and ready for just such an occasion. He opened his safe and removed a few tightly bound stacks of cash which he shoved into his shoulder bag along with his laptop, three sets of fake identification, and credit cards in those names. He figured his home was being watched and was grateful for the secure underground parking. He would drive out of there and they could follow. He didn't care just yet. He dropped a letter addressed to his niece into the mailbox containing the key to the apartment, and safe combination. She could have whatever she could grab before the feds took it all.

Twenty minutes later he was waking Nikolai, or at least getting him up. The house alarm had awakened him as Vasili let himself in. He too collected items similar to those of Vasili. While he was getting packed, Vasili removed the hard-drives from all the computers in the house.

Nikolai left a note for Mrs. Wessels explaining that he would be gone for several weeks. Since she got paid by direct deposit he did not have to worry about her immediate loyalty. He made one call to Dr. Hye, from his home phone, using their prearranged code to tell the researcher to leave the country. For the rest, his businesses would run themselves. His legal clients would be farmed out to the other lawyers in the firm and there would be a couple of mistrials he was sure.

They waited on Anatoli who arrived very promptly at five 'o clock and immediately left the house. Nikolai was whistling and Vasili marveled at his cousin's great mood considering they were on the run. Something must be up, he just didn't know what.

Lebedev did not call for his limo. Instead, the three men climbed into Lebedev's Rosso Folgore, Maserati Ghibli. The magnificent, dark red car roared to life and Lebedev peeled out of the parking and down the road taking one sharp after another. He twisted and turned around the dark streets. He was not sure if he was being followed but was determined to shake a tail if he was. They also had to assume that a tracking device may have been affixed to the car. Never the less, they needed time to put the escape plan into action, and this was the quickest means to an end.

Vasili called ahead on a brand new disposable pre-paid cell phone that he pulled out of the glove compartment. He booked and paid for three tickets to São Paulo on the seven-thirty am flight out of Newark, NJ. Lebedev made it into the short term garage parking in thirty-one minutes.

The three men raced to check in and pass through security. They waited nervously in line, expecting to be apprehended at any moment if they had already made the TSA no fly list. As soon as they were safely through security, they circled down and out through the baggage claim area; but only after entering a men's room and reemerging unrecognizable.

The tallest and shortest men left the terminal
returning to the Maserati wearing huge sunglasses,
and fedoras pulled low, careful not to look in the
direction of cameras, to collect their extra bags.
These they took to the curb outside arrivals.

Lebedev, now Neville Levin, stopped at the
rental car stand, and in a very convincing, and
extremely common Cockney accent rented a large
white Chrysler with his British passport and driver's
license. He took the keys, and drove to the arrivals
concourse where he collected David Morris, and
Matthew Rindell. The three drove sedately out of
the airport and headed west on I-76 and then across
to I-80 westbound.

CHAPTER TWENTY-THREE

The dungeon

Back at the dungeon Mack Brewster's abductors had not reappeared through either passage in over an hour. Mack called to the injured young woman, asking her name.

"Missy Beth Layton," she told him in a very thick Southern drawl.

"Who are you, and what are you doing here?" was his next question. Missy moved her jaw.

"I'm thirsty and my jaw really hurts, almost more than my hand."

"I'm sorry," Mack said. "I'm sorry I can't do anything to help you. I need to figure out what's going on here, so if you can, please answer my questions." Missy looked at him suspiciously.

"Who are you?" she asked him.

"My name is Dr. Mackenzie Brewster, I am an FBI agent working on a case against Nikolai Lebedev." He figured what the hell; Gruzdev already knew that much and he wanted to gain the girls trust. "How old are you?" he asked her.

"Nineteen, I gone done it now, am I in deep

shit?"

"No sweetie," he answered as kindly as he could. "You are not in trouble, in fact if you help in any way, the District Attorney will give you immunity from anything you may have done illegally for Mr. Lebedev or Mr. Gruzdev."

"Who is Mr. Lebedev?" she asked and Mack explained the relationship between the two men. Missy nodded. "Oh, the lawyer that sometimes helps some of the girls who get accused of turning tricks. He is not a nice man. He likes the girls to pay him with favors and they say he likes to hurt people." Mack was struggling to understand the girl her accent was so thick.

"Where are you from? he asked her.

"Lilian, Alabama. I ran away from home because my step-daddy was fucking me more than mamma. If I'm gonna do that, I may as well get paid the big bucks and the advertisement in the Penny Saver said we wuz gonna make big bucks. 'Cept they did say foh moddlin, not strippin and sluttin. I done sucked moh dick in this city than there's people in Lillian."

Mack wasn't sure what to say now. Obviously she was not paid to open her mouth to speak. He now knew who this unfortunate creature was and just how dispensable she obviously was to the human traffickers who owned this place. Something else to add to the indictment if they ever got out of here.

"Missy, I need you to listen to me. Those men want information from me. Once they have that information they will kill us both. I cannot tell them what they want to know. I have to try very hard not to tell them, so enough time can go by, so the police can find us. Do you understand what that means?" Missy shook her head confused.

"Missy, they are going to come and do stuff to us much worse than before. Much, much worse. I want you to know that I do care about you but I can't tell them no matter how much they hurt you. If I do, we both die." Missy started to cry again. This time she had no gag and the wails were loud enough to wake the dead. Not a good sign, Mack thought. If they are not worried about us making a noise, obviously no one can hear us.

He wondered where the hell they were. He figured they were trapped underground and he wondered if they were at Lebedev's country home in Connecticut or his summer place in Montauk. He looked at his wrists; they were raw from him thrashing around when he was electrocuted. He imagined Missy's were worse but did not ask.

"Missy, do you know where we are?" he asked the poor girl when she eventually stopped crying. He was surprised to hear the answer, and was not sure if this was a good or bad thing.

Mack tried reaching his restraints with his teeth but his head was still duct taped against the back of the chair. At least the tape on his eyes had come loose. He called to Missy to try using her teeth to loosen the leather strap. He was impressed that she was limber enough to actually get close. Her mouth could just reach the nearest edge of the strap. Missy started chewing on the thick, stiff leather trying to get a purchase with her teeth.

Mack was somewhat disappointed, this was

going to take a while and he wondered how much time they had before those two bastards returned. He had absolutely no idea what time it was. He was more tired than he had ever been.

Occasionally. he would have a terrifying dream and he didn't think he was asleep. He figured he was hallucinating as a result of whatever they had used to drug him. Running through the list in his head, he felt certain he had been incapacitated with Ketamine. That would explain the weird dreams.

It had taken the NYPD two hours to get a judge to sign the search warrant for The Pole Vault. They were still working on warrants for the homes and businesses of Nikolai Lebedev and Vasili Gruzdev. The team was assembled and en route to the strip club.

The FBI agents from New York were already on scene, and those from Washington had landed and were on their way. All entrances were covered. A SWAT team member approached the big red, awning covered doors at the business entrance. The intercom crackled, and a voice asked who it was and what he wanted. The SWAT member shouted,

"NYPD we have a search warrant open up!" The voice on the intercom said he'd be right there and after a short wait, the door swung open, revealing a sleepy looking Brent Farber. Farber asked to see the warrant. He perused it and stated that he would have no problem letting them in if they could just await the arrival of Mr. Gruzdev's attorney whom he had already called. Detective Talbot stepped forward, and informed Farber that they would not wait, and Farber stepped aside as the officers and agents filed inside.

Farber was told to collect all people present at the address and assemble them in the club. Since a little birdie had warned them of the search all the girls were long gone; as were all the bar staff, bouncers, kitchen staff, and even the club's manager. Only the cleaning crew remained, hard at work getting the club ready for the opening at noon. Scrubbing, polishing, doing laundry, and restocking. All very reasonable and legitimate practices were occurring here this morning.

The employees were assembled in rows of chairs against one wall. One by one they were taken into the convenient lap dance booths and questioned by police. Nobody knew anything, nobody had seen anything. Most had been working there for years, all paid taxes on time, and presented valid identification.

Agents started in the offices of Gruzdev, and the club manager, working on to Farber's office and so on. Nothing seemed out of place. Everything appeared to be related to a very 'normal' strip club operation if there is such a thing.

Other agents searched every last corner of the building and the basement. Walls were banged on looking for secret hiding places. They found nothing. A heat seeking monitor was brought in and this too found no hidden hidey-hole with the missing man.

The employees were sent home, and Farber was taken to headquarters for questioning. It was mid-morning, they had nothing, and the suspects were nowhere to be found. If the latest intel was to be believed, Lebedev, Gruzdev, and Dubnovsky were in the air on the seven-thirty am flight to São Paulo. This was rapidly deteriorating into a disaster and Mandrake was furious with himself for not placing these men on the TSA no fly list before he left DC.

Down in the dungeon, Mack watched Missy chew away at the now very gooey leather binding her right wrist. Eventually, she managed to get a good grip and wiggled her head back and forth as much as she could trying to get the strap to slide toward her and out of the double keepers.

It took many attempts, over more than an hour, to get the strap out of the keepers. She then fought hard to pull the strap tight enough for the metal tongue to slip out of the hole. Three times it went straight back in the hole as she released the strap. Frustrated, on the fourth try she shook her head violently in an attempt to move the end of the tongue away from the hole. She released the strap and yelled out triumphantly when she felt the strap loosen against her wrist.

She got really quiet and stared toward the passages, terrified that her shout would summon the abusers. She wriggled her hand free, crying in pain as her damaged fingers dragged against the strap. She gallantly set to work freeing her other arm. Not as easy a task as it would have been if she wasn't down the very fingers that help one grasp. Once both hands were free, she loosened the straps on her legs. As she stood, Mack gave a triumphant but muffled whoop, cheering her on.

Missy came over and unwound the duct tape from his head, yanking out tufts of hair in the process. He tried not to call out. Her pain was real so he felt foolish whining over some pulled hair. She undid one hand, and he quickly did the rest. His very first deed was to unclip the vicious little clamps from his swollen testicles and pull up his pants. Missy looked away.

She followed him as he cautiously went down one passageway only to meet a very solid door with a key hole and no door knob. He could not see a way to open it. They returned to the main room and went down the second passage, only to run into exactly the same problem. Once again they returned to the main room.

They went down the wider hallway at the back of the room. Cell like rooms projected off each side of the central hall. The first two rooms were the most stark with single metal framed cots bolted to the floor, a thin hard mattress covered in a stiff plasticized gray material, and a thin, dark gray woolen blanket.

Each room also had a crude bucket toilet. The first room on the left was covered in puke, and smelled awful Mack realized that this must be where he was before being dragged unceremoniously to the chair. He barely remembered the room. There were five rooms on each side. The other eight rooms had heavy wooden bunk beds on one wall and two lockers on the other, either side of a small desk with mirror.

At the end of the hall was a military, or prison, style latrine. A row of open stall toilets on one side and a communal shower area with four shower heads across the room. On the wall on either side of the door were a couple of hand basins. Not a single window in the entire place.

Mack used the facilities, grateful that he could actually urinate. Then he rinsed his mouth. Missy waited for him to turn and walk back down the hall before she, too, used the toilet and tried to rinse her face with one hand. She was so thirsty she bent her head to the faucet and drank until she heard a shout. She quickly turned off the water and ran down to the main room.

Mack had a refrigerator open. Inside was mainly bottled water but there were also a few sodas and one lonely beer. The refrigerator also contained bottles of various condiments, some well past there sell by date. He took a better look around. The wall with the refrigerator was set up like a kitchen in a studio apartment. Just a line of counter-top with sink, hot plate, microwave, and refrigerator.

In the cupboards above he found paper cups, paper plates and canned goods; below were pots, none with long handles, floppy plastic cutlery, dried goods including rice and pasta, and a first aid box. At the end, closest to the 'rooms,' was a closet full of an assortment of second hand clothes.

On the opposite wall was a washer and dryer, a large metal trash can with lid and a long table with an equally long bench as seating. Obviously people were periodically kept down here in fairly large numbers. Well, at least they wouldn't starve.

Mack wondered why Gruzdev and Dubnovsky had not returned. He also wondered if this was a scare tactic or if they had been abandoned underground to die a slow death. He tried not to think about dying in this hole. He collected the first aid kit and called Missy over to the table. She saw the kit and sat down offering her swollen fingers. They were huge but did not look red or infected yet.

He collected a bowl washed it with hot water and dish soap; then filled it with bottled water before placing it in the microwave to heat. He put a hefty serving of salt in the water to act as the disinfectant and he returned to the table.

Mack soaked the hand for about five minutes, and then dried it gently with a sterile swab. He covered the small wounds with triple antibiotic ointment from a tiny plastic sachet. He told her to close her hand, and pressed the damaged fingers down, curling them to match the middle finger and then wrapped gauze dressing around the three fingers to keep them folded. This would bring the severed tendons' ends closest to each other. He was hoping to closely approximate the tendons so that they would have the best chance of healing especially if they didn't see a surgeon any time soon.

When he was done, Mack told her she could open her hand and just her index and thumb unfurled. He covered the gauze as best he could using the duct tape that had been left lying next to his torment chair and taped the edges to her bare skin.

"Now try not to get it wet," he told her. "If you want to take a shower, I will wrap your whole hand in a plastic bag so it stays dry. He was hinting that she may need to shower because she smelled pretty bad having obviously voided in fear and pain at some point during her torture. There was a small assortment of pain pills in the kit but he had also seen a bottle of Tylenol in the cupboard above the microwave. He took three regular-strength Tylenol and handed them to her with a bottle of water.

Mack revisited all the rooms looking for reading material. This was going to be a harsh confinement if there was nothing to read. He found a tattered bible, English on one side and some funky writing on the opposing page. Well, he wouldn't be learning a foreign language down here when he couldn't read the fucking script. There were a few old, tattered fashion rags, two People magazines, so old that Brittney Spears still looked cute. Obviously, nobody down here was big into reading.

He chose a room midway down the hall on the right. Halfway to the john, half way to the beer. He laughed at his own stupid joke, and settled down to read. Missy came in with a bag and the tape. He taped her up and she went off to take a shower. She had helped herself to a towel and some 'new' clothes. Mack stank like puke but he figured he would shower after Missy was done.

While the two in the dungeon set up house to await their fate, the men and women of the NYPD and FBI, completed their search and left the building, sealing all the entrances with crime scene tape. Mack and Missy were effectively buried in a huge, and very expensive coffin. Mack set the time on the microwave to 12:00. He had no idea what time it really was.

CHAPTER TWENTY-FOUR

Flight to Brazil

Riana was awakened by Yuri asking to go to the toilet. She got up and took him back to the restroom near the galley. She also used the facilities and they went back to their seats listening to the captain telling everyone to fasten their seat belts and place their seat backs in the upright position, with tray tables stowed for landing in São Paulo.

By seven am she was standing in front of a monitor looking for flights. Unfortunately, the flight she wanted was at six pm. They would have to spend the entire day in the airport as there was no way in hell she was taking the chance of leaving the secure area within the airport.

She was terrified of using the credit card to buy the tickets because she was pretty sure someone would be monitoring the card and would shut it down as soon as she made a suspect purchase.

Riana approached a currency exchange and innocently asked the man if he could check the cash back balance on her card. The man smiled, taking the card and swiping it through the machine. You have a ten thousand dollar per day limit he said.

Riana gasped, trying to turn it into a cough, that turned into a real cough as she choked on inhaled saliva. The agent looked at her with concern and she apologized stating that she was just getting over the flu.

She swiped the card again and put in the pin, and requested nine thousand dollars as the tickets she wanted at the last minute where twenty-seven hundred dollars each. The agent placed the money in one hundred dollar bills into four individual envelopes and cautioned her against taking the money out in public.

Riana rushed over to the airline representative and bought the three tickets in cash after showing the agent her passport and the letter authorizing her to have the children traveling with her. When asked about the intent of the travel, she stuck briefly to the truth only in that she explained that they were in the Bahamas and then taking the children to vacation in Brazil with their parents. Then she delved into fantasy telling the agent that she had just been informed of the severe illness of their mutual grandmother. She explained that she was the boys' nanny but also their cousin and that the children's mother was already en route home.

After receiving their boarding passes, she took the boys to a large duty free shop with iPads and other electronics. Yuri and Demmy could not contain their excitement. She bought them each an iPad and took them over to the digital center that allowed purchase and download of Apps, games, and movies. She figured this would keep them quiet most of the day. She found herself a good book to read and then they went in search of a restaurant for brunch. After a safe meal of burger, fries, and ice-cream, they settled onto the floor near the power outlets along the wall near their gate and Riana closed her eyes and prayed nobody would find them before the flight at six.

After another round of fast food, this time pizza and more ice-cream, their flight was called. Riana logged onto the airport WIFI and on the FBI website she left an anonymous message that read. " Re Nikolai Lebedev and Vasili Gruzdev, the Pole Vault has a hidden basement." Forty five minutes later the plane took off, and Riana felt a flood of relief. Now she was sure that the boys would be safe. It would be very difficult for anyone to scramble and intersect them before she delivered the boys, even if they did figure out this late on a Friday night, where she was taking the children.

CHAPTER TWENTY-FIVE

On the run

Nikolai, Vasili, and Anatoli drove west. The DOJ informant had said that she was only getting bits and pieces of information. The communications from Special Agent Hammer were still being received via France but it was believed that he was somewhere in the Midwest so they were headed for Chicago, a nice busy city where they could hide out in plain sight while they waited for news.

Just beyond Clearfield, Pennsylvania, they were listening to the news on the satellite radio when they heard the updated news about the kidnapping of a nanny and her two charges, the death of an FBI agent and the apprehension of the suspect in the Bahamas. Nikolai swore, he had hoped to hear that the boys were in Brazil not this bad news. Mason wouldn't talk, but the Feds might get the boys before he could make sure they were safely hidden.

It was going to be impossible to clean up this mess. His life in the United States was over. Now he just wanted the pleasure of killing Isabel, the life destroying bitch, before heading to Brazil to pick up his sons and then perhaps back to Russia.

Nikolai was also very grateful that the cloned two-year-olds were all owned by the corporation that had no direct link to him. After the Kentucky Derby he would ship most of them overseas. He would have to make some plans for the horses. Definitely get some plastic surgery so that he could safely return to watch one of his Secretariats win the Triple Crown. He was very confident his colts were that good. At least his boys would be safe, and waiting for him on his ranch in Brazil by tonight if Riana followed Mason's directions. Thank God for offshore banks and desperate girls.

As they drove west with Anatoli at the wheel, the three men discussed strategy. Sasha was waiting in Chicago, the four of them would make a formidable team in the hunt for Isabel and, the now much hated federal agent, Mitchell Hammer. They whiled away time imagining horrific tortures just for fun. Suddenly Nik shouted,

"Damn it, her dogs. That bitch sure loves those fucking dogs. It would have been grand to gut 'em in front of her." This brought renewed inspiration to their plans of horror and Vasili started scouring Craigslist, in each town they were due to pass through, looking for a Fox Terrier or Saint Bernard that even remotely resembled Isabel's dogs.

In Akron, Ohio they found a Saint Bernard. She did not look particularly like Emma but she was the only Saint Bernard they could find and she would have to do. It pissed Nikolai off that it cost almost three hundred dollars to 'rescue' the stupid mutt. Vasili had played the part of the doting father from

Chicago, taking home the best birthday present his daughter had wished for. The young dog was hyper active and drooled constantly. Vasili, stuck in the back seat with the overgrown pup, became more and more irate as he got wetter and wetter. In less than an hour he ordered Anatoli to find a secluded area.

Near Lodi, they located Hidden Hollow Park and took the dog for a walk, following the stream through the park as far away from obvious habitation as they could. The poor unsuspecting pup bounced and strained, thoroughly enjoying the walk. When they reached a good sized tree with convenient strong low limb, Nikolai put his gun to the dogs head and shot her, killing her with one bullet.

They quickly hung her in the tree by her back legs and cut her throat catching some of the blood and smearing it over her coat to disguise the difference in color. The rest of her blood pooled on the ground beneath the dog as she hung in the tree. Nikolai took many photos from various angles, some with Anatoli holding the knife, and gutting the dog, pulling her intestines out to hang toward the ground.

Nikolai intended to tell Isabel they had gutted the dog before cutting its throat. When they were done, they dragged the carcass under some bushes hear the stream and used the stream to wash the dog's blood from their hands and arms before returning to the car. Only ten minutes later Vasili whooped.

"Wow, it's our lucky day. There is a breeder of Wired haired Fox Terriers in a town up ahead called

New Washington. I'll call and make an appointment." He called the number on the web page and spoke to a woman who agreed to see them at six-thirty pm.

With almost an hour to spare, they stopped for an early dinner at the only place they could find, Pete's Cafe where the Thursday special was forty-five cent wings. They ordered two dozen hot wings and, at the suggestion of the flirty young waitress, the sweet potato fries. Since there was not a drop of liquor to be found in the place they settled for diet cokes.

At six-fifteen they went in search of the breeder. Nikolai saw the dog they wanted immediately. Vasili thought they all looked the same but Nikolai knew Zippy well enough to recognize his 'twin.' The woman did not particularly want to part with the young male, as she was prepping him as a show dog with the plan for him to perhaps become her new stud. Nikolai asked her what a fair price was for a show dog of that quality and immediately offered her an extra thousand dollars.

"My wife has been searching high and low for the right dog to start showing with, I just know this is the dog for her," he told the poor woman. "Perhaps you can teach her, she can come to you and we pay you for lessons." The breeder looked pensive, now she had a really good sale and the prospect of getting good money out of this obviously rich idiot, so she made the deal and accepted thirty-five hundred dollars for the dog.

Hoosiers Mister Twister, kennel name Tug, trotted out to the car with his new owners sporting the collar and leash that the breeder threw in when she realized they had none. She also gave them a small plastic bowl and a Ziploc baggie full of kibble. Nikolai quite liked this dog, no drool, well behaved, and very attentive, cocking its head back and forth as you spoke to it. This one might actually last long enough to cause the bitch some real pain up close and personal.

The three men headed for Toledo. It was nearing eight pm and it had been an exceedingly long day. They would find a decent hotel and get a good night's sleep. Vasili looked for pet friendly hotels and found the Ramada to be the best bet in town. Not a single upscale hotel appeared to take pets. Oh well, the Ramada it would be.

Vasili booked two rooms, he and Nik would share and Anatoli could keep the damn dog. When they pulled into the hotel, he reminded the man to walk the dog later so that they wouldn't have to pay for a new carpet. Anatoli gave him a dirty look. He was accustomed to being expected to walk Isabel's dogs; it happened often enough in new York.

They left the dog in the room during dinner, and Anatoli took the meaty bone from his T-bone steak for the poor doomed Tug, that Nik now insisted they call Zippy.

Back in the suite, Nik turned on the television to see if there was any more news on the events in Orlando. It did not take long. The ten o' clock news reported an update. The man who had been arrested in Nassau in the Bahamas in connection with the death of the FBI agent in Orlando had been identified. Agents were en route to interview the suspect, named as Jackson Mason, an investigator for the law firm of Lebedev, Cohen and Kennedy.

It was believed that the missing children were in fact the sons of Mr. Nikolai Lebedev who had been in protective custody at the time of their kidnapping by Mr. Mason. The whereabouts of the children were unknown but police were searching Freetown and surrounding areas based upon an anonymous tip.

The FBI had reason to believe that Mr. Lebedev and two acquaintances, his cousin Vasili Gruzdev, and personal bodyguard, Anatoli Dubnovsky had not fled the country, as previously reported, and where being sought in connection with the kidnapping. Any information into the whereabouts of the children, or the men shown, should be called into 1-800-CRIMESTOPPERS. The news said nothing about Isabel.

Nikolai was angry and as usual Vasili just waited him out as he ranted and raved about the injustice and misfortune. Again Isabel bore the brunt of his anger. Vasili marveled at how his cousin never took any responsibility for his self-induced troubles. It was always someone else's fault, always someone out to get him. Nikolai calmed when Vasili pointed out that Riana and the boys were obviously no longer in the Bahamas.

"Don't worry Nikolai. We were leaving anyway. No one is looking for us here and by Monday we will likely be with Yuri and Demmy on the ranch. Mason won't say a word, you know that. He has absolutely nothing to gain as long as he thinks we are gone. He knows you will pay him very, very, well to take the fall with his mouth shut. Also, he knows what you will do to him if he does talk. I will upload the dog photos to Isabel's fake Facebook account and get her freaking out. You sleep now we need to leave early."

CHAPTER TWENTY-SIX

Earlier that morning in Milwaukee

Mitch had woken late on Friday morning. He opened his email to find that there were three emails from Mandrake. In the first, from last night, Mandrake informed him that the FBI had received a call from the Nassau police department in the Bahamas. On an anonymous tip, they had apprehended a man called Jackson Mason. Mason just happened to be an investigator for the New York law firm Lebedev, Cohen and Kennedy.

According to the tipster, the children had been dropped off in Freeport to rendezvous with their father. Mason was accused of throwing the captain of a charter boat overboard about thirty to forty miles north and both the Bahama authorities and the US Coast Guard were engaged in a search and rescue effort.

Allegedly, again according to the tipster, Mason had murdered Bob Sanders when he took the kids and the nanny. No sign yet of the boat captain. An agent was en route to the Bahamas to interview Mason. There was no sign of the boys or their nanny.

The second, from hours later, recounted the events in Saratoga and the disappearance of Mack. This was a harsh blow, and Mitch's mind was racing. The third, from only minutes before, was even worse. Lebedev, Gruzdev, and Dubnovsky had apparently evaded the FBI and had left the country on a flight to São Paulo. Lebedev's car had been impounded when it was located at the Newark International airport. This meant he was likely off to rendezvous with his children.

On a positive note, the Cyber division had run a tracer and the mole was an IT guy called Bill Franks. He was in custody so they could resume normal channels of communication. Alexei Lashkov, aka Sasha, had been released from the hospital, against medical advice, by the time the local PD showed up to arrest him. Lashkov had taken a taxi to the nearest BMW dealer, received a new key and been dropped at the Truck Stop. It was presumed he was driving east until Lebedev went missing, now they had no idea. There was a BOLO issued to law enforcement, in three states, for his vehicle.

With Lebedev out of the country, the kids missing, and the mole in custody, Mitch decided to call Mandrake. He slipped out of bed as quietly as he could and took himself outside to make the call. Mandrake quickly filled in all the details. Mitch gave Mandrake their current location and informed his superior that he thought it would be best for them to lie low in the house and keep Isabel away from the news while they tried to locate the children before they slipped out of the Bahamas; if, of course, that had not happened already.

Mandrake agreed after suggesting that Mitch contact the Milwaukee FBI office and have an agent cover the property around the clock until they were sure of Lebedev's arrival in Brazil. Mitch agreed and signed off. He was dreading the scene when Isabel found out he had lost her kids. She was going to come apart at the seams. He called the Milwaukee FBI office to request the round the clock cover before heading in.

Back inside Mitch could hear Isabel in the shower. He turned on the television to see if he could catch the footage of the events relayed by Mandrake. Mitch flipped through the channels trying to find a news network. Greta had Time Warner so he found CNN on channel 44 and Fox News Network on channel 48,

He was switching back and forth between the news channels when they ran the story of the events in Saratoga. He watched in amazement as the newscaster recalled the events, and he watched the various clips roll by, seeing that poor little dog hooked up to tubes and the scene of Cathy being placed in the squad car. At least she wasn't in cuffs although they did say she was held overnight and remained in police custody.

They replayed the fiery crash and mentioned the names of the deceased. They had moved on to other news so Mitch quickly turned off the TV when Isabel came to the door, rubbing her wet hair vigorously with a towel.

"Your friend Cathy killed a man last night when

he tried kidnapping her." Mitch informed her. Isabel went quite pale. For a moment Mitch thought he may have to jump up and catch her. She sat down on the edge of the bed and he narrated the excitement of the previous night.

"I hope dear little Dodger is going to survive," she said quietly,. "Poor Cathy, she will be so sad if he dies and it will be all your fault." Mitch took the blame without comment since it was true.

"Nikolai must be getting pretty desperate. I wonder what gave her away," he mused. We better get our affairs in order this morning and then hole up for a while until things calm down and I can get you back to New York. Oh, that reminds me, I forgot to tell you that Nikolai and his cousin left the country this morning on a fight to Brazil."

Isabel smiled, "Good, then maybe you can bring my boys back," she countered. Mitch's mind raced, he needed an excuse yesterday already.

" I want us to hole up here for a couple of days; just until we have eyes on the ground in Brazil telling us what he is up to.

"I suppose that makes sense," she replied. Mitch was tremendously relieved since right now the boys were probably also en route to Brazil and it was going to be a bitch trying get them back.

Isabel offered to make some eggs on toast or pancakes while he did whatever he thought necessary. Mitch gave her a wry grin and asked for both.

"You don't deserve to be rewarded for this disaster," she snapped. "You have endangered my friends and family with your gung-ho approach to the law."

"Maybe, but I need my strength to keep you safe, Nikolai might be on his way to Brazil, but his 'security' as you put it are still here somewhere and we cant find Alexei Lashkov," he retorted. Almost immediately he felt like a real shit-head for scaring her all over again. Isabel looked pale and glum as she turned and left the room.

After a very subdued breakfast, which had included both eggs and pancakes, for which Mitch thanked her profusely, he had her run through the attic drill. Still around forty to forty-five seconds. That was probably as good as it was going to get.

In an effort to keep her away from the televisions, Mitch told her that he wanted her to sit at the table with pen and paper and write down everything she could remember from the past twelve years that seemed out of place to her.

"Just don't mention anything about the stuff you were involved in. You will cover that later after you have a signed immunity from the feds." With Isabel safely ensconced at the dining-room table, Mitch sat down with his laptop to write his report. A little after midday, he looked up to see Isabel stretching.

"Wow!" he commented, "Nikolai must have been a very busy boy to keep you writing for hours." Isabel grinned, and lifted the stack of papers.

"Well, once I got started, I kept remembering little things that were said here or there, so I started trying to make connections, these pages all have lines connecting them to other pages. It is quite a mess really but I think that it might be helpful once you guys fill in times and places of the stuff you were investigating." Mitch walked over and gave her a hug.

"Brilliant idea. You need the reward that I don't deserve. How about pizza. On the refrigerator I see there is a specialty pizza place about two miles away and they deliver. No chain store pizza for my newest co-conspirator. I'll pull up their menu."

Isabel took a quick potty break and joined him in front of the computer to choose her authentic thin crust Neapolitan. Mitch chose the Four Seasons with tomato sauce, provolone, prosciutto, mushrooms, black olives, artichokes, and Isabel went with the oven roasted vegetables and provolone. When they couldn't decide on desert, they got the Tiramisu and the flour-less chocolate cake. Isabel cleared the papers off the table, and handed them to Mitch and then set it up for lunch. Within forty minutes they were tucking into the best pizza she had ever tasted.

After their late lunch, while Isabel was clearing away the remains of their feast, Mitch contacted Mandrake for an update. The news was not good. It appeared the men had never actually been on the flight, despite checking in and clearing security. Video footage from the airport showed Lebedev, Gruzdev, and Dubnovsky entering but never leaving the airport building. Facial recognition software could find no matches exiting. The parking structure video showed the three men leaving the Maserati. Sometime later two strange men approach the vehicle and remove bags from the trunk. They appear to leave the area and go out onto the arrivals pick up zone, however, they found the only blind spot and there is no indication that any one of the vehicles that slowed within the blind spot specifically picked them up.

So, Lebedev was probably en route to the Bahamas by private plane or boat. They were checking radar and satellite images. However, there was a small possibility he was actually still in the US and hunting for his wife.

"Be careful, Mitch," his boss warned, "Be very, very careful. He is cornered now, so he is a supremely dangerous man."

The news about Mack was equally bleak. The raid of the Pole Vault had not found him. They had no idea where he was. The only evidence found, during the search of the premises to date, was inside a black utility van belonging to Gruzdev's strip club. It consisted of an empty syringe containing traces of Ketamine, and traces of dried saliva. They were running the saliva for a DNA comparison.

The van did come up positive for fingerprints of Anatoli Dubnovsky, Brent Farber, head of club security, and Mack Brewster, so Mack was definitively in the van at some stage. Brent was in custody, but denying any recent use of the van despite his cell being used at the time and location of the suspected abduction. Currently, other than the two dead men, the only missing club employee was a teenage stripper, not likely involved.

They disconnected and Mitch called the agent on the Milwaukee FBI surveillance detail who was watching the cottage. He warned him to expect at least three men if any were to show up. He was not sure how that bastard would find them but he was sure that the man could. Surely there is no way he would have risked staying in the country unless he knew where to find Isabel. Of course he could be on his way to the Bahamas, but it was too dangerous to believe that without proof. He told the agent that he expected to hear from him every half hour and requested that he drop a secure two way radio in the mail box within the next fifteen minutes.

Just then the back door opened next door and a very noisy Weimeraner came charging out barking like crazy. The young man, from whom he had collected the house keys apologized and yelled at the dog, Zola, to shut up! but of course the dog ignored him and bounced around at the fence like a lunatic. He smiled, greeting his neighbor and went back inside. He didn't mind having a paranoid dog next door.

Mitch went to the computer to check the camera feeds. He set an alarm to go off every time motion activated the record function. With such a small perimeter, they were not going to get much warning. He checked his Glock, made sure he had a full magazine and another in his pocket. He strapped a second holster onto his ankle and checked the smaller nine mm he placed in it. He preferred his fourth generation Glock 22. The forty caliber weapon was his favorite, never jammed, and very little recoil for such a powerful pistol.

He loaded a second nine mm Glock and chambered a round. He would place this one up in the attic for Isabel. On his other ankle he strapped his dive knife. This was going to be nerve wracking.

If Lebedev had started west out of New York early this morning, he was going to be in the area by about nine pm at the earliest. However, he expected the man to do surveillance first so the attack would likely come during the night. He also collected the two way radio from the mail box and checked in with the agent.

Mitch thought that he was really going to have to do something special for Greta. He was using her house, drinking her wine, and was quite likely going to cause some serious damage if Lebedev showed up guns blazing. He wondered if they should go to a hotel.

He had a thought and wandered through the kitchen into the small rear bedroom. He pulled the dresser away from its position in front of the window and dragged it to the mud room door. He maneuvered it through the door and down the small step and then dragged it onto the closed hatch over the stairs that led down into the basement.

There were just too many damn windows in the basement. Then he pulled the utility shelving in the mudroom across the back door, effectively blocking that entrance. Now anyone coming in would have to use the front door or the master bedroom window as all the others were well off the ground and would make a speedy entry impossible.

Isabel had finished in the kitchen and watched him silently until he was done, and had grabbed a beer and seated himself at the table. She joined him and cocked her head and just said,

"So?"

Mitch told her that the FBI no longer believed

that Nikolai had definitely left the country.
Somehow, he had eluded security cameras at
Newark International airport in New Jersey and was
possibly headed to Milwaukee if he knew their
whereabouts. "The FBI believe he is traveling with
Gruzdev, and Dubnovsky. Alexei Lashkov had
checked out of the hospital in Erie by the time the
FBI got there so there was no reason not to think
that he, too, may be coming in this direction," he
said as he watched her face crumble with fear.

With a feeling of dread, Mitch realized that the
latter man might already be here. The thought sent
chills down his spine and he said nothing to further
spook poor Isabel who now appeared quite ill. To
try and set her mind at rest, he told her about the
FBI agent watching the house as well as the
increased police patrols in the neighborhood,
especially the streets on either side of them.

Mitch showed her the smaller Glock and they
climbed into the attic and secured the gun to the
back of the wooden trunk to the left of the small
dormer window. While Isabel watched from behind
the now drawn curtain, Mitch took the hose and
watered the garden, taking the opportunity to do a
careful surveillance of the visible surroundings. He
found no sign of Alexei Lashkov.

When Mitch came back in, he reset the alarm on
the surveillance software that he had paused while
outside. He told Isabel not to open any curtains or
touch them to cause movement when she looked
outside. He turned off the AC in the south wall that
could be seen and heard from the street or next
door, and left only the bedroom AC running. The

house would get a little hot but they could try and make it appear unoccupied. No lights on at all except for the front porch. He dimmed the computer monitors so that the glow would not be apparent through any curtains.

Isabel commented that she was feeling rather useless and asked what she could do to help. Mitch asked her to prepare food to be refrigerated so that they would not have to make dinner in the dark. He also unscrewed the light bulb in the refrigerator, and unplugged the microwave. Isabel got to work preparing a salad, and sandwiches to eat later.

When she was done, she informed Mitch that she was going to write to her sons just in case she didn't make it out of this fiasco alive. Although Mitch wanted to tell her everything was going to be alright, he encouraged her.

"Great idea, he told her. I'm confident we will find your husband and you will get through this just fine but it will still be a great letter to give your kids one day when you eventually tell them what really happened this week in history." He thought that this would keep her busy and away from the news from any source.

Mitch went back to writing up his report so that his superiors would know everything if anything happened to him. He also looked through Isabel's notes and added comments here and there. He photographed all the pages and once he was done, he sent his report and the attached photos to Mandrake.

A couple of times the camera alarm was triggered, once by a cat, the other was two squirrels fighting near the bird feeder. Mitch adjusted the sensitivity of the motion detection. He did not need to have heart failure every time a small animal invaded his domain.

By early evening they were both done with their tasks. Nerves were getting frayed and she snapped at him when ever he spoke to her. Mitch grabbed a couple of beers, feeling bad that Isabel was reduced by fear to following him around the tiny house like a puppy with separation anxiety. He led her through to the sitting room, and handed her a beer. After getting comfortable on the deep leather couch he said,

"Isabel, they can not get here before nine at the earliest. There is no indication that any small planes coming this way are unaccounted for, so he will be driving if he is coming. We have FBI surveillance out front, regular police patrols and we have the three cameras with alarms. You must try to relax or you will make yourself sick and you wont be any good to me if we do need to fend off Nikolai and his team. If the alarm goes off once it is dark, you will hurry into the attic. In fact, I'll go drop the ladder right now and leave it down." Mitch left the room briefly and was back in a minute. "There, done." She gave him a wan smile.

"OK, can we play cards of something so my mind stays busy?" Mitch nodded.

"Yup, lets do it in the bedroom so I can keep one eye on the monitor." The two went through the now darkening house and into the bedroom. Mitch located some cards while Isabel fetched the food, a couple of plates and forks, some salad dressing and two more beers.

Mitch asked her if she knew how to play poker and when she said no, he got busy trying to teach her a game that would really keep her mind off of anything other than winning his money. After her second beer and winning a few nickels and dimes, he got her a glass of wine and moved the stakes up to a dollar. He wanted her just drunk enough to relax and fall asleep. Once she was giggling and was down eleven dollars, he asked her,

"Strip poker or Seinfeld?" She gave him the evil eye and chose the comedy.

Isabel went off to use the bathroom in the dark while he got the Netflix running on the laptop under the covers. One last check in with Mandrake revealed nothing new. Mitch spoke to the agent on the surveillance detail and asked that he just use the buzz function overnight, and Mitch would buzz back unless the either man saw anything to warrant talking.

Mitch and Isabel settled in under the blankets to watch Seinfeld and soon she was sleeping peacefully. Mitch watched the camera feed looking for any sign of trouble. He dozed fitfully between the buzzing and trying to watch the monitor.

SATURDAY

CHAPTER TWENTY-SEVEN

Toledo, Ohio

Vasili checked his email just before five am. He was instantly very angry with himself for not checking it late the previous evening. There was a message from the mole with the location of Isabel and the FBI agent. He immediately called Sasha and told him to get to Milwaukee and check out the information. They were about six hours away depending on the traffic. He woke Nikolai and Anatoli and they packed the car, and stopped for coffee and breakfast sandwiches before hitting the highway westbound with happy little Tug curled up on the back seat..

Alexei 'Sasha' Lashkov was driving north within a half hour. He arrived in Enderis Park a little after seven. He parked his car in the parking area near the park toilets and walked over to Seventy-second Street parallel to the cottage that Isabel was supposed to be staying in.

He made his way through the garden of the home that backed onto the house across the street from the cottage. He stuck close to the residence so that the occupants would not see him. Lashkov had checked the Google maps satellite picture to access the terrain. At the corner of the house he quickly ducked around the cars and followed the fence line to the corner of the property behind the garage, checking the trash bin on his way by. He scaled the fence and approached the next garage. Creeping around it, he stared at the house for signs of movement.

Just then, a door opened on the side of the house facing the driveway, he ducked back behind the garage as a dog ran out on a long lead and did its business just feet away from where he lay as motionless as possible. The woman called to the dog and the two disappeared back into the house.

Lashkov waited behind the garage watching the back windows. He could see the woman busy in the kitchen. No one else appeared before the woman exited again through the side door, this time alone. She appeared dressed in scrubs so maybe she was going to work. That would be a bit of luck. The woman went into the garage and within a couple of minutes, pulled out of the yard in a nineties model Honda.

Lashkov quickly moved across to the back of the house and looked back toward the house behind him and those in view to either side. He used his binoculars to peruse the visible windows but saw no movement. It was likely that most people were either sleeping late or had left for work. He knew from some quick Internet research, and the mail in the trash can he had peeked into on his way through that yard, that a very fat, older woman lived in the house. He doubted very much that she could see him over the fence and through the good tree cover.

Alexei Lashkov cut a small hole in the glass and opened the window. As yet, the dog had not made a sound. He quickly jumped up onto the window frame and climbed into the kitchen closing the window behind him.

Lashkov moved quietly through the house, he saw the dog sitting on a chair staring out of the window in the living room. He moved back to the kitchen and looked for something smelly and tasty. He found some left over chicken in the refrigerator and carried it through to the bedroom, and placed the chicken and a bowl of water on the bathroom floor, and then proceeded to make some scratching noises. Soon the dog barked and ran toward the kitchen, he scratched again and the dog came sliding into the room. It saw, or smelled, the chicken and raced into the bathroom. Lashkov quickly leaned in and pulled the door closed.

He left the hysterical dog and went into the sitting room. He could easily see the house across the street even without approaching the window. He climbed the stairs to the minute upstairs room and found a small dormer window looking down on the house across the street. This would be a great vantage point. The window was made of many small panes of tinted glass that would effectively break up the view of the room as seen from the street. It would be difficult to spot someone sitting behind the glass.

Lashkov went back downstairs to the kitchen; made himself a sandwich, grabbed a can of diet soda, and returned to the upper room to watch the cottage across the street.

Lashkov called Gruzdev to update him. There was a car in the drive, but otherwise the house looked deserted; porch light on, curtains drawn and no sign of movement. The yard was very overgrown. He definitely identified one cop of some type watching the house from a van parked in the driveway of the house on the corner a few houses south of his location. He had not seen any other surveillance, but a patrol car had cruised past slowly which he did not think was a coincidence. Despite the deserted look and feel, he was sure they had found their mark. Vasili told him they were still about four hours away.

CHAPTER TWENTY-EIGHT

Nassau, Bahamas

Justin Porter was the man on the ground in the Bahamas. With the most incredible luck, the boat captain had been picked up alive. He was at Doctor's Hospital in Nassau in the intensive care unit. The unfortunate man had sustained a cracked skull, a small subdural hematoma, bad sunburn, and severe dehydration after nineteen and a half hours floating in the ocean.

The doctors were reporting that he was doing well after more than twenty four hours in an induced coma and would likely be able to talk to the police as soon as the sedatives wore off. He had been sedated to protect himself from harm as he was extremely delirious and combative on admission.

Porter had stopped by the detention center, on Friday and was informed that Jackson Mason was refusing to say anything. Porter had asked to listen to the 911 recording. The voice had a heavy guttural accent and Porter was convinced it was the nanny. He had them search flights for her name, then the

names of the children in case they were headed
back to the States or on to Brazil although that
seemed less likely now that it was confirmed that
Nikolai Lebedev never left the country.

Nothing came up which he found very odd. Why
would she call from the airport if she didn't fly out?
Maybe she was trying to make it look like she did
and perhaps she and the children were right here on
Nassau and not in Freeport. He expressed this to the
local police who had immediately broadened their
search for the missing children.

He had requested video footage from the airport
surveillance cameras. The local police had called
the airport and requested that all footage from two
hours either side of the 911 call be presented as
soon as possible. It had been at least an hour before
they received the footage and then it had taken a
few hours to go through all of it. Porter was very
frustrated with having so little control. This
morning he had one witness unconscious, one
suspect uncooperative, and a trio of youngsters that
had vanished into thin air.

In New York, the FBI office was in high gear.
Late last night there had been a very credible tip on
the website. Based upon the IP address, the tip was
from Brazil so perhaps another message the nanny
if she had indeed taken the children there. Her role
was becoming confusing, she was ratting out her
boss, yet taking his children to what they had
thought was a rendezvous in Brazil. An agent was
en route to São Paulo.

Meanwhile, someone was trying to find building
plans for the building housing the Pole Vault; the

NYPD were interviewing Pole Vault staff; and Mandrake himself went to interview Brent Farber.

Initially Farber was uncooperative but when he heard that the nanny had told them about the hidden basement called the dungeon, a small misrepresentation of the actual facts since they did not know who left the tip, Farber realized he was about to go down hard if he did not cooperate. He had no loyalty to Lebedev and knew that the man would shoot him as soon as not; so he asked for an attorney and agreed to help as soon as his attorney and the prosecutor came to an understanding.

Mandrake knew what that meant and called the Justice Department to establish just how much he could offer this witness. He was told to offer total immunity and witness protection for full cooperation and testimony against Lebedev and Gruzdev. The deal would be void if it came to light that he had committed murder, however, if he confessed to such crimes prior to trial, he would receive fifteen years with possibility of parole.

Mandrake went back to the interrogation room and presented the offer to Farber and his attorney. They conferred for a few minutes and Farber agreed. He had committed many egregious crimes for Gruzdev, with the sex trade and he had killed for him. He knew that it was likely these crimes would come to light as the investigation progressed, that they might even find some of the dead girls. He knew exactly how these things worked.

Farber demanded a maximum of ten years in prison with the availability of early parole in exchange for his testimony. He also wanted to be incarcerated out of state under an assumed name. He knew Gruzdev and Lebedev would put out a hit. He also asked for the witness protection program on release. Mandrake realized that they had an opportunity to blow the case wide open and begged the district attorney to accept the deal.

Within the hour Farber had explained how to enter the hidden section of the basement. Mandrake left the rest of the questioning to another agent and departed to find Mack Brewster. En route they called for police back up as well as medics on scene. There was always a chance that Lebedev was hiding in the basement.

As soon as the Swat team was in place, the bolts that held the steel shelving in place across the door in the basement garage were removed and the shelving pulled back. The key retrieved from the magnetic key holder under the front bumper of Farber's SUV opened the heavy door and Mandrake used a bull horn to call into the passage.

Within seconds they could hear footsteps and Mack called out that they were unarmed and alone. The Swat Team did not stand down but entered the passage as soon as Mack and Missy appeared. The paramedics quickly loaded them into the waiting ambulances and Mandrake rode with Mack getting the details of his detention and torture.

Once back at FBI headquarters, the team, including Mack who had refused to stay at the hospital for observation after an ultrasound confirmed normal blood flow in his still slightly swollen scrotum, reviewed the progress and had to admit that for all action of the last few hours, they were no closer to finding Lebedev and had no clue as to his whereabouts. Farber worked for Gruzdev in what had been an almost legitimate position and had no direct knowledge of Lebedev's activities unrelated to the club prior to the kidnapping of Brewster. However, the team had no doubt they could connect what he had done for Gruzdev to the unsolved mysteries surrounding Lebedev.

The girl, Missy, was still in surgery. The team also received an update from Porter. Unfortunately, the tapes reviewed the previous day did not reveal the boys or their nanny. It had, however, shown Mason entering and then exiting the airport just before four forty five on Thursday and leaving only minutes later without the luggage he had taken inside.

The local police were still searching the airport for the two suit cases. It seems that Mason had not purchased any tickets. There had been a no show of a party of one female adult and two male children for a flight to Panama. So it was presumed this was a smoke screen to make it appear as if the trio had left the Bahamas. Until they received the tip from Brazil, it had seemed like the children were still somewhere on the islands. Porter was staying to interview the boat captain as soon as he could.

Using the information received from Isabel, the team up in Montauk had retrieved the GPS unit from the boat owned by Nikolai Lebedev. The computer forensic team was sure they would be able to locate potential dump sites unless someone had thought to wipe the memory. This was unlikely because nobody put much thought into the GPS unit unless they were actively using it. The rest of the time it remained on in the background tracking the boat's every move.

The Montauk team also had cadaver dogs and was searching a grid in the state park behind the Lebedev summer home. Within two miles, there had been a hit and the crime scene unit was en route to start excavating. If they managed to secure even one DNA match to a missing witness within range of the Lebedev home, they would have cause for a search warrant to take the contents of all his homes, storage facilities, businesses and law office.

For the first time in this case, there appeared to be a shot at credible evidence to convict Nikolai Lebedev and send him to prison for the rest of his life. Now they just had to find the man.

Mandrake spoke to Mitch and they exchanged the latest news. Still no sign of Lebedev, or the children anywhere at all. Bill Franks was still denying any involvement or personal knowledge of Lebedev. He denied any knowledge of the regular deposits to his account. He even denied any knowledge of the actual account itself.

He was fiercely proclaiming that he had been framed so Mandrake had called in a favor at the NSA to get outside help investigating the possibility of a much more insidious and sneaky mole without alerting the potential mole. Mandrake and Mitch agreed that if the mole was still in play, Mitch and Isabel had been compromised and Lebedev was likely on his way. Mandrake and his team were heading for the Gulfsteam before the conversation went cold.

CHAPTER TWENTY-NINE

Nowhere to Run

In Milwaukee, Isabel and Mitch were up just after seven. They worked together in the small kitchen fixing breakfast. Mitch had slept fitfully, Isabel not much better. Mitch kept expecting the alarms to go off warning of an imminent attack, but nothing happened all night. Not even a stray cat or raccoon set it off, just the damn buzz from the radio check in every half hour.

After breakfast Mitch logged in via the VPN, he did not want to attract unwanted attention even if Bill Franks was not the mole, and they had been compromised. He considered the elusive Lebedev situation and reasoned that perhaps Lebedev was still monitoring Isabel's Facebook account. She was reading out on the couch.

He called for her to come to the computer and asked her if she would be willing to log in. "You could even leave your folks a message." Isabel was quick to agree. Mitch paid the small fee to route his connection through a very busy underground Internet cafe in Paris, before letting her input her user name and password. Isabel screamed and was sobbing hysterically as soon as the page loaded. The page was filled with graphic color photos of a disemboweled dead dog.

"Emma, Emma, poor, poor Emma, she keened over, and over, as she sobbed, tears running down her cheeks. The photos were posted by the Grim Reaper, and captioned with just one short statement. 'Nowhere to run, nowhere to hide. Guess who is next?'

There was also a short, slightly blurry video of a tricolor wire haired fox terrier on a leash in a parking lot. Not a single license plate was legible. Isabel cried harder if that was even possible.

"He's probably going to kill Zippy in front of me before he kills me," she said in a small voice interrupted by hiccups. Mitch was holding her tightly, wrapped in his arms; he rocked her gently, making conciliatory noises as she spoke or sobbed. He felt so helpless at that moment and so despicable for bringing this heartbreak to such a sweet, wonderful, kind, and beautiful woman.

Once she calmed down, he asked her if she wanted to return to New York and be with her family in protective custody until Nikolai was apprehended. Isabel considered this but was unwilling to place her family in jeopardy. She knew than Nikolai would hurt everyone with her when he found her.

"We stay here." If he knows we are here he will come and you can shoot him." Mitch nodded, he did not have the heart to tell her that he would have to take the man alive if at all possible. He was not about to be judge and jury, that's not how the system worked. Even if the system was somewhat broken, it was the system until further notice.

He saved the photos to his computer with a copy of the Facebook account and then he deleted the photos. He hoped her family had not been on Facebook yet this morning. Isabel left a short message telling her family that she was safe and well, and then Mitch logged off. Isabel was crying again. She curled up on the bed and cried and cried. Mitch suspected she was crying for more than a dead dog at this point. He was wracked with guilt for his part in destroying her life.

With nothing left to hide from her, Mitch did not leave the room when he checked in to give Mandrake this latest turn of events, he was just careful not to mention the children after making it obvious to Mandrake that Isabel was in the room..

After he disconnected the call, Mitch went out and sat on the couch for a while to plan the day. When he returned to the bedroom, Isabel had fallen asleep again. He was relieved. They were both exhausted from both lack of sleep and heightened tension.

He sat and monitored the cameras, nothing but squirrels and the occasional passing car. He was sure that Lebedev and his men were here. He spoke to the agent up the street every half hour. The man denied any suspicious activity. All tags were run and none were from out of town or from a car rental company, and none, other than local traffic, had been by more than twice. At this point, Mitch did not want to be seen outside. He didn't even dare to move the curtain.

At lunch time, Mandrake called with the next update. Mack was secure and medically fine. Missy was in surgery, and the forensic team was in Montauk. They discussed increasing the security presence in Milwaukee but Mandrake said that the local FBI was understaffed and did not want to increase the presence during low threat daylight hours. They had agreed to cover all four street corners from ten pm tonight until eight am. As soon as Mandrake and the team arrived from New York, they would move Isabel to a safe house in Chicago. Mitch agreed that it was unlikely that the fugitives would attack in broad daylight.

Mitch went into the kitchen and made a plate of sandwiches and poured two glasses of lemonade from the pitcher that Isabel had made. She really was a wonderful woman, smart, beautiful, and so thoughtful. He realized that he was getting unprofessionally attached to his mark and chided himself. He placed a few ice cubes in each glass. The house was getting hot despite the small air conditioner running in the bedroom window. He placed the small meal on the dining room table and went through to the bedroom. Isabel was awake staring up at the ceiling and did not move when he walked in.

"You OK?" he asked. She nodded. "Come have a bite to eat. I know you probably don't want to eat, but we need to stay strong." He took her hand and drew her up. She followed meekly and they sat and ate in silence. He was relieved to hear her resilience shine through when she commented,

"Wow, what a woman has to go through to get a guy to feed her." He grinned and squeezed her hand.

Once they were done eating they cleaned up in the kitchen, Isabel washing, Mitch drying. As he placed the last item in the drawer, Isabel grabbed him and hugged as hard as her small body could. Mitch, despite his recent chat with himself, kissed the top of her head as she mumbled her appreciation for his efforts against his broad chest.

Without warning she lifted her face, her lips meeting his. He froze as her tongue explored his lips and then teased at his tongue. Yearning got the best of him and he kissed her back, hard, and demanding. Within seconds he was mentally bitch slapping himself and pulled away apologizing profusely. Isabel grinned a sly grin and winked, then roared with laughter as Mitch's face colored with a blush.

Mitch tried changing the subject, reintroducing reality while trying hard to ignore his raging emotions. He told her that they would have much more security that night and would likely be going to a more secure location in the morning as they still had no hint of Nikolai's current whereabouts. The longer they remained in one place, the more likely he was to locate them. She nodded in agreement. All fight was gone at the moment, replaced with the remnants of whatever had just passed between them. She tried hard not to think of Zippy, but she kept seeing him with Nik and she just prayed that the poor little dog was OK. She took her mind off of the dogs by thinking of the horses.

"Mitch, do you suppose the FBI could slow walk

the horse part of the investigation, after all, it was never on your radar and you wouldn't know if it wasn't for me telling you. I think that having the two Secretariat clones face off in a huge Graded stake like the Breeders Cup or the Derby would be monumental for the field of genetics as well as for understanding what makes a great racehorse. Those two will never be allowed to breed; they would eventually have to be gelded to ensure that; not that it would really matter because he was not such a great sire of graded runners anyway, although he was a good broodmare sire."

Mitch thought about it for a moment before replying, "Well, we have a ton of far more important stuff to investigate first. As the other stuff comes to light I suppose we would do a thorough DNA comparison between the cloned horses and their registered parents to prove the clones were in fact not the babies of those horses."

"They are called the progeny of those horses," she corrected him

"What ev..."

Just then the alarm went off. He pointed upwards as he grabbed his Glock off the table. He rushed to see the footage as Isabel disappeared up the ladder disappearing into the ceiling securing the hatch after pulling up the ladder.

Mitch saw two men approaching up the front path, he did not have time to rewind the rear footage. He rushed into the dining room and placed himself up against the wall behind the bathroom door next to the internal window between the dining room and the sitting room.

There was no knock, the front door just burst inward after a heavy kick to the lock. Mitch subconsciously registered a silenced pistol on the man diving through the door and instinctively took him down with a double tap. The second man did not appear.

Mitch heard the back door glass shatter, and then a crashing thud as the shelving was tipped over. He had to push the bathroom door away to turn and face the kitchen. Again he fired as soon as he had a target. The glass above the air conditioner shattered and Mitch felt the round hit him in the chest before the whoosh of the silenced weapon fired through the side window even reached his ears.

Mitch crashed to the floor. He had been shot through the right side of his chest and his Glock went flying across the floor. He tried to reach down to his ankle to get his second pistol but he was kicked in the stomach with such force he could not breathe. The man coming in the window had been too quick.

Vasili Gruzdev searched Mitch retrieving the gun and knife. He called out for Nikolai to join him. The two men were very rough as they pulled the bleeding Mitch up and onto one of the dining room chairs. Mitch was barely conscious and was struggling to breath with a collapsing right lung and the pain in his gut.

Gruzdev pulled Mitch's arms around the back of the chair and secured them with duct tape found in the second drawer Nikolai opened in the kitchen. Next he checked Anatoli and Sasha but both men were dead. This increased Gruzdev's anger and he smashed his fist into Mitch's face relishing the sickening crunch of the nasal septum as it was crushed by the force of the blow. Mitch screamed but the sound was muffled by the lack of sufficient air flow.

In the ceiling Isabel could hear the men abusing the injured Mitch. She heard her husband say that Mitch wouldn't last long with a bullet in the chest and that much blood loss. They would have to torture him fast if they were going to find out where he was hiding her. She could hear one of them dragging the chest of drawers off the basement steps and then nothing from him.

She heard Vasili below her shouting at Mitch so Nikolai must be down in the basement searching for her. Isabel was terrified that Nikolai would notice the fine line of the square in the kitchen ceiling that was all the evidence of the hatch from below. She heard Gruzdev asking Mitch questions and then doing things that made him scream. She considered opening the hatch and trying to shoot the two men but she just knew that would be suicide.

Isabel grabbed the Glock from behind the trunk and moved as quietly as she could to the dormer window. She was certain there was no one outside to worry about as she tried to open the small window without a squeak. She wished that they had tested the window yesterday. Slowly, oh so damn slowly, she turned the four knobs holding the window in the frame.

When all were open, she put the gun into her waist band and then immediately took it back out and placed it next to her. A Glock with a round chambered was not a healthy choice jammed into one's pants. She grabbed the two handles and wiggled the window. Thank God it was the height of a hot summer so the wood was not wet and swollen in the frame. It seemed like forever before the little window was free and she placed it on the floor, She grabbed the gun and climbed out onto the flat roof of the sitting room.

Isabel stood and looked over the edge on the side of the house above the outside basement hatch but it was too high to jump down safely. She was praying that neighbors had heard the gun shots and called the police. Keeping her hands on the roof she climbed onto the steep pitched section over the bedroom and moved around to the back deck. She tossed this out too because although it was fairly low, she might be seen through the bedroom window or the mudroom door. She continued around to the flat roof over the back bedroom and looked down into the narrow alley where Mitch had erected the hidden escape over the fence.

Isabel turned and lowered her legs over the edge of the roof; she was not sure how she would get the gun down. It was fairly high here and she did not want to drop the gun in case it fired accidentally. She placed the nine mm in her mouth biting down on the grip as hard as she could while keeping the muzzle facing left of forward. She wiggled backwards gripping onto the gutter and hoping like hell that it didn't break under her weight. Isabel lowered herself over the edge and hung down, her feet were only about three feet from the ground when she looked down so she let go and dropped, absorbing the impact on bended knees.

Immediately, she scaled the fence and started running. Isabel did not care who saw her at this point. She was not sure if the FBI agent down the street was still alive. She suspected that he was at least incapacitated, so she ran to the nearest house and banged on the door.

There was no reply so she ran to the next house and tried again. Again there was no reply, and Isabel was starting to panic. She tried the house across the street with a car in the drive. A young mother, with a toddler on her hip, answered the door, so Isabel hid the gun behind her back.

"I need to call the police," she said breathlessly. "Please may I borrow your phone? The young woman unclipped her cell phone and handed it to Isabel through the door. Isabel dialed 911 with her thumb and began speaking as soon as she heard the operator.

"Gunmen have invaded a home on Seventy-third street near the park." She looked at the young mother, "What is the name of the park?" On receiving the answer she continued "Enderis Park. They have shot an FBI agent called Mitchell Hammer, he is very seriously wounded. It is the house with the solid wooden fence, I don't know the number. There are two armed men in the house, one is the wanted fugitive, Nikolai Lebedev." Isabel handed the phone to the young mother without disconnecting the call.

"Keep them coming, my friend is dying in that house, I need to help him," she said pointing to the roof visible between two houses across the street.

As soon as the young mother acknowledged the operator, Isabel turned, no longer caring if the woman saw her gun and ran back toward the cottage. She hoped that neither man was in the bedroom looking at the computer as she climbed back over the fence. As she looked down the south side of the house she saw Zippy lying against the wall. His legs were taped together and his muzzle was taped shut to keep him quiet. She fought her emotions in order to abandon her dog and go around to the back door.

Isabel walked in through the open back door and peeped around the door frame into the small bedroom so she could see into the dining room through the kitchen. She was so angry seeing poor Zippy treated this way, and then seeing the brutally beaten man slumped in the chair in the dining room sent her into a rage. Neither man facing Mitch had a gun in hand so she boldly stepped into the kitchen pointing the gun directly at Nikolai.

"Step away from the agent," she screamed and both men spun toward her in surprise. "I dare you to go for the gun," she said. "Just fucking do it because right now I want to kill you fucking animals for what you did to Emma." Nikolai held his hands up slowly, and she tried not to focus on either one so that she would not miss the other reaching for a gun.

"I've got our kids and Zippy, put down the gun or you will never see them again," Nikolai said in a hard, cold voice. He started walking toward her.

"Stop or I will shoot you," she warned, but he continued to approach. Isabel knew the eight foot rule and with no warning she fired a shot right into Nikolai's stomach. He roared and fell to his knees.

Vasili, spun and dove right out the window, landing on the fence separating the two houses. Nikolai was between her and the window so she was unable to follow and stop him. Through the kitchen window, she saw Gruzdev taking off across the next two properties and over a wall out of sight just as the immense wail of many sirens approached the front of the cottage.

Isabel motioned for Nikolai to move to his right but he would not move. Through the broken front door, she could see men in SWAT gear advancing up the path. She screamed for them to hurry, and that she had a gun and please not to shoot her, yet they did not seem to hurry. At the door one pointed his automatic rifle at her and told her to put the gun down.

"I am covering Nikolai Lebedev, so hurry once I put it down." She slowly placed the gun on the floor and stood back up just to find herself grabbed from behind. The police secured the scene and the paramedics were beside Mitch in seconds.

Within a minute he was intubated and she was horrified to see them punch a large needle into his chest after sticking bandages over the entrance and exit wounds. Within another minute they were wheeling him out the door, intravenous fluids running into both arms. The medics had been in the room less than five minutes. More paramedics placed Nikolai on a stretcher. He was cursing her and everyone around, mostly in Russian. He screamed in pain as they jostled him out through the door and down the steps. Isabel tried to follow but the man holding her didn't let go.

"Please," she said, "My dog is dying outside. That bastard has him hog tied next to the house with his mouth taped shut."

"Wait," the man said, 'There are two dead here, who are they?"

"Inside the front door, that is Anatoli Dubnovsky, in the kitchen is Alexei Lashkov. There was a fourth man here, Vasili Gruzdev, but he took off through the neighbor's yard." she said pointing to the south. The man barked some orders and some of the SWAT team took off out of the yard, others over the fence. There was a lot of radio chatter as a BOLO was issued.

"Please can we get my dog now?"

"With that man loose, you are not safe outside. Billy, find the dog and bring him in."

The addressed man hurried out and was back with the poor squirming dog before she could even protest. As soon as they placed the dog at her feet, Isabel realized that this was not Zippy. She hurried to get the tape off and said nothing about the wrong identity. That sick bastard was going to torture a random almost identical dog, just to break her heart. As soon as he was free, the cute young Fox Terrier was dancing around and then peed on the table leg.

"Shit, we are messing up the crime scene. OK everyone out and secure the perimeter for the crime techs. I want a wall of bodies around Mrs. Lebedev as we get her out of here." said a detective with the Milwaukee PD who was securing the scene. They hurried her out into the street and into an arriving

FBI SUV with tinted windows, Zippy number two followed, happy to be free, jumping in with her. Whomever this pup was he certainly was a forgiving and friendly little soul she thought. The man who climbed in with her introduced himself as Special Agent Gabe West; and told her he would be delivering her to the FBI office on Kilbourne Avenue in downtown Milwaukee.

CHAPTER THIRTY

Truth hurts

Isabel had argued, then begged to be allowed to go to Froedtert Lutheran Hospital. She felt that she needed to be there when Mitch awoke from surgery if he had survived long enough for surgery. She really didn't care whether Nik lived or died. She thought it would be a lot easier to live with him being dead but he was the father of her children and she did not want them hating her for killing him.

Her pleas fell on deaf ears and she was transported to the FBI office in the tall towers on Kilbourne. There she was placed in an interrogation room and offered tea, coffee, or other beverage of her choice and something to eat if she was hungry. Isabel accepted some unsweetened hot tea and declined anything to eat.

She was left alone for more than a hour before an agent entered, read her the Miranda Rights and charged her with conspiracy to commit a list of felonies so long that she stopped listening. At one point she asked how many charges there were in total and he replied sixty seven. She was asked if she waived her right to an attorney.

Isabel immediately declined the waiver. She knew that Mitch had said that they were going to give her immunity for testimony but she didn't even know if he was alive. The agent explained to her that, since they could not question her at this point, she would be transferred to the custody of the US Marshals Service and that they would likely house her at the Milwaukee County Jail pending arraignment and acquiring an attorney.

Isabel remembered her boys. She asked the agent, whose name she did not bother to recall at this point, where they were keeping her sons, how they were doing, and when she would get to see them. The agent told her that he did not know but would attempt to have that information to her before she left with the U.S. Marshals.

Isabel knew right away that something was terribly wrong when the agent returned with a tall, lean, black man whom he introduced as Dr. Taylor, a forensic psychologist from the Chicago office. Dr. Taylor sat down opposite her and took her hand in his.

"Mrs. Lebedev, your husband had your sons kidnapped during the week and taken out of the country. We have traced them to the Bahamas, where the local law enforcement has arrested the kidnapper. We have the children's nanny on the nine-one-one recording stating that the boys are fine and were delivered to their parents in Freeport.

An extensive search of the island has been unsuccessful at this time. Since you and your husband are both in Milwaukee, we think that she is obviously lying to protect the children. She is the one who alerted the Nassau police to the kidnapper so we think that she still has the children in her custody.

We have video footage of the kidnapper entering and leaving the airport, however, we have not yet identified the nanny or the children entering, even though the call came from within the departure hall. However, we are fairly sure that they flew out, we just have not received the flight manifests.

At this time the Bahama authorities are telling us that, per the various airlines, no tickets were sold to anyone with the nanny or the children's names. We have no other information as yet, but we will let you know as soon as we know anything new at all. On behalf of the US Government, the Department of Justice, and the FBI, I offer sincerest apologies as we were trying, at all costs, to keep your children safe during the final days of this investigation. Do you have any questions for me?"

Isabel said nothing. She was at once horrified, depressed, angry, and felt so betrayed by Mitch. He had been lying to her for days telling her that Demmy and Yuri were fine and she realized that she had been falling in love with him. Hatred engulfed her soul. She turned away from the men watching her and refused to cry. She would cry later in private but she would be damned if she would cry in front of these hateful people who played fast and loose with lives. Ha, Fast and Furious all over again. The DOJ had so much to answer for and the American people just let it happen. Now she hoped both of those bastards would die under the knife at

Froedtert Lutheran Hospital.

She ignored the men as they attempted to get her to speak. Eventually they left the room but she knew that they continued to watch through the glass. She walked over and did the finger to glass test, just so they would know that she knew they were watching.

It was probably late evening when the US Marshals arrived, took custody of her and drove her over to the county jail. She was stripped, searched, photographed and fingerprinted just like on TV. She felt numb. It was hard to comprehend this was actually happening to her.

She was offered one phone call and she called her step-father. Liam, listened through the sobs and told her that they would be there as soon as possible and that he would get her the best attorney money could buy. She cried with relief when he informed her that Emma and Zippy were safe and sound at his feet. She begged him to get the new Zippy out of the pound as soon as he got to Milwaukee.

She could hear her mother crying in the background and it broke her heart. As she was forced to end the call, she called to her mother and both women yelled affirmations of love as the call was disconnected.

After the phone call, she was escorted by two correctional officers to a cell in the solitary housing unit known as the SHU. Since she was a high profile federal inmate, she would not be sacrificed to the potential dangers of the general population.

Isabel saw her attorney, Graham Short, on Sunday. He informed her that her parents were in

Milwaukee and would be in court the next day for
her arraignment. They also had the little dog, whose
microchip revealed that his name was Tug.

Isabel told Mr. Short everything from the
beginning, including the physical assaults by Mitch
early in the abduction. She also mentioned the deal
that he had promised would come. Graham Short
was incensed. The damn feds acted like they were
above the law. In fact, cops in general these days
were getting away with too much. He promised her
he would see her before the hearing the following
day.

After he left, Isabel suffered alone, with no
telephone, and no television to keep her company.
Her imagination was running wild and she tried
really hard to talk herself out of the endless
speculation. 'Que Sera, Sera' she reminded herself.
Granny always sang it. 'What will be will be'.

MONDAY

CHAPTER THIRTY-ONE

Lost and found

On Monday morning, at eight am, a young woman with two young boys entered the U.S. Consular building at 1 Sandton Drive, Sandhurst, a suburb in Johannesburg. After some trouble convincing consular staff that she was legitimate, she and the children were taken to see an official who listened to her story.

After a brief call to the FBI in Washington DC and receipt of FBI photos via encrypted email, she officially handed the boys over to the U.S government. She hugged the boys who both started crying when they realized she was leaving.

Completely unsure of her future, crying openly herself, Riana rushed back out to her cousin who was waiting to call the South African police had she been detained.

EPILOGUE

MONTANA

First Saturday in May

Isabel sat on the huge rustic couch in front of the television in their log home in Darby, Montana. She could hardly believe that in a couple of hours she was going to watch the Kentucky Derby and that two of the five cloned three-year-olds were running. She wished she knew why they were still racing but she didn't dare ask and ruin everything. Perhaps Mitch had never said anything about the cloning to protect her. She certainly had not been indicted on any related charge. Yesterday, one of the two fillies had won the Oaks. Not very impressively she admitted, but who really cared. A win is a win.

From their new home in the witness protection program, she kept as close an eye on the clones as she could. The one filly had been retired, her health issues had not improved and she had continued to be weak. Isabel did not expect her to survive long enough to breed. Sometimes clones just did not do well. In general, they certainly had not yet proved to have the longevity of an original.

The John Henry colt was just starting to come into his own having raced once for third place. The two Secretariats were going to run head to head for the first time today. Only the slightly smaller of the two, the Hopeful winner from Saratoga, had run in, and won, the Breeders Cup two-year-old mile.

The other colt had been injured in shipping and had been sidelined until his win in the Holy Bull. Both colts were unbeaten to date and this afternoon was shaping up to be an amazing first Saturday in May. It was not as exciting as it would have been if American Pharoah had not won the Triple Crown so recently, but if these two colts were as good as their blood brother, this was going to be an epic five weeks.

Isabel, known around town as Mrs. Caroline Odie, wife of Eugene Odie, was enjoying Montana and the beautiful surrounding mountains despite missing her parents and her brothers. The boys loved the life of fishing and riding that their 'step-daddy' offered.

Of course they were initially very suspicious of this huge blond haired blue eyed man who had whisked them away from the lives they had led in New York City. She had told the boys, now Ben and Ian, names they had chosen for themselves, that their father had been arrested and charged with many crimes including murder, and that Uncle Vasili was still a fugitive and was trying to harm them. She explained that later, once the trial was over, they would be able to visit their father but until then it was terribly, terribly important not to talk about their old life, or names.

Isabel tried to equate their current situation with a secret spy story, maybe like one of the Bourne movies the kids had loved. Ben and Ian, now happy to be spies on the lamb, enjoyed the pretending, and practiced their new back ground story with glee. Eugene was very nice although his size was intimidating. She grew to appreciate how hard he worked to make the boys happy and help them forget their worries.

Darby was only thirty minutes from Missoula and so they got to enjoy the country life without a total disconnect from civilization, such that it is in a small western city. She had a job teaching biology and biochemistry at the local college. It was slightly dangerous to work in this field but she felt the sacrifice worth it for her sanity

The U.S. Marshal Service had chosen her location well. They had hooked her up with a local man who had very solid roots in the community. Anybody researching the new lecturer would find her married to a well liked, born and bred local, and therefore not likely in the witness protection program. Even Isabel herself had no idea that he was an ex-Navy SEAL and fellow team member of one Mitchell Paul Hammer; so she couldn't figure out how the DOJ had convinced a local sheriff to pretend he had found the love of his life on eHarmony.

After seven and a half months she still did not know what had happened to Mitch. As expected, she had been offered the full immunity that he had mentioned. Her attorney had advised that she take it and answer all questions honestly, but not to offer unsolicited information. They had not asked about the horses and she had said nothing in return.

Nikolai had recovered and was in a maximum Security Prison somewhere awaiting trial. He was deemed a flight risk with significant assets in Russia and was thus denied bail.

Vasili was in Brazil and was fighting any attempts at extradition. Turns out the sly, hideous, bastard had a wife and kids in Brazil. Isabel wondered how much it cost him to buy that kind of insurance. It was apparent that he was a master of disguise and it was suspected that he had snuck back into the US at least once and was the chief suspect in the orchestration of the gruesome death of Brent Farber, his former head of security. Farber had been found in his cell, his tongue cut out and bound in such a way that he drowned in his own blood. Hence the extreme caution with her. Other important witnesses, including Riana, who had voluntarily agreed to extradition, were all in protective custody pending the trial whose date kept being postponed by Nikolai's attorneys.

Between watching the races on the Derby undercard, Isabel glanced out the window and idly watched Maris chop wood. Maris was the handy man who was conveniently around whenever Eugene was busy at 'the office'. She enjoyed the easy way Eugene teased her with silly stuff like calling his police work 'the office'. She appreciated the decency with which he had accepted this horrible invasion of his privacy. Isabel now knew that he was divorced, with a bitter wife in Moses Lake, Washington. Occasionally he went over to Moses Lake to visit his young daughter. Sometimes he brought the ten year old Belinda home to play with the boys. The kids were all turning into little cowboys.

Allegedly, this woman had cheated on him while he was away in Afghanistan during a military deployment of some type. He wasn't absolutely certain the child was his but he was not about to ruin the best thing to come out of his marriage by finding out that she was not.

Maris was not local, and had shown up looking for work a few days after she had moved in. She suspected from the camaraderie between the two men, that they knew each other well and had served together in the military. Maris was a strange man and although courteous, he was certainly never chatty. He was a thin, wiry, deep olive skinned man about five feet nine inches with very cut muscles, who had grown up in Mozambique. She suspected that despite his small frame, he was quite likely a deadly weapon if he was there to keep her safe.

Isabel's eyes shot back to the television as the Bill Mott filly, Souper Sue, owned by the All Irish Soup Co.'s CEO, Susan Clair Waugh, powered down the stretch to win the Churchill Distaff Turf Mile. Only three races till history is made, she thought.

Her mind wandered back to Mitch. As soon as she had received the news that the boys were safe at the U.S Consulate in Johannesburg, South Africa, she had stopped being mad at Mitch. After that she just worried. Even her attorney had not received any news. The specific charge against Nikolai, related to Mitch, had remained attempted murder so she figured he must be alive. Other charges had been mounting regularly since then, and he had some murder charges related to the testimony from Brent Farber and the remains found in various locations. Surely Mitch was alive but nobody would tell her anything.

Sometimes she would depress herself by imagining him in a coma at some horrid acute care facility in Milwaukee on life support. Whenever this happened she would get really mad at herself and change the subject in her head.

All three dogs lay around on the rug between her and the television. Emma and Zippy had accepted Tug as if he had always been part of the pack. Her parents had told her the story, as told to them by the breeder, of Nikolai's three and a half thousand dollar purchase. She could not believe that she had ever fallen for an evil man who could pay thousands for a dog to kill out of spite.

Isabel's thoughts wandered to Montauk and all the horrifying evidence her attorney had shared with her. In the state park, within two miles of the summer home, the authorities had found the corpses of five young females in various states of decay. With the help of information provided by Farber, Riana, and other women questioned about the illegal girls trafficked through the 'dungeon,' and with the help of Interpol, three of the women had been identified as Eastern European girls who had answered ad's for work in the United States.

Using the information gleaned from the GPS on-board their boat, several weighted cylindrical items had been found out in the Atlantic. These were discovered using a camera on a small, remote controlled submersible. Since the items seen were merely tarp covered, somewhat human shaped cylinders, attached to concrete building blocks, they did not yet have conclusive proof that these items were actually human remains. The suspected remains were due to be recovered as soon as the weather in the area permitted.

Isabel was drawn back to reality by the horses breaking from the gate for the ninth race on the Derby card. Her stomach was starting to knot. She was allowing herself to get far too excited about the upcoming Derby.

Mike Maker took the seven furlong race for four-year-olds and up, worth half a million dollars, with a horse called Head Shaker. The connections were jumping up and down like girls gone wild on YouTube.

She looked up, and out of the window, as Eugene and the boys rode past in the direction of the barn. She was really going to miss this place when the trial was over. It was so amazingly beautiful with the river to the east and the huge mountains to the west.

By the time the horses lined up for the tenth, and final, race before the Derby, Eugene and the boys had joined her on the huge couch with its gorgeous polished wood arms. Eugene's dog was met with excitement by her three and there was a lot of noisy shouting to 'lie down' and 'shoosh' as the horses broke from the gate.

Not unexpectedly, this race went to the five-year-old Irish horse, Stoned on Clover, trained by Todd Pletcher. Feeling her excitement, Ben and Ian were on their haunches whipping their imaginary mounts down to the wire and screaming with glee at the win. They had been told never, ever, ever to use their own names and she was getting used to calling her boys by their chosen designations.

Isabel rose and went over to the large open plan kitchen that was part of this huge open living area. She inquired as to everyone choice of beverage and poured drinks for them all. Eugene came over to help.

"Carol, you doing OK?" he asked. She smiled,

"Pretty good, this is an exciting day; I just wish I knew what happened to Mitch. I can't help being sad at the thought that he is in a coma, dying slowly all alone." One little tear escaped and ran down her cheek. Eugene pretended he hadn't noticed and picked up the tray of cold drinks and took it over to the coffee table. Isabel composed herself and came over to watch the Derby contenders as they paraded over from the backside - as the barn area is known on the track.

Both colts looked magnificent. Considering the huge noisy crown and more action than either had ever seen before, they were remarkably well behaved. Isabel could see that Alistair Brown had stuffed their ears with cotton, a common way of blunting the tremendous roar of such a large crowd.

Secret Man and Proletariat stood well for their saddling and paraded in the ring prancing a little after the 'Riders Up' call came. Alistair and his assistant each lead a gleaming chestnut colt through the tunnel under the grandstand and out onto the track.

The crowd, as expected, went wild, the roar reaching the magnitude of an F18 on the flight deck. Pony boys took the lead rope of each and the colts moved past the grandstand for the first pass. They came floating by on their gallop down to the gate. Isabel found herself holding her breath, the most exiting two minutes in racing was about take place.

Secret Man had drawn post position four and Proletariat post position sixteen. The horses loaded, some acting up, others being gentleman, all held firmly by the gate crew.

"And they are off and racing in the Kentucky Derby!" The horses broke from the gate and Isabel screamed in horror as Secret Man stumbled coming out of the gate. Her eyes darted across to watch Proletariat being chased from his outside post making it into fourth place, two off the rail, as they went into the first turn.

She sought Secret Man; he was third from last on the rail and at least fourteen lengths off the leader. Down the back stretch she watched as Proletariat maintained his position just two and a half lengths off the lead. The horse in front was setting killer fractions, going the quarter in twenty-three, and the half in forty-six and change.

Secret Man's jockey was no fool and he didn't chase the pace, choosing instead to pick off horses one by one up the back stretch. Proletariat challenged the leader going into the far turn and was immediately challenged himself by the three horse as the leader lost ground.

The two horses were head and head around the far turn while Secret Man, now running a little wide drew into fourth place as they approached the quarter pole.

As Proletariat fought off the challenger alongside, starting to gain the upper hand, Secret Man, like his prototype before him, came powering down the center of the track drawing alongside his stable mate by the three sixteenth pole.

The boys were going wild, whipping their imaginary mounts and Isabel had grabbed her hair with balled fists, pulling hard on the unfortunate clumps as she rose from the couch, not breathing as she watched the two fight down to the wire.

Proletariat, having run too hard early, and with the serious challenge on the far turn, was just no match for the fast finishing Secret Man who appeared to be in cruise control. After a quick glance over his shoulder and assured of second place, Proletariat's jockey, obeying the instructions of his trainer not to break his mount's heart with a beating, allowed him to cruise home, under a hand ride, beaten a half-length by his powerful brother, the third horse trailing in another seven lengths behind.

Isabel was shaking; she took a huge breath, realizing that she must have been holding it for the whole two minutes. She felt light headed and was stunned to hear the track announcer declare a new record time for the Derby. In fact he stated, the first two horses past the post have broken the record held by the mighty Secretariat since nineteen seventy-three, with a winning time of 1:59.22.

Suddenly she felt sick. With Nikolai in prison, she was technically the principle owner of their racing syndicate. She had just run one-two in the greatest race in America. She watched with a mother's pride in her heart as her 'son' received his garland of roses amid a barrage of flashes and clicks emanating from the throngs of racing's greatest photographers including the famous Dan Dry and her own good friend Tibor Szlavik.

That night, after putting her tired young sons to bed, Isabel looked forward to her sleep. She was exhausted from all the excitement, worry, fear, dread, and anticipation of the reality of her day and existence. She prayed that the case would go to trail soon. She was just sick and tired of the endless waiting and uncertainty.

As she lay her head down on the pillow, she noticed a framed photo next to her on the night stand. She picked it up. There was no mistaking the giant Eugene in his battle fatigues. She curiously looked at the other faces in the photo and froze. Standing next to Eugene, dwarfed by his size and almost obscured by his shadow, was Mitch. Her heart exploded with joy. Through it all Mitch had found a way to keep her safe. That meant he was not just alive, but also OK. Now the trial just could not come fast enough.

Isabel seriously doubted she could sleep a wink she was so wound up. She reached over, picked up the small bottle of over-the-counter sleep aids and took one of the little blue pills, with a few sips of water, to help her fall asleep.

She turned off the light and noticed the moon, occasionally huge and bright. The night was cloudy with a howling wind, and the thick clouds raced across the sky. As one crossed its path, the moon glowed dark, and she wondered if Mitch was also looking up at the dark moon and thinking of her.

Isabel had a wonderful dream that night. Mitch was there with her, telling her that all would be OK and that one day they could be together again. He had caressed her sweetly, and kissed her softly, and had held her tight in his arms promising to return as soon as he could.

Isabel awoke early, it was still dark outside and she was bursting with hope and happiness. Awesome dreams could really bolster the spirits. She buried her head in the pillow next to her and breathed deep. She swore she could smell his scent. Isabel wondered what time it was and turned to look at her alarm clock. There, in front of the clock, lay a single red rose.

THE END

Translation of the Afrikaans song.

Oh, I have a horse, a shiny chestnut horse, with an absolutely brand new saddle, and I mount my horse, my shiny chestnut horse, and and I'm coming to get you. Because you said, if I want you, then I must come and get you, on my lovely riding horse, my shiny chestnut horse, with the absolutely brand new saddle.

Made in the USA
Middletown, DE
06 November 2020

23459212R00198